FROM THE BESTSELLING, AWARD-WINNING
AUTHOR OF

THE TALLCHIEFS

COMES THE POWERFUL STORY OF
NICK PALLADIN,
DECEMBER'S MAN OF THE MONTH,
IN
THE PERFECT FIT
by
CAIT LONDON

**"Living on the borders of his brothers and the
Tallchief family, Nick glimpsed how love could
be cherished and last. The dark Palladin legacy
hadn't stopped Joel and Rafe from finding
happiness, but Nick doubted love was meant for
him...until he met Silver Tallchief."**

Romance readers all over the world have fallen in
love with the Tallchief family and their legends.
Now, Cait London, the Tallchiefs and the Palladins
invite you to spend Christmas with them,
Silhouette Desire style.

**"Cait London is one of the best writers in
contemporary romance today."**
—*Affaire de Coeur*

Dear Reader,

All of us at Silhouette Desire send you our best wishes for a joyful holiday season. December brings six original, deeply touching love stories warm enough to melt your heart!

This month, bestselling author Cait London continues her beloved miniseries THE TALLCHIEFS with the story of MAN OF THE MONTH Nick Palladin in *The Perfect Fit*. This corporate cowboy's attempt to escape his family's matchmaking has him escorting a *Tallchief* down the aisle. Silhouette Desire welcomes the cross-line continuity FOLLOW THAT BABY to the line with Elizabeth Bevarly's *The Sheriff and the Impostor Bride*. And those irresistible bad-boy James brothers return in Cindy Gerard's *Marriage, Outlaw Style*, part of the OUTLAW HEARTS miniseries. When a headstrong bachelor and his brassy-but-beautiful childhood rival get stranded, they wind up in a 6lb., 12oz. bundle of trouble!

Talented author Susan Crosby's third book in THE LONE WOLVES miniseries, *His Ultimate Temptation*, will entrance you with this hero's primitive, unyielding desire to protect his once-wife and their willful daughter. A rich playboy sweeps a sensible heroine from her humdrum life in Shawna Delacorte's Cinderella story, *The Millionaire's Christmas Wish*. And Eileen Wilks weaves an emotional, edge-of-your-seat drama about a fierce cop and the delicate lady who poses as his newlywed bride in *Just a Little Bit Married?*

These poignant, sensuous books fill any Christmas stocking—and every reader's heart with the glow of holiday romance. Enjoy!

Best regards,
Joan Marlow Golan
Senior Editor

Please address questions and book requests to:
Silhouette Reader Service
U.S.: 3010 Walden Ave., P.O. Box 1325, Buffalo, NY 14269
Canadian: P.O. Box 609, Fort Erie, Ont. L2A 5X3

CAIT
LONDON
THE PERFECT FIT

SILHOUETTE *Desire*®

Published by Silhouette Books

America's Publisher of Contemporary Romance

SILHOUETTE BOOKS

ISBN 0-373-76183-X

THE PERFECT FIT

Printed in U.S.A.

Books by Cait London

Silhouette Desire

*The Loving Season #502
*Angel vs. MacLean #593
The Pendragon Virus #611
*The Daddy Candidate #641
†Midnight Rider #726
The Cowboy #763
Maybe No, Maybe Yes #782
†The Seduction of Jake Tallman #811
Fusion #871
The Bride Says No #891
Mr. Easy #919
Miracles and Mistletoe #968
‡The Cowboy and the Cradle #1006
‡Tallchief's Bride #1021
‡The Groom Candidate #1093
‡The Seduction of Fiona Tallchief #1135
‡Rafe Palladin: Man of Secrets #1160
‡The Perfect Fit #1183

Silhouette Yours Truly

Every Girl's Guide To...
Every Groom's Guide To...

Silhouette Books

‡Tallchief for Keeps

Spring Fancy 1994
"Lightfoot and Loving"

*The MacLeans
†The Blaylocks
‡The Tallchiefs

CAIT LONDON

lives in the Missouri Ozarks but loves to travel the Northwest's gold rush/cattle drive trails every summer. She loves research trips, meeting people and going to Native American dances. Ms. London is an avid reader who loves to paint, play with computers and grow herbs (particularly scented geraniums right now). She's a national bestselling and award-winning author, and she also writes historical romances under another pseudonym. Three is her lucky number; she has three daughters, and the events in her life have always been in threes. "I love writing for Silhouette," she says. "One of the best perks about all this hard work is the thrilling reader response and the warm, snug sense that I have given readers an enjoyable, entertaining gift."

To all the wonderful readers who have enjoyed the
Tallchiefs, and especially to Melissa Senate, my editor,
for her enthusiasm, expertise and guidance.

Elizabeth Montclair-Tallchief's Legend

"He'll be a fine beast of a man, haughty and proud and strong as a bear, gnawing at the maiden's shields, testing her, claiming her with wicked eyes and the pearls nestled in his hand. If he places them upon her, warmed by his flesh, and gives her a sweet kiss, the pearls will be her undoing. Then their hearts will join forever."

One

He'd come after the temperamental, spoiled woman who had just pushed him back out of the shop's door, and he was getting her. At thirty-four, the survivor of a scarred life and the trouble-shooter for Palladin, Inc., Nick Palladin wouldn't be stopped by a closed door. He wrapped his hand around the antique brass doorknob, jerked open the door to the tiny perfume shop for the second time and stepped inside. The rain, typical of late May in Seattle, misted against the door's glass, forming tiny rivulets and creating shadowy snakes in the shadowy interior of the small shop. He locked his legs and folded his arms across his chest. The owner and creator of the exclusive Silver's Signature Fragrances was his to deliver to his grandmother…and he would.

Silver Tallchief, a top perfumer called "The Nose," had just placed both hands on his chest and had pushed him out the door. Nick forced himself to breathe slowly, methodically. She was under contract to Palladin, Inc. and knew that a representative would collect her. Without knowing who he was, she'd shut the door in his face and had drawn down the fringed blind and the Closed sign. The shop, located on an artsy, hilly street in Seattle, was tiny, fragrant with women's scents and cluttered with packing boxes, wooden crates and luggage. Now, inside the shop, Nick locked on to the woman he wanted and stood quietly in her path as she came soaring back to run him out again.

Nick braced himself for a second attack; she'd surprised him the first time—women usually liked him. He was ready for her now, and he was getting her, he repeated. Her long platinum hair swung out from her shoulders, silk fanning on air as she swept up to him, dressed in a loose, silky cranberry red blouse and slacks that clung to her slender body. Her finger shot out to punch him in the chest, long red glossy nails contrasting with his pinstriped gray suit jacket. Her gray eyes flashed at him, reminding him of iced, slashing steel. "I'm closed. The shop is already leased to someone else. You're too big and taking up too much room. Don't look at me that way, all dark and stormy. I cannot abide off-the-shelf masculine scents amid my exclusive ones— they clash. There is no way in Hades that leather and pine trees and man blends with the essences I use. You'll ruin my nose. What is that awful animal essence?"

Her nostrils flared delicately, and she leaned closer to his throat. Her next sentence dripped with scorn. "Do I detect ironing starch?"

"This is a *business shirt,*" he explained tightly. "It's washable, but the collar needs extra stiffening." The lady was getting to him, and Nick regretted the gravelly edge to his usually smooth tone. He showed his teeth in a cool smile. In his job as a troubleshooter for his family's company and in his private life, Nick knew how to cover his emotions with a smile.

"I cannot abide household cleaning scents." Her finger punched his chest again, and Nick caught it in his hand and continued his cold smile as he eased it away from him. The woman's eyes flashed, smoky with anger. "*O-U-T.* Now."

Her hair fanned out from her shoulders again, feathering the fragrant air like a silky fringe as she pivoted and swept back amid the valley of boxes and luggage, retreating into her lair. She waved her hand, dismissing him airily and leaving him in a wake of feminine scents. He recognized a subtle musk and a bite of citrus.

Nick inhaled slowly, slightly uncomfortable in the tiny shop with *Silver's* artistically scrawled across the window. The jingling, whimsical angel bell over the door he had just closed went silent.

Outside, the rain stopped suddenly and sunlight poured through the window, labeling him with a shadowy *Silver's*. A man who had escaped his grandmother's matchmaking efforts for years, Nick edged slightly away from the elegant scrawl across his chest, unwilling to be labeled as Silver's property.

The van he had rented to transport Silver's most precious essences to the airport gleamed in the cloud-filtered sunlight outside the shop. Palladin, Inc.'s new acquisition, the creator of Silver's Signature Fragrances, was bossy, rude and knew what she wanted. Silver's lengthy list of demands lay crumpled in Palladin, Inc.'s new Amen Flats branch offices. The lady wasn't a sweetheart.

"She's temperamental, just like all good noses in the perfume business...give her some slack. She knows what she wants and how to get it. I like that. She reminds me of me, in a way, determined to succeed and not taking guff off of anyone. We need her talents to launch and package a unique Palladin scent," Mamie, Nick's employer and grandmother, had said.

According to Nick's research, the protégée of a playboy perfumer twice her age, Silver had the endorsement of Monsieur De LaFleur. Living in Cannes and retired, Jacques remembered Silver fondly, warmly, and told Nick to give her a kiss.

Silver's glossy red lipstick covered a generous, sassy mouth and sharp teeth—Nick wanted his skin intact, and kissing Silver wasn't on his menu. She lacked the Tallchiefs' friendly manners.

Nick sniffed through the feminine fragrances for his own slandered scents. Silver, at thirty-one, a top "Nose" in the perfume business, had been accurate. He hadn't had time to shower before putting on his business suit. Before driving to Denver and stepping into Palladin's company jet, he'd taken his baby nephew for a horseback ride on Montoya.

Nick pinpointed his lime-scented aftershave. A gift from his new relative, Elspeth Tallchief Petrovna, it was understated and

did what it was supposed to do—the mild astringent tingling after
his shave.

A loner wary of attachments, Nick realized that his left eyelid
was twitching slightly. At the moment, the reflex was to the tall
blonde's orders to get out of her way and her insult to his aftershave. She had even managed to insult his horse's scent.

Nick forced the tense muscles in his shoulders and neck to
relax; hours of flying had lodged stiffly into them. Mamie, his
paternal grandmother, wanted him to marry Silver Tallchief. Still
spry in her eighties, Mamie had hand-selected Silver, who was
now gliding quickly down the narrow aisle of boxes. She looked
like a moon witch in flight as strands of her straight white-gold
hair flew out around her shoulders and a healthy thick length
swayed in the middle of her back, the tips catching the dancing
light.

Her hips were curved and all woman—

Nick's fingers moved just once, the reflex surprising him. For
just a heartbeat, he'd wanted to reach out and collect that thick,
gleaming moonlight-colored mass into his keeping.

A man in control of his emotions, Nick stepped back into his
control, gloving himself in it. With his shoe, he eased aside a
crate marked Fragile. Glass. Bottles and Stoppers. His family's
fate was entwined with the Tallchiefs, and Silver wasn't his pick
of a lifetime mate. His business telephone conversations with her
had left him uneasy; her husky low voice had curled around him
sensuously, until the matter of the contract dollars arose—Silver
Tallchief was a capable, shrewd businesswoman with a cash register for a heart.

Though Nick enjoyed puzzles, he didn't enjoy a woman with
too many secrets. He eased through a narrow passage of stacked
boxes, marked with Fragile. Essential Oil. Each scent was listed
neatly—Rose, Sandalwood, Bergamot, Clary Sage, Oakmoss,
Frankincense, Lavender, Myrrh, Patchouli, Ylang-Ylang, Lemon,
Lime, Geranium, Vetiver—My Jasmine had a big heart drawn
upon it.

A man who appreciated women, but rarely let them enter his
life, Nick's gaze locked to the flowing cranberry silk slacks covering Silver's hips. The matching tunic's hem fluttered gracefully,

adapting to the tall woman's feminine sway. Silver had the height and lithe, feminine build of her Tallchief cousins, Elspeth and Fiona.

A subtle, feminine citrusy scent curled around him, and he edged through a sweeter, sensual musk to find himself enveloped by a light floral blend. He shook his head slightly to clear it and continued easing through the scents. Silver Tallchief had accepted the business offer from Palladin, Inc. too easily…almost as if she were waiting for a chance to go to Amen Flats, Wyoming.

A man who was born into a predatory family, Nick recognized Silver's tendencies from their first business conversation on the telephone.

Nick inhaled slowly, caught a darker, softer scent blended with roses and studied Silver's shapely backside. In constant motion as she went—stooping, checking boxes—Silver's energy swirled around her, her hair swaying, gleaming almost like iced silver in the shadows, sliding sensuously around her cranberry clad body.

The Amen Flats Tallchiefs, descendants of a Sioux chieftain and a Scots bondwoman, shared the inheritance of black straight, glossy hair. Una Fearghus, the Tallchiefs' great-great-grandmother, had given the Tallchiefs gray eyes—

Over her shoulder, Silver's cool gray eyes skimmed the aisle of stacked boxes back to Nick. In the shadows, her full lips gleamed in a red gloss that matched her loose tunic and slacks. She casually leaned against the door frame. "You realize that if you break anything, you'll pay. The ingredients for perfumes are very expensive, even the synthetic ones."

Above the crystals on her layered gold necklace, Nick recognized the Tallchief features immediately—skin that could tan easily, high cheekbones, black brows winging high and pride tilting her chin. She folded her arms across her chest, one perfectly manicured berry-shaded nail tapping her sleeve as she studied him. A spray of colors shot from the rows of diamonds on her fingers.

Beneath the tufts of hair spiking up and out from the top of her head, her black eyebrows and heavily mascaraed straight lashes were all Tallchief, and a narrow margin of dark roots said her blond shade came from a bottle. There wasn't anything innocent about the stormy shaded eyes boldly scanning Nick's six-foot-four body. In the small confines of the shop, the punch of her sexuality slammed into Nick's gut, stunning him. But then, a woman who had lived with the famous French playboy would be experienced at gauging what lay beneath his gray business suit.

"I am—" Before he could introduce himself, Silver's long legs were taking her deeper into the shadows of the small shop.

Nick tensed, eased around a small wooden crate marked Amber and followed her through a citrusy scent. He'd flown Palladin, Inc.'s business jet into Chicago from Denver to baby-sit Mamie's spoiled brat, who would be the creator of Palladin's new Silver's Signature line. After two months of negotiating with Silver to secure her talents and trademark, Nick had been dismissed—

Nick almost stepped on tiny wooden crates marked Musk and Amber No. 1. He nudged them gently aside with his foot. Mamie had personally researched Silver and her career, and his grandmother wanted Silver's talented nose under contract to Palladin. She also wanted Silver to be receptive to Nick as a future husband. "It's all coming together…she's a loner, like you, Nick, and she needs the warmth of the Tallchiefs—maybe I do, too. I can see real potential in Silver living in Amen Flats, working to develop Palladin's Silver line," Mamie had said. "If she wants a laboratory in more of a homey setting, find her a place—some cute little ranch where she can be influenced by the herbal and flower gardens. Your place will do nicely."

Nick hadn't trusted the too innocent gleam in his grandmother's eyes. His brothers, Joel and Rafe, had married Tallchiefs, and a computer addict, Mamie had been sorting lists to find Nick a prospective Tallchief bride. "Unmarried ones are scarce as hen's teeth," Mamie had muttered darkly, before pouncing upon Silver Tallchief, custom perfumer.

Mamie also wanted Nick to marry and to have her required great-grandchildren. His brothers had already made her extremely happy by producing babies. According to Mamie, Joel and Rafe had "left Nick in their dust."

Because his grandmother had raised Joel, Rafe and Nick, and

because she was the head of the corporation he worked for—Palladin, Inc.—Nick's troubleshooting talents were assigned to capturing—securing—one Silver Tallchief—for Palladin, Inc.

Nick was also designated to see to Silver's needs, and to make her happy during the contract. The contract would last until Silver's unique essences were blended into a "liquor." She would design the packaging and promotion for bath salts, powders, candles and soaps that Palladin would market exclusively.

Nick rotated his stiff neck slowly and released the breath he had been holding. Silver Tallchief was talented, temperamental, driven by success and power, and Mamie saw her as an asset. "The Nose" also had fashion-marketing style; she could design exquisite bottles, stopper designs and packaging.

A delicate ruby red glass perfume stopper, etched with white roses and disturbed by an accidental nudge of his shoe, rolled from a crate into his hand. He ran his thumb across the fragile and dangerous pointed tip. With Palladin, Inc.'s new remote offices in Amen Flats, Silver would be in the nest of her Tallchief cousins.

The bell over the door jingled as Nick opened the scarred office door wider. He scanned the tiny, cluttered office, sunlight dancing in the crystal, knife-cut edges of the tiny bottles and stoppers near the window. Amber, wine, lemon and clear shades caught the sun, drinking from the filtered light. A blue-gold, blown-glass bottle looked as if a genie would step from it at any moment—maybe she already had, in the person of one Silver Tallchief.

The fronds of a delicate hanging fern caressed Nick's cheek as he found Silver stretching in front of a window, her body arced taut, the cranberry silk clinging to every feminine curve. Silver braced one leg on her cluttered desk and placed her hands on her foot, slowly bowing her forehead to her knee. The sunlight gleamed on her toes, tipped in cranberry shades, pale and slender, escaping the strappy high-heeled sandals.

Nick swallowed the rise of pure male appreciation as the silk stretched tautly across her bottom. His throat dried as the softness beneath the silk shifted lithely. If there was anything he didn't need, it was to mix business and pleasure with a calculating, demanding woman like Silver Tallchief.

The first shocking sound of her voice two months ago had instantly caused him to tense, focus and—

Nick straightened. He tossed out Mamie's notion that Silver would appeal to him. *Marriage to that manslayer wouldn't be sweet.*

Silver's moon white straight hair flared out from her shoulders, spilling around her and into the shadows as she turned, and straightened. She slashed a dark look at him, reminding him of the Tallchiefs when their tempers were up. "I'm busy. Move along, will you? I'm expecting a moving man with knuckles that drag the floor. I'll probably have to take all day explaining 'duh' to him. So get lost. And really, I have to protect my nose. I make my living by fragrances. That animal scent is awful."

She left Nick to deal with that insult as she grabbed the continental-style telephone, which had just jingled Christmas music rather than ringing. She answered it impatiently, "Silver's."

Her gray eyes darkened, narrowed and she turned from him. "I'm moving. I want this…no, I can't come and discuss it with you and Father.… John is worried about me? Mother, he is almost twenty-five. He can deal with life. No, I am not going to reassure him. I've done all I could, so have you and Pop. This move will put distance between us, and maybe that will be good."

Nick leaned his shoulder against the door. Mamie wanted him to marry this cold woman, to bring her into the bosom of the loving Tallchief family. Mamie had forbidden him to research the years prior to Silver's eighteenth birthday. Nick's grandmother sometimes had odd requests, which he honored meticulously. Mamie's obscure reference to Silver's painful youth reminded him of his own and that sometimes secrets were better left uncovered.

The pieces didn't fit. Nick fingered the ruby red stopper and placed it on the desk beside a cool mint green one. He retraced his telephone conversations, picking over the contract's clauses.

Why would a successful businesswoman with an exclusive clientele accept the Palladin contract so easily? Why had the offer she was about to turn down suddenly interested her, once the Tallchiefs in Amen Flats were mentioned?

The nails weren't real and neither was the hair. Silver had city girl written all over her. Why was she so interested in the Tallchief family, their land and legends? The woman was a hunter and Nick had immediately recognized her stealthy questions— Silver wanted to live in Amen Flats, and she had a reason.

Silver turned to the window, the sunlight pouring over her blond hair, catching in the varied shades. She toyed with the silken tassel of a mauve antique perfume atomizer. Her voice slid into steel and ice as she spoke on the telephone. "I'm not into guilt trips anymore. You make your life. I'll make mine. No, nothing can change my mind, Mother. I can't...won't come home to visit before leaving. Goodbye. Stop crying."

She replaced the receiver to the cradle, then leveled a cool look at Nick as she swept a stack of empty deli cartons into the trash. "Well?"

Nick had the feeling she wanted to dump him in the trash as well, impatiently clearing anything that disturbed her to get on with her life. Too bad. He was sticking and doing the job he was sent to do—

"A little rough on your mother, weren't you?" the tall, powerfully built man drawled as he moved from the room's shadows into the myriad of colors created by the sunlit crystal atomizers. The delicate muted shades did not soften the rugged contours of his face, his narrowed hunter's eyes. "I'm Nick Palladin, the knuckle dragger, and the animal scent you don't like is called eau de horse. I took my baby nephew for a short ride before getting on the plane. You'll smell a lot of horse perfume in Amen Flats, Wyoming."

"Nicholas Palladin, of course," she noted quietly, studying him more closely. On the telephone, his voice had been smooth, sexy and charming; now it held a muted lash of anger, like vetiver fighting amber. "I thought I detected a baby. Their scent is distinctive, quite marketable, but the essence didn't fit. You look hard enough to send babies crying for their mothers. Let's get this straight—how I handle my family is my business."

Establishing walls protected emotions too ready to unravel. She ached for her mother and father and brother. Years of shielding her emotions never prepared her for the way her mother looked at her, as if searching for someone she had loved with all her heart and suddenly lost—

A reflection of her face danced across the wavery window glass and a sword reached up to slice her heart. That familiar pain, which had never lessened, shot through her, snaked around her heart and squeezed.

Lost. Gone. Silver shivered, then slapped the stack of papers on her desk, her formulas, which she would personally carry to Amen Flats. Her entire family had been shattered, torn apart, when her twin sister died years ago, of a disease that love couldn't stop.

Jasmine… Born only minutes after Silver, Jasmine had lived to all of seventeen, and Silver's life—her family's—had come unraveled. They were just teenage girls, dreaming of their princes' awakening kisses—when suddenly Jasmine was wasting away in a hospital room. Then she was gone. A cog of the close, loving family was always missing, never quite gone. Silver had to do something, anything, even though it was wrong to break the wall of pain—and now she had a desperate plan. She'd find the Montclair-Tallchief pearls, tear them from the past and find peace. The legend that Elizabeth Montclair Tallchief had given the pearls circled the tiny office—

"He'll be a fine beast of a man, haughty and proud and strong as a bear, gnawing at the maiden's shields, testing her, claiming her with wicked eyes and the pearls nestled in his hand. If he places them upon her, warmed by his flesh, and gives her a sweet kiss, the pearls will be her undoing. Then their hearts will join forever."

Silver jerked herself into the present, and studied the man looking at her. He was even more interesting than an ancient Egyptian blown-glass perfume bottle, and few men in Silver's experience could compete with antique perfume bottles and stoppers. A fierce pride ran in the rough edges and the lock of his jaw. She studied the sunlit jade green of his eyes. Though filtered by dark brown lashes, the shade was almost too brilliant and hard to be real. Brittle, tough, competent—this was the dark knight that Mamie had sent to secure Silver's talents—shoulders that took up too much space and a scowl like a fighter ready to punch. Power and sensuality ran through him, his scent—the unidentified base layer—slammed into Silver. This was a man as wary and determined as herself and primitively appealing. "Nick Palladin. The family's baby. Mamie's pride and joy."

He nodded and there was nothing friendly in his expression. The sunlight glinted in his dark brown, neatly clipped waves as he nodded. Myriads of color from the crystal stoppers lit his harsh face, glittered in the emerald depths of his narrowed eyes. However smoothly he handled business on the telephone, resisting slightly when she had pushed for more perks, Nick—in person— was a man who could be dangerous. "At your service."

After a fresh encounter with her mother, riding on nerves, desperation and a dream about to come true, Silver didn't want any problems as she settled into the Tallchiefs, explored them and grabbed the information she needed. Nick, taking up most of her office and looking as movable as granite, could be a big problem.

Silver tried a small smile, the tempting one that she allowed to warm her lips after licking them—the sultry knowing smile that a man as masculine as Nick Palladin would certainly...

He frowned, his dark brown brows separated by a harsh line. There was nothing tempting about his mouth, and Silver sensed that his relaxed pose covered an athletic body ready to pounce. She recognized that look of a predator, of a hunter—

She straightened and slowly studied his body, from broad shoulders to narrow hips, to those long powerful legs and expensive, braced apart shoes—as if he wasn't moving until he got what he had come to collect. She slowly lifted her gaze upward, exploring his expensive, perfectly tailored business suit, and met his dark green eyes. The essences were all there, the top layers, the "keynotes," were instantly recognizable. The "core note," or the essences, which give the scent character was more interesting, and the "basic note" which blended the combination together was fascinating—potent, dark, moody, private, stormy, and at the moment all the notes spelled "trouble."

This was the centurion, the guard dog, who wanted to know why she was so interested in the Tallchiefs' legends, the journal their great-great-grandmother, Una, had left and why she wanted to read Elizabeth's letters to a Tallchief relative.

This was the protector of the Tallchiefs, of his brothers' happy lives and children. Mamie had described Nick as sweet and caring, addicted to family life and babies, and had poured out the Palladins' dark secret.... Lloyd Palladin, Mamie's son, and father of Joel, Rafe and Nick, was a spoiled brat turned criminal. He'd mistreated his sons and finally was sent to prison for murdering the Tallchiefs' parents.

There were five Tallchief children, left to survive and cling together, and Mamie and the Palladin sons had tried to compensate for Lloyd's crimes.

The other Palladin brothers were now married to Tallchiefs and had children to occupy them. Silver would coo and cuddle the babies, win their wives with scents and gossip and girl-talk, and the Tallchief secrets would be in her fist.

Nick was another matter; his questions had been too keen, too carefully phrased. "Are you done looking?" he asked in a voice that lifted the hair on her nape. There was just a touch of arrogant male, nettled by a woman's bold examination.

"Not quite. I'm trying to decide if I should trust you with my essences."

"If they are packed well, they are safe." He smiled tightly, giving her nothing. "In our agreement, Palladin, Inc., did not agree to take responsibility for packing."

Silver tapped her cranberry tinted nail on her stack of formulas. *If she had to seduce him to get what she wanted, she would.* She had him all to herself until Amen Flats—by the time they landed in Denver she would know what he liked in a woman. Silver shrugged mentally. She could be cuddly, sweet, wholesome, innocent—her virgin state was no lie, she'd been too busy—surviving, succeeding and planning—to have time to waste indulging in affairs.

She studied Nick's closed expression and smiled. She picked up a cut-glass, iridescent vial of white fluid marked Silver's Jasmine and caressed it. Whatever she had to do to get the incredible gray Montclair-Tallchief pearls, she would.

Nick took a step, reached near her and dragged the old wooden office chair from behind the desk. It protested his weight as he eased into it and braced his long legs on the desk, effectively blocking the doorway. He studied the fingernails she was tapping on her formulas and folded his hands over his stomach. "You tap your nails when you're thinking and planning how to come at something, to get a fix on what you want and how to get it. I recognized the sound from our telephone conversations."

Silver jerked her hand away, picking up an envelope opener. She eased around the desk and braced her hips on it. *This guy is a real problem.* She stabbed the envelope opener into a soft ball of red velvet and left it there. "You're very shrewd—intuitive, aren't you? What do your senses tell you about a day's moving work ahead of you? Is there anything about, 'shall we hurry'?"

He leaned back, tipping the chair against the wall, his hands behind his head, as he studied her. "I thought we could have a little chat before packing your things into the jet."

His "little chat" rang of setting the ground rules; Silver intended to have her way, regardless of the tall, powerful man sprawled casually in her office. "My personal belongings have already been shipped. They should be arriving in that cozy little country home you got for me, equipped with a laboratory, isn't it? I did want those meadows of wildflowers, and an excellent air-filtering system in my laboratory."

"Your four-poster bed and your exercise toys are waiting. You have everything you asked for—a view of Tallchief Mountain and Lake, and why, I wonder, would you want that specifically?" This time, his gaze slowly moved down her body to her strappy heels and glossy toenails. "You do that, too. Tap your feet when you're impatient and want to get on with whatever you want. You want, Miss Tallchief, and that is the problem. Exactly what do you want out of this? Not money, or the success of the Palladin Silver line. You're successful, on the rise, and any corporation would count themselves lucky to have your blends exclusively. Briefly your price was high, but a bargain for what you could have gotten for an exclusive contract. Bargains make me uneasy. Why do Amen Flats and the Tallchief legends, especially Elizabeth's letters, intrigue you?''

His gaze moved upward, meeting her frown. The warmth that men usually returned to her was not there. Silver braced herself and repeated what she had practiced—not into a mirror because Silver meticulously avoided her own reflection. "I am related to the Tallchiefs—Duncan, Calum, Birk, Elspeth and Fiona. It's only natural that I would want to visit and study the place where my ancestors met and loved, that I would want to know about the legends about Una's dowry, sold to protect Tallchief land. Each of my relatives went in search of that dowry, and according to the legends attached to the dowry, each found love. It's all very romantic, don't you think?''

"Glynis, isn't it?'' Nick asked after a long, thoughtful pause. The name dropped like an ice block into the shadows.

His tone caused fear to skitter, icy cold, across her skin. Nick Palladin had been researching her, finding a life she had buried long ago. He was too thorough to please her; that meant she had to disarm him. "It was. I had my name legally changed.''

"Mmm. Interesting.'' Nick's chair came down with a thud and Silver forced herself not to shiver. He stood slowly, his body coming up close to hers, his eyes too focused, penetrating, foraging for Silver's motives. He reached for a strand of her hair and studied the color and texture, a pale contrast to his tanned, slightly scarred skin. "Silver, you're creative, but you don't have a romantic bone in your body. You are entirely directed toward your personal success. I've just heard you speak to your mother, and that shatters any illusions of family love. You're out for something from the Tallchiefs, and I won't let you hurt them.''

"Hurt them?'' Silver pushed down the anger that had begun to rise in her. Who was he to care, to prowl through her life, her pain and accuse her of hurting the Tallchiefs?

Two

"Get this—you won't," Nick murmured, leaning very close to her. "You won't hurt them or my grandmother, who seems to like you or she wouldn't have let you drive the contract price sky-high and met all your whimsical demands. She's worked hard, running an empire after her husband died, putting up with my father, and finally raising my brothers and myself. We weren't an easy ride as teenagers, and she kept us in line. She's paid enough for my father's crimes, and nothing, but nothing, is going to hurt her, if I can help it. That includes you, Silver."

The impact of his level stare and his low, carefully spaced tone sent a shiver skidding up Silver's back. She'd underestimated Nick. His telephone voice, businesslike and yet friendly, had sent her off the track. He'd easily agreed to her list of demands, and now, after meeting him, Silver sensed that Nick made the rules. She couldn't have that in her life, not now. "If you are Mamie's sweet, lovable, playboy bachelor, baby grandson, I'd hate to meet the others."

A fond flicker coursed over Nick's lips, though not quite a smile. "Mamie thinks of me like that. I'd like to let her keep that image, and I'd like her to have that designer perfume line she wants to add to Palladin, Inc. I have strict orders on how to handle you, and that precious nose of yours. You were very specific. Not too dry air, et cetera. On a business level, your demands will be met. On another level, you step over the line and it won't be pleasant.''

"You're frightening me," she returned in a lie, and knew that she would not allow him to stop her. "You want unofficial game rules."

"Precisely. I don't like surprises." He studied her lips, which she had just moistened, and Silver, who made certain she was always in control, realized her heart had just kicked up into overdrive.

"Don't," she managed to say as Nick reached to flick the dangling crystal beads at her ear. She wasn't accustomed to being backed into corners, protecting herself from a powerful man— this one was too potently male.

His finger stroked the strand of hair that webbed across her shoulder, and toyed with it. He leaned closer and a sudden awareness of his masculinity surprised her. She fought the quiver running through her, the shocking sense of her body awakening— He brought the silky strand to his nose. "Whatever scent you're wearing is very…nice."

"I don't wear scents. They would ruin my nose. I've been packing essential oils—" She arched back as he eased closer, towering over her. The leather and pine scent enfolded her, and she picked through the other scents—baby, dry cleaning, plain, unscented soap, coffee, black and strong—to his body's original scent…smooth, clean, dark, a touch of exotic, a drop of experience and a new, masculine indefinable edge—a scent of a wild, free river, dark secrets and moonlit magic—

The essence of magic and male startled her…and the need to leap upon him, to discover how to reproduce that scent as she had Jasmine's. Nick's base notes were too hard, too volatile, unsettling as mountain thunderstorms.

Nick tensed, the tilt of his head rising. Something live and hot moved beneath the slumberous depths of his green eyes. "Why, I believe you're sniffing me, Miss Tallchief."

She eased back, too aware that she had been leaning toward him and hiked up her defenses; Nick Palladin was too potently male. "It's usually not that obvious, but it's what I do, Mr. Palladin. I'm very good at it. Scents are like people. There are interesting little nuances, blends and drops of this and percentages of that. I can almost smell the 'don't do this and don't do that' pouring off you."

"Don't is the appropriate word. I don't want to see you upset the Tallchiefs in any way. They've had enough to deal with."

She realized that Nick's business suit was a veneer for the strong, primitive man it covered. She could picture him in buckskins, taking what he wanted…the hunter foraging and taking—she couldn't afford to be dissected or held captive under his thumb.

Silver had always made her own rules, and a male moving into her life, threatening to dominate her and put limits on her private plans, infuriated and excited her.

He was very good, but so was she— Turning the play, she eased slightly against Nick, lifted her face to his. She dived into the flickering male acknowledgment of her power as a woman, her excitement jerking up by miles as Nick's expression settled warily, grimly, his eyes narrowed.

All those lovely spiky male edges, lovely craggy angles and tense powerful muscles challenged her. A creative woman who followed her impulses, Silver wanted Nick Palladin's lips on hers more at that moment than she wanted the Montclair-Tallchief pearls. She wanted to test the heat beneath that firm line of his mouth, test the hunger that she had sensed before it was shielded, fling herself into the challenge and win. She sensed that if she couldn't handle Nick Palladin, she wouldn't be able to complete her goal—he might even be useful, once on her side. There were pluses to collecting Nick, a cautious, mind-prowling hunter of a man.

Then there was her own need to taste him—to see if all those wary edges could be smoothed into a problem-free path, leaving her free to concentrate—

A natural competitor, leaping to challenges, Silver liked games and she always won.

"Let's get this over, shall we?" she whispered before lifting
her lips that fraction to his. She inhaled delicately, bringing all
that was Nick Palladin into her, circling his essence—sandalwood, cedar, oakmoss, contrasts of man and baby, protector, danger, predator...

This isn't going to be easy, she thought as her prey didn't
respond, his eyes narrowed warily.

Because she was on tiptoe and still didn't complete the distance to his mouth, Silver reached for Nick's pin-striped gray-
and-navy-blue tie and tugged slightly. He remained immovable,
though something banked and dangerous flickered beneath his
lashes. Then there was that cleft in the center of his chin, a dark,
tasty little piece of magic—

Fascinating eyes, Silver thought, studying the unique dark
green shade. As cool as a mountain stream, shady with secrets,
and just enough primitive threat to entice her; Silver had never
liked an easy game.

She tugged his tie again and this time, Nick's hand came up
to circle her wrist, capturing the bells on her bracelet. "Back
off."

Only the slightly uneven edge to his deep whisper salved Silver's uncertainty. She eased her wrist from his callused fingers,
noting the way he resisted freeing her. The slight caress of his
thumb upon her inner wrist and back again did wonders for her
damaged ego. There for an instant, Nick Palladin had wanted to
kiss her, and for now that was enough.

He wanted to protect his family and for that, she admired him.
If she could have protected her family from its pain, she would
have died trying. The Tallchief family meant a great deal to Nick;
his response ran deeper than mere affection.

It was almost too bad she had to step into that perfect Tallchief
nest and walk over Nick Palladin to get what she wanted. He
was adorable, in his way—nettled, wearing over-the-counter but
respectable aftershave. The wary angle of his jaw proved that she
had gotten to him, so her first foray into petting the Tallchiefs'
guardian warrior wasn't a total loss.

Impulsively Silver stood on tiptoe to gently bite the hard line
of his jaw—just to test his reaction. She followed the bite with

a flick of her tongue. She wanted him distracted and unaware of her real purpose.

The taste and texture of his skin lingered on her tongue, as intriguing as his scents.

This time she got what she wanted—that flick of heat and desire, quickly shielded. "This is going to be very interesting, Mr. Palladin. By the way, I can't have my sense of smell contaminated by woodsy, male scents, not if Palladin is going to get that exclusive all-woman essence liquor they want. If you're going to be involved with this project, and in my vicinity, you will shower often, and please use unscented soap."

When the telephone rang, Silver impatiently ripped it from the cradle, her eyes stormy and locked with Nick's. "Silver's."

Nick pushed his aroused body back into control. Silver knew just how to arouse, how to tempt, and that bite had sent a jolt of pure sexual need coursing through him. He used her current distraction to push away the temptation of her mouth, the warmth of her lips against his skin disturbing, tormenting.

She reached to crush the layers of tissue paper, which she had been using to wrap and pack perfume bottles. Her lean, impatient body tensed as she focused on the caller. She half turned from Nick, the array of antique bottles framing her, filled with sunlight and shadows, her taut body in silhouette. A shield of white-gold hair slid across her face, lingered on her cheek and spilled like liquid moonlight onto her shoulder. "Pop, Mom will have to live without me for a while. She can do that, can't she?"

There was more mockery in her tone than love. The shelved bottles seemed to dance with the emotions vibrating from her. Every word was spaced, wedging a distance between her family and her heart. She tossed the wadded tissue onto the desk as though she wanted to discard something—someone—in her life. "I'm fine. I'll call."

Nick leaned against the wall, studying the woman he would bring to Amen Flats. Steel ran through her, and fear, her emotions tumbling, conflicting, and he glimpsed pain, quickly shielded. Silver Tallchief was very good at shielding, protecting herself. This family cared about her, yet Silver wanted to be cut free. Why?

A slender finger reached to touch the pointed top of a cerulean blue stopper, tapping it briskly. "Sorry, Pop. I can't stay. I've signed a contract. I'll try to write. Uh-huh. Bye."

Silver replaced the telephone and scrubbed her face with both hands, like a person wearily trying to remove herself from a bad dream. Her fingers trembled as she pushed back a length of hair webbing her cheek. She focused on Nick, lightning and thunderstorms in her gray eyes. "Look. I've got a family that doesn't want me to leave them, okay? Don't stand there looking like a brooding warlock. You're not a part of this, and there is no way I'm listening to anything you have to say about my family."

"Just as long as you don't hurt the Tallchiefs in Amen Flats—"

"You and I are not getting off to a good start. What if Mamie knew that the Tallchiefs' guardian was making me uncomfortable and that I couldn't create under his nose?" At the next ring of the telephone, she jerked it to her ear. This time her impatience snapped across the shadows. "Silver's. John, handle it. It's about time you started dealing with what happened. I am. Take it easy on Mom and Pop, because they're all you have. Do not call me a 'Scent Vampire.'"

Nick settled back into the shadows and allowed the lacy fronds of a fern to seductively brush his cheek as he settled into his thoughts. Silver was extracting herself from the family circle, placing her cranberry-tinted toes firmly outside their love and contact. There was just that silvery, damp rim below her eyes before she swallowed, straightened and started briskly wrapping her collection of bottles and stoppers in tissue paper, lining them up like soldiers on her desk. The moving process was slowed by a number of male callers, and there was no denying Silver's sexy, inviting tone. "I'm off to the ball, Ron. Sorry. You can't visit. I'll be back before you know it. Thanks for the great going-away party last night—loved your hors d'oeuvres, and no, you can't visit me."

She glanced at Nick, her smile intimate. "I'll be very busy."

Mark rated a chuckle and Dan, who called next, a long, slow wistful sigh. "Mmm...I'll call you when I get back. I'll collect my stuff then. You'll keep it for me, won't you? How are those cooking lessons going?''

Jacques De LaFleur was next and Silver's tone changed to an intimate, warm seduction. ''You've taught me well. I miss you, *mon cher.*''

A flurry of soft, intimate French followed and Silver laughed huskily, warmly.

Nick stripped off his tie and jacket, tossing them over her chair. She'd lived with De LaFleur for five years, traveled with him to perfume shows, and he'd paid the bills. Their relationship was intimate, from publicized dinners to sailing trips, and the bikini-clad photo of Silver, sitting on De LaFleur's lap, said the pair had shared a bed. The lady had lovers, and they weren't happy that she was leaving them hungry.

Nick's life rule was to keep inside the boundaries of his own life, and his family's—the Tallchiefs included. He opened the top buttons of his dress shirt and rolled back his sleeves. He treasured his brothers, and now the unique Tallchief family. Silver's lovers were apparently drooling, and she hadn't missed a beat.

The perfectly aligned, wrapped-in-tissue rows of bottles and stoppers were exactly how the lady did business: neat and cold. When she hung up the phone, he asked, ''Are you certain they can live without you?''

She shrugged and slid him a glance beneath her lashes. ''Is this a problem with you?''

Nick hefted a crate to his shoulder; the woman thrived on challenges, seeking them. ''As long as you give Mamie what she wants, there's not a problem.''

''Mamie and I understand each other, but I have a feeling that you could be real trouble.''

''I can be.''

Six hours later, Nick circled the tiny landing. A bossy woman where her beloved essences and laboratory equipment were concerned, Silver had paled as Nick moved her boxes from Palladin's luxury jet into the smaller cargo plane. She had hurried beside him, her hands reaching out to touch her precious essences and more than once she'd left him with the fragrant, disturbing brush of her fingers along his cheek. The hair on his nape had lifted warningly, nettling Nick who controlled his body and his senses with a tight rein.

The flight from Denver had been smooth, the turbulence over the Rocky Mountains minimal. Despite Silver's tough attitude toward her immediate family, she had been too quiet—except for a few questions about the women in his life. Nick gave her nothing but silence.

Framed in the cockpit by the dying sun, the white-gold color of her long straight hair blended with her silver leisure suit and windbreaker, dragging across her shoulders as she leaned back against the seat. In the shadows of the cockpit, Silver's high slanting cheekbones had glistened suspiciously before she swiped away the moisture.

Nick braced himself against the helpless fear that swamped him when a woman cried. Every move Silver made was designed to suit her own purposes and she was hunting—

While the cargo hold stored the crates, Silver had never released the traveling bag with her formulas. Her fingers had gripped the leather tightly as if everything she wanted or would want was in the bag.

When she glanced at him, there was nothing in her gray eyes. Nothing. As if an essential piece had been vacuumed from her soul and could never be replaced. The circles beneath Silver's eyes gave her a haunted, lonely look. Then the steel slid through her, her mouth hardening as she looked out into the beautiful mountains studded with trees and colored by red jutting rock.

"You're acting doomed, you know. But once I'm settled, you can be on your way. I'll dismiss your services. You can fly away, fixing things for Palladin, Inc." There was that cocky, challenging look at him as she placed her silver boots over a layer of notebooks and flight plans. Without missing a heartbeat, he reached to circle her ankle and tug it away from his notebooks, just as he wanted to remove her from his life.

Nick almost muttered his curse before his lips clamped tighter. Shaken by just that sliver of an insight into the woman next to him, he checked his controls. He didn't want to feel anything for Silver, his senses telling him that something was very wrong—

Maybe he'd seen too much loving in the last years, since his brothers had married into the Tallchief family. Maybe he'd cradled too many smoky-eyed Tallchief babies on his lap, because his senses were telling him to hold Silver tight and safe.

Maybe he wanted to place his cheek along her smooth one, nuzzling it. Maybe he wanted to finish that kiss, taking it beyond the limits she had set.

But Silver was an illusion of a woman, and beneath the incredible female fantasy was ice.

To dive into that image, even temporarily, would be a complication, and Nick didn't like human puzzles. He inhaled sharply. In a quiet, pensive mood, Silver was even more dangerous than when she was bossy and feminine. The dusk blanketing the ground, the blue sky above, only heightened her unusual coloring—not the pale skin of a natural blond, but the creamy light skin of a complexion that would darken easily in the sun. The straight sweep of her lashes was all Tallchief, the smoky gray of her eyes marking her as a member of the family.

"Tallchief Mountain...and look, there's the lake, just like Mamie said," Silver whispered, looking out her window. "A treacherous dark lake, capped by white waves, looking moody as my Tallchief," Silver murmured.

My Tallchief. The hair on Nick's nape lifted, the passage familiar. Elspeth Tallchief Petrovna had read similar words from Una's journal.

Silver leaned closer to the window, her body tense. "Yes, that is the castle where Rafe and Demi live. See, on the other side of that hill. Montclair Castle, brought from England by the wealthy owners—the castle where Liam swept Elizabeth and their son back to America. Every one of the Tallchiefs retrieved an item of the dowry and found love. Your brother Rafe fell in love with Demi and the legend of the crystals came true."

"You've done your homework." *Why?* Nick's senses quivered just as they did when he sensed danger.

The engines hummed under Silver's too quiet, almost reverent tone, as if she were speaking to herself. "Yes. Every legend was true, the descriptions of the items vivid in Una's journals. Tell me about Elspeth, Nick...how she seems to sense things before they happen. With a Celtic seer ancestor and a shaman from the Tallchief inheritance, she's a natural. I like naturals."

"You'll meet them soon enough. You can see for yourself." Nick tapped the glass gauges, an old habit developed from his early days of piloting poorly serviced or renovated planes. Nothing about Silver was natural. Whatever she was after, it was not exclusively to develop a top line of scents for Palladin, Inc. She was too interested in her relatives, in how Elspeth had worked, just as her mother had, with Una's journals, preserving and examining them.

He glanced at her. With the same features as the Tallchief family, she could have inherited other traits. "Do you ever feel sensations, like Elspeth?"

"Because we're both descended from a Celtic seer and a Sioux shaman? Sometimes…no, I'm positive that isn't in me. I don't want anything like that in me," she said firmly, placing her open hand against her reflection in the plane's window.

"Cleaning fluids," he said automatically as she inhaled delicately. "I had the plane cleaned for you."

"I expect my directions to be followed. My nose is my best asset—and at the moment, it's a Palladin investment. That leather jacket you're wearing could use some oil. It looks ancient. Better yet, why don't you buy a new one?" She leaned over, peering down at the shadowed emerald field below. "What's that?"

Nick glanced at her. "So far, you don't like my scent, my horse's and a gift of aftershave from a woman I respect. This jacket is my favorite."

"The jeans and T-shirt are nice," Silver offered after studying his body as though assessing a potential lover, her silvery gray eyes lit with humor. "The crease in your jeans is old-fashioned, but very nice. You starched them, too, didn't you?"

Nick decided to keep the conversation away from his jeans and ignored Silver's smirk; she'd gotten to him. He didn't like his cruising lanes filled with turbulence, or the knowledge that his mouth had dried at the sight of her in the metallic jumpsuit, hair flying around her as she strode toward the plane, wind pasting the jacket to her body—there were more curves than he'd expected, concealed by her loose silky outfit. "That square on

the meadow is a parachute landing for the Tallchief women—
Talia, Lacy and sometimes Fiona, when she's testing my brother
Joel. That's Elspeth wrapped in the shawl—the Tallchief tartan—
and the rest of the family beside her. They've been waiting for
you."

Silver's long slender fingers splayed, opened and flattened on
the glass as though reaching out to grasp what she wanted. "You
didn't radio our arrival time, did you?"

"Elspeth always seems to know, and this plane is hard to miss.
Amen Flats doesn't have a public airport—this is a private landing."

"Elspeth Tallchief sounds fascinating. She would know more
than the rest, her senses coming into play. She took her mother's
place after the shooting—I'm sorry, Nick. I didn't mean—"

"My father made a career of ruining lives. I don't understand
why the Tallchiefs aren't bitter, but they've accepted us. It's a
healing time." Nick fought the bitter taste crawling up from his
stomach. He was only six months old when his father had sold
him and Rafe, and Mamie had interfered. As a child, Joel had
battled for Rafe and Nick, and somehow the three brothers had
survived. Then when Lloyd—Nick's gaze involuntarily shot to a
small mirror, reminding him of his likeness to Lloyd—when
Lloyd killed the Tallchiefs' parents, Mamie had collected the
three teenage toughs and shoved them into school.

Nick studied his hands on the controls. They were big like his
father's, and Nick learned early that big hands could hurt; Nick
trembled when he held the Tallchief children, fearing his dark
inheritance—

Women. He preferred women who didn't reach into him, dragging out his fears, making him give too much, and he didn't like
female puzzles. Joel and Rafe had settled their demons, but Nick
held his passions, even while making love—nice, clearly defined,
surface relationships had suited him well. Cruising through life,
traveling where he wanted, which now seemed to be back to
Amen Flats when he could— He inhaled Silver's feminine, understated scents and realized that it had been years since he'd
made love, and the last kisses he'd been given were ones from
the Tallchief and Palladin children, all innocence and lollipops.

After five years with Jacques De LaFleur, Silver's innocence was doubtful.

"A healing time," she repeated softly, looking out to the clouds layering Tallchief Mountain like a cloak. "You're lucky to have that peace."

Nick didn't want to feel that tug of tenderness for her, for whatever secrets she hid. He skimmed the rugged, snowcapped outline of the Rocky Mountains. The small plane slid through the sky, the mountain winds calm, air pockets and turbulence at a minimum. He liked to cruise through life the same way. Single life suited him—no complications, doing what he wanted, leaving when he wanted... He glanced down at his leather bomber jacket, a favorite one purchased with his first pilot's paycheck. He didn't like interference in his life—no turbulence, no air pockets, no sweet-scented women revving his temper.

He'd been too aware of Silver's every movement from the moment she slid into the cockpit, those long graceful legs and the restless adjustments of her body. Unused to confinement, Silver wasn't a woman to sit still, and in constant motion, she'd unzipped her jacket to reveal a tight T-shirt. Beneath the scrawled *Fun Girl* her breasts were— Nick had fought not to stare. Fun Girl wasn't wearing a bra; she was all soft, flowing, rippling woman, the cloth tight against her.

Nick exhaled, pushing the air from his lungs. Silver was not only tall and lithe as her loose clothing made her appear—but she was also the proverbial stacked Venus, a whole lot of woman, curved in all the right places. A physical, dynamic woman who recognized a man's interested, aware look.

Eyeing him, Silver arched, arms above her head and stretched.

Desire slammed into Nick's lower body, his heart revving up.

Then she smiled, slowly, seductively, and he knew that the movement was meant to rattle him. "Don't worry. I'm not in Mamie's bride and groom, happily-ever-after picture. I make my own life-as-I-want-it pictures and marriage isn't one of them. However, it could get real boring in Amen Flats, even with mountain climbing and diving in the lake."

She'd tossed the sensual ball into his lap, waiting for him to begin the play. At the moment, his lap had an uncomfortable problem. Her finger cruised down his neck. "You're tense, baby. Does little old me bother you?"

"Not a bit. Did you learn that from De LaFleur?" Nick took her wrist and eased her hand away. Her scent clung to him and the silky soft stroke of her finger packed enough electricity to flip the plane.

"Jacques said you were investigating me. He had the impression that you were suspicious. He's a lovely man. I learned everything I know from him—the unique, small essences that bring out a woman's sensuality. I could even mix a man's love potion for you, if I wanted. A little jasmine, a few drops of patchouli and black pepper…a very dark, sensual scent and a nice mix for your natural scents. You need not be lonely, ace."

She watched him, waiting for him to respond to her taunt. Nick refused to be drawn into her web, returning to the safe details of the scenery. "Thanks. I'll pass. Tallchief Lake isn't for scuba diving, if that's what you mean. The currents beneath the surface are strong enough to kill. It's fed by an underground stream, and so far the bottom hasn't been found."

"I see. You said that the Tallchief women skydive." Silver's dark brow arched. "Do you fly them?"

"Sometimes." Nick smiled briefly, remembering how Calum Tallchief, Talia's husband, had given him specific instructions and had personally checked Talia's parachute. Fiona, Joel's wife, loved to land perfectly in his waiting arms. Birk Tallchief was a sizable pain in the rear, referring to the petite mother of his children, Lacy, as "maddening…this is positively, absolutely the last time she's playing she's a snowflake drifting down into my arms."

Nick had had a glimpse of that tiny snowflake plummeting down toward the white, terrified face of her tall husband. The parachute that had fallen over them both had been very quiet for a long time. "They dive when they aren't pregnant and their husbands aren't brooding and storming about women falling from the sky. The wind currents from the mountains can easily send a parachute off course. The Tallchief women are unusually good athletes, or they wouldn't be allowed to dive."

"I see. Their husbands call the shots. How quaint. And you

prefer to stay outside marriage, protecting your adopted family and your brothers. 'Uncle Nick' is just fine with you, am I right? A lot of men come into my shop, hoping to make their loves happy, but I can't see you doing that. You're a buy-off-the-shelf sort of guy."

Nick avoided the subject of marriage and realized that he'd never wanted to share his life with anyone. "Their husbands love them, but I wouldn't say they are obeyed."

"Just how good are the Tallchief women?"

"The best athletes I've seen."

Silver peered down at the ground. "Even in wind currents, like today?"

"They can handle wind currents. But there aren't any today."

"I like my relatives. Families should be like that, even though they've been touched by tragedy. They should grow together, not apart," Silver said quietly. "I know. You don't want anything happening to disrupt their lives. I think I'll just step to the back for a minute and check on my boxes—to see that they are still strapped safely. Would you mind circling slowly? A little bit lower? I'd really like to get the overall feel of the land."

Nick lowered the plane's altitude, cruising slowly. At dusk, the shadows moved down the pine-tree studded mountains, the lake was quiet, almost waiting for a wind to toss its waves.

For a time, he'd found what he wanted, here amid the Tallchief family, with his brothers, Rafe and Joel. Mamie, uncomfortable too long away from her luxury penthouse in Denver, still seemed to ease when she came to visit. Though Nick preferred working from his home office, the company's remote Amen Flats office worked well with the Denver one and—

"Slower," Silver called from the back. She thrust her head into the cockpit, and a strand of white-gold hair caught on the stubble on Nick's jaw. She grinned when he brushed it away, disconcerted by her fantastic scents. "Look what slipped out of your briefcase—hmm, not bad."

She placed the photograph in front of Nick. A tall, shapely brunette sprawled gracefully in a leopard bikini thong and nothing else. Above Whitney's glossy smile, she had written: Hungry For You.

Nick tucked the panoramic photo into the clip near him, with Whitney facing away from him. Whitney wasn't giving up, though their short affair had been over five years ago. She'd wanted too much, all the tethers of a relationship headed toward the altar. Whitney also wanted a hefty marital portion of Palladin, Inc. "I usually zip my briefcase. Interesting how this picture could have slipped free."

"Yes, it is. Mamie told me you hold on to your single status like it was a lifeboat in shark-infested waters. Poor baby. She tried to make it sound like a challenge to me…it wasn't. You've got 'traditional male player' written all over you. You're the kind to like well-orchestrated courtship periods…a very predictable guy. Here. Watch this," she ordered as she plopped her formula bag into the empty seat. "Let me know when you want me belted in for landing, okay?" she asked with a grin, and bent to kiss his cheek. "You're a pretty good pilot, aren't you? I mean, you can handle unexpected currents, emergencies and all that, right?"

A soft kiss, a brush of her breast on his shoulder and Nick damned his rising temperature. "I'm experienced—"

She laughed softly, knowingly. "I'll just bet you are, ace."

Nick jerked from the second impact of that sudden, unexpected, soft playful kiss. He eased back, slowly uncurled his fingers, one by one, from the controls, and stretched in the seat, listening to the drone of the engines as he cut them, cruising and circling for the sight-seeing passenger. With the Tallchiefs around, the bossy woman in the rear of the plane—

He appreciated predictable women; there was nothing wrong with a natural sequence of steps. Miss Nose was getting to him. One minute he fell into whatever haunted her, the next rattled the cool control he preferred to keep around a manslayer like Silver. That tempting offer in her office had nagged at him and there was no way he was getting involved with—

The light on his panel flashed—the side loading door had just opened—there was a brief jerk and swerve as wind invaded the plane. Nick adjusted the controls, leveled and glanced down to see the dying sun gleaming on Silver's body.

Her helmet matched her jumpsuit, all silver, bulleting toward the shadowy earth— Poised in a free-fall position, her arms and legs splayed apart, Silver suddenly curled into a ball, somersaulting downward before angling her body, turning on her back and waving up at him.

Just as quickly, she turned into proper position and freed the silver parachute.

Nick's short curse shot into the cockpit. He understood now why Silver had insisted on positioning and double-belting her precious crates. When he got his hands on Mamie's spoiled acquisition, he—

Nick wasn't certain what he would do. A controlled man, a predictable one, he'd be prepared for her taunts when he landed. He put the plane on autopilot, secured the opened cargo door and returned to the cockpit. He'd handle Silver coolly, methodically, a temperamental woman who was nothing but a troublesome business associate. He'd be smooth and calm; she wasn't getting to him. Not a bit.

Three

At last standing on Tallchief ground, Silver unharnessed the parachute, ripped off her helmet, shook her hair free and grinned at her relatives. She felt as though they'd waited forever and it was her destiny to come to them. They'd survived, just as she had, and in their childhood play had given themselves special names. They were as beautiful as their story, fighting to stay together as orphaned teenagers. In the light between day and night, Elspeth "the elegant" stood wrapped in her tartan, and a child sitting upon her husband, Alek's shoulders. Duncan "the defender" holding his wife's hand with a toddler upon his shoulders and another resting in his arms. Emily, Sybil's daughter, a leggy twenty-year old, and Birk "the rogue" and Lacy with their babies. Talia and Calum "the cool" with their two and Joel and Fiona "the fiery" with Cody and Ian, and Rafe and Demi—

All the essences were there, love, tenderness, protection and unity that had lasted for generations and would go on.

"Perfect," she heard herself whisper as the plane droned overhead, preparing to approach the thin lighted runway.

It was Elspeth who first moved from the family, sweeping

through the thigh-high sunflower meadow to meet Silver. "I've come so far, Jasmine," Silver whispered quietly and walked to meet the woman whom she instantly loved.

Elspeth's sleek black hair shimmered in the dying light, bound into a long, thick braid. The fragrant lavender bouquet in her arms blended with the earth scents. Her smile was more of warmth and inner light than of beauty as she handed the bouquet to Silver. "Just as I pictured you.... We look alike. Almost twins."

"No, not twins," Silver stated more sharply than she wanted. She caught the wary darkening of Elspeth's gray eyes, and tried for a gentler tone. "But we do look alike. I'm the fully packed model and have you by a few pounds."

The friendly jest slid by Elspeth. She looked straight into Silver's eyes, as if seeing deeper into the shadows of her life. "You'll find happiness here."

"Will I? How do you know?" Silver accepted Elspeth's hand, sensing the instant bond between them—Silver couldn't afford one more obstacle that could stop her, and yet meeting Elspeth's steady gray eyes, she knew that more than blood ran between them.

The answer came softly, firmly. "I just know you'll find what you want right here."

There would be no running from this woman who saw into hearts and lives; there could only be honesty between them. "I have to."

"Yes," Elspeth whispered solemnly. "I'll help you."

Then the rest of the family circled her, and Silver claimed them, one by one. She would use them and she would keep her heart apart from their tethers. *Use them.* She uneasily glanced at Elspeth, who was watching her quietly. *I'll help you,* she'd promised.

Silver had everything in her grasp that she needed... sunflowers and earth, sky and dew, and scents, wonderful lavenders and rose, and basil and savory mixed with bread and— soon she would be free. Silver let her emotions enfold her, barely noticing the plane gliding down for a smooth landing.

Through Elspeth's introductions, and the juicy kiss of the toddler, Ian, Silver took in the essences of each of them, loved each individual scent—she turned to the tall men standing side by side, with dark brown hair and laughing green eyes, and matching clefts in their chins. "Don't tell me…Joel and Rafe."

Nick's hard, wary lines weren't there, the secrets cloaking him. His older brothers looked like happily married men, arms encircling their wives.

Over the lavender bouquet she clutched close to her, she noticed the third tall man with dark brown hair and a cleft in his chin. His green eyes lashed her. Silver took a step backward as his angry, male scent slammed into her. From the top note to the bottom characteristic, his scent was primitive, ragged, frustrated and volatile. "You're upset," she said, angling her chin up at Nick. She'd led an adult life free of restraint and orders, and the nettled man in front of her wasn't interfering— "I'm very good. There was a challenge. I took it. So what?"

"Aye," a Tallchief male murmured, the word a reminder of their Scots heritage. "That's the one."

"No." Nick glared at the family, who grinned back.

Silver reached up to pat him on the head. "He's so easy."

"Am I?" That flat male challenge slammed into her before he nodded grimly to the Tallchiefs. He latched a big hand gently on Silver's nape, his fingers firm as if he were claiming a playful kitten who had gotten too close to the fire. "Miss Silver needs her rest. She'll see you all tomorrow."

"Lunch tomorrow at Tallchief House. It's the original homestead, but Duncan has added on to it," Sybil said. "You come too, Nick. Duncan needs help laying that new fence. I'll feed you for your time and then let you baby-sit."

"Right. I'd like that." Nick dipped just enough to toss Silver over his shoulder. Then he was striding toward the sleek Palladin pickup truck parked near the plane.

"Are you unhappy for some reason?" Silver managed to ask as she waved to the Tallchief family and held her bouquet away, keeping it from being damaged by Nick's long stride. She reached out to pluck sunflowers, adding them to the bouquet. "You just made me strip the petals from that lovely sunflower."

"Unhappy isn't the word for it."

Silver pressed her hand to his inner thigh as she peered between his legs. The hard muscle bunched immediately, quivered and Nick stopped abruptly as though stunned. A small but detectable shudder ran through his taut body as Silver ordered, "Move a little to the left. There's a huge, perfect sunflower that I must have. You want me to have the scents I need, don't you?"

She grinned when Nick hesitated, then swerved to the left, and she collected the sunflower. Silver smiled as she bruised the petals of the sunflower, releasing its perfume; Nick could be managed. He realized the importance of her work, and gathering the scents into her. A company man to his bones, Nick would do what would serve Palladin's best interest. "Perfect. Your brothers, Joel and Rafe, look like you. At the moment, they seem much sweeter."

After a pause in which Nick didn't answer, Silver placed one hand on his belt, and braced upward before she lifted to wave the bouquet to the Tallchiefs. "Let's try for a little dignity, shall we, Mr. Macho? After all, I am the professional perfumer who is going to make big bucks for Palladin, Inc. I'll tell Mamie you manhandled me. You could get fired."

Nick savagely jerked open the pickup door and thrust her inside. "Get that seat belt on."

"Touchy. Yes, sir," Silver muttered as she gave one last wave to the Tallchiefs.

Nick geared the pickup and soared down the dirt road, passing a herd of grazing deer. Silver settled back to enjoy dusk creeping across the fields, the cows and calves grazing in the lush fields. "Oh look, there's a fawn...see how tiny and leggy—"

Nick's hard green gaze slashed at her as she pushed a sunflower stalk over his ear. A glowering male, wrapped in frustrated anger, was too tantalizing to resist. He ripped the sunflower away and discarded it through the open window. "Do you do just what you want, when you want?"

She shrugged. "Usually. It pays off not to let someone else determine what I should do, and I can't resist a challenge. You shouldn't get uptight. From what Mamie has said of you, you should understand independence. Your essence is unsteady now, volatile and bristling, and I've got enough to cope with. A nose has to be careful. How will I work with all that dark aura storming around me? A happy worker is a good worker," she singsonged.

Nick expertly slid through the gears, a cord tightening in his jaw. "Careful? You haven't been careful since you were eighteen. Then you started racing cars, skydiving and taking white-water kayak trips. That was just for starters. From the frequency of the men calling at the shop, begging you to stay in touch, I'd say you had a few training partners along the way."

"They're just like my brothers—except John isn't athletic. And darn, those dance contests do call for a male to be involved—most of them at least. I'm an active girl, the challenges were there, and you've done your research. Where are we going?"

When Nick didn't answer, Silver settled back into the seat with her thoughts. She was frightened she would fail. At least while she was free-falling and meeting her relatives, and teasing Nick, who responded beautifully, she wasn't being squeezed by fear.

Jasmine…I'll do this and we can both rest.

The small ranch cottage was exactly what she had wanted. A new building addition shot off to the side, viewing Tallchief Mountain and Lake. While Nick carried the crates into the house and laboratory, Silver stood watching the night enclose the mountain and blanket the lake.

The India pearls had been Elizabeth Montclair Tallchief's, only part of a small jewelry chest she had brought with her to America, when Liam had claimed her.

In the last part of the 1880s, Liam and Elizabeth had first met high on Tallchief Mountain. Liam, son of Tallchief, a half-blood Sioux, had been staked to the ground by renegades. Elizabeth, an English lady, had been touring the West. Faced with her sister's death and dishonor—and her own—Elizabeth had placed herself upon Liam, and given him her virginity. Later, he had claimed her and their son in England. Kidnapped and married now to Liam, Elizabeth had moved to Tallchief land and had happily found her destiny.

Elizabeth had written in her letters to an English friend: "I would not have my own dear Liam shamed by my wealth, though he would not say it is so. The pearls are from my dowry, given to me by my grandmother, and dear to my heart because of her and because I wore them when Liam and I first met, so shockingly. But nothing is so dear as Liam, my husband, my heart.'' Elizabeth had confided in her letters, ''Because I have my love, and it is true, I give these pearls to another and pray that the legend will come to be as it has for me, to the woman who wears the pearls and finds her love.''

Elizabeth's letters had been purchased from an antique dealer. Bound with a red ribbon, they were stashed safely in the same tiny chest as a collection of blown-glass perfume bottles. Dreaming of their princes, Jasmine and Silver had pored over the letters, filling themselves with dreams of true love.

A creative woman, Elizabeth had established a new legend to serve the Montclair-Tallchief pearls: *''He'll be a fine beast of a man, haughty and proud and strong as a bear, gnawing at the maiden's shields, testing her, claiming her with wicked eyes and the pearls nestled in his hand. If he places them upon her, warmed by his flesh, and gives her a sweet kiss, the pearls will be her undoing. Then their hearts will join forever.''*

As girls, Jasmine and Silver had made a solemn, whispered midnight pact, each holding a candle, that they would seek and find Elizabeth's pearls. For years, they dreamed of the moment they'd hold the pearls, and the princes would claim them. They'd been invincible in their dreams, until Jasmine lay ill, fading away. Then, holding that frail, limp hand, Silver had cried and promised to carry on the search alone.

But now, *Jasmine was gone.* Silver shivered with loneliness, her bones cold with it. She wrapped her arms tightly around her and wished she had her ancestors' shaman and seer powers. The pearls' legend had been so strong, binding Jasmine and herself, and Silver had to complete the dream, to finish that portion of her life, of girlish whims and princes who awakened with kisses and love forever more.

Nick had come to stand behind her, the night wind bringing his scent to her, enfolding her. He'd come to set the rules to tame her, and she couldn't let him spoil the moment when her heart had settled into a tenuous peace, when she was finally so close to settling her shadows.

Without looking, she sensed that he was brooding, ready to start defining his rules. She lifted her head, inhaling the pine and earth scents of the country, blended with the animals'. "Say what you must tomorrow…not tonight. I couldn't bear it."

"You're crying." The words were harsh, uneven.

"I never cry. Leave me alone." Silver closed her eyes, and suddenly realized how tired she was, how many hours she had planned for the start of the hunt…and now the time had come.

Fear returned to chill her, and when she turned, Nick was gone.

Silver awoke to the morning sun slanting across her face and the tantalizing scent of fresh coffee. She stretched and blessed the god of automatic timers on coffeepots.

Last night, she'd left Nick to deal with locking the house as he left; she'd found the bathroom, flung a towel over the mirror and took a luxurious shower with her requested unscented soap. She had poured herself into the sunshine-scented sheets on the antique bed she had purchased with the money from her first big sale.

The quilt laid across Silver's carved, walnut 1880's four-poster bed was handmade and old—the note that had been resting on it from Elspeth, gifting Silver with a pioneer woman's handwork. The Tallchief tartan at the end of the bed was Elspeth's work, a gift bringing Silver into the family.

She stretched, enjoying the fresh cotton sheet against her naked body, yawned and stretched again. The house, what she had seen of it last night, was spacious, plainly furnished, and her crates would be waiting to be unpacked in the lab.

Silver threw back the sheets, leaped out of bed and wrapped the Tallchief plaid around her. The soft merino wool had been woven, no doubt, on the same loom Una had used, and had given to Elizabeth. The tartan settled around Silver like a homecoming caress.

If the laboratory requirements were handled as well as the rest of the house, Mamie had reason to be proud of Nick, Palladin's troubleshooter. In her bare feet, Silver padded across the varied topaz shades of the hardwood floor toward the scent of the coffee.

Following her instructions, her weights and workout bench were placed in front of an open window, overlooking a vast wildflower meadow. Her climbing and scuba gear and mountain bike rested in a corner and Silver couldn't wait to use them.

All in good time. She had to make her visit appear as if she were honoring the contract, though she'd already blended the fragrance to leave her more time for hunting the pearls. She had a full day ahead of her, setting up the lab, making contact with Mamie and visiting the Tallchiefs. Sybil Tallchief was a top genealogist and an heirloom hunter; Elspeth had senses that Silver could use; and liaisons with both women could prove to be profitable. Jacques had taught her how to hunt, to seek the essences she needed and to call forth her instincts. He'd said those seer and shaman instincts were in her, and she would need them now to free herself…and Jasmine.

Silver glanced in the mirror, the shadows capturing her image. Slanting cheekbones, an oval face, bruised gray eyes—a skeletal image lying in a cold white hospital bed swept over Silver's. Jasmine…

"I specifically said, no mirrors," she muttered and whipped off the plaid to walk to the mirror. She reached to lift and stand it on the floor, silvered surface against the wall. She pulled the plaid up around her nude body, not ready to let her anger take away the pleasure of the gift. On her way to the delicious scent of coffee, Silver smoothed the soft merino wool caressing her body. "Mr. Ladykiller will hear about this. I gave him direct orders that my living quarters would not have mirrors."

The man in her kitchen wasn't wearing a shirt. He was wearing well-worn jeans and no shoes. Nick looked over his tanned and muscled shoulder. His slow, thorough gaze skimmed down the tartan covering her to her bare thighs, down her legs to her feet and then slowly rose to study the rounded line of her breasts above the cloth.

"You!" Silver gripped the counter while he poured her coffee. His slow, interested, downward gaze locked on her cleavage, and instinctively protecting herself, Silver jerked the cloth up to her chin.

That look was enough to make her want to— She fought for air, and hated the shiver that coursed down her body. Nick was very experienced at looking at women, while she—

While she had to find the Montclair pearls. She battled her unsteady emotions as she adjusted the huge blue-and-green tartan closer to her body, tucking one corner in as though it were a sarong. If Nick Palladin thought he could make her run from a room— She glared at Nick, who lifted a so-what eyebrow. Giving herself room to form exactly what she would say, she stalked to the refrigerator, retrieved ice cubes and plopped them into her coffee. She wanted to be fully awake before she started laying out the rules to Nick. He shoveled bacon and eggs onto two plates, poured coffee into a pottery mug that matched hers and sat down at the sturdy pioneer table as if he served her breakfast every morning. The familiarity rankled. Silver had kept her life apart from possible intrusion for years.

Silver sipped her coffee with one hand, gripped the tartan firmly with the other and eyed the intruding male. "You don't need to play watchdog now, Nick. I'm here, and I know how to lock a door. I know how to set up my laboratory, and a call to Elspeth will help me find Tallchief House. There's another pickup outside, the four-wheel drive, which I wanted, so logically I have means to travel when I want. Or I can ride my bike. I'll get to work as soon as I can— Just exactly, why are you here? In my house?"

"Breakfast," he explained and dived into his food, ignoring her. He fought inhaling her freshly bathed fragrance, the musky and citrusy undertones that subtly rose from her skin. Last night she had taken herself into another time and he had been an intruder. Now, with her eyes flashing like steel, he wanted to enjoy the battle. "And this is my house."

"I thought my list specified a leased, isolated ranch. I require quiet and privacy. My reports to you on the progress of the project can be made to your Amen Flats office," Silver stated tightly after a moment.

A meadowlark trilled in the morning sunlight, and Nick took

his time in answering, fascinated as her eyes slashed at him, the color rising in her cheeks. "This was the only available ranch meeting your requirements near Amen Flats."

Nick gave her credit; she'd jerked the blue-and-green woven plaid up to her chin like an innocent and blushed when she'd seen him. No doubt the blush waited to be called forth at will, but it and the fast flurry of her hands, gripping the plaid to shield her body, still intrigued him. And now the furious smoky gray of her eyes said she wasn't backing down; she was settling in to fight.

In the brittle morning sunlight, stripped of her rings and bracelets, the false nails and cosmetics, Silver's walls were high, her temper raging. Nick's emotions weren't exactly calm. The sight of a naked woman—all honey shaded curves and long legs—adjusting mirrors in his home had jolted Nick, especially since she'd cried out so painfully during the night. Why did she refuse to have mirrors around her? What did she want?

Silver's trembling fingers gripped the mug and, locking her gaze to his, she sipped the coffee. While she replaced it carefully on the pioneer table, scarred from years of use, Nick tried not to look at the smooth sunlit curve of her hip, bared by the plaid.

She wasn't backing off, and Nick reluctantly admired that distinctive Tallchief quality. She flounced gracefully into the chair opposite him, the movement of an athletic female in a snit. He admired the time she took to collect herself, glancing outside to the sheep grazing in the meadow before speaking. "You've had your little joke. Now get out."

"Let's go at this easy, okay?" Nick asked as he pushed his empty plate away. He knew instinctively that neither he nor Silver were easy people. When they clashed, it would be wild, lightning and thunder, primitive at a level he'd never experienced.

Did he want that experience? Just once, to enter the circle of fire as his brothers had?

Not with this woman, all ice and steel beneath the curves, that lazy, inviting smile she had spared the Tallchiefs.

She stared at the plate he had placed in front of her. After one bitter glare at him, Silver jerked a fork into her hand and began eating. Nick waited, fascinated as she devoured the hefty meal. "More?" he asked as Silver sighed and pushed her plate away.

Her look at him was petulant, simmering. "I was hungry, okay? I suppose you enjoy hitting me with this first thing in the morning, don't you? I suppose you enjoyed playing Peeping Tom while I fixed the mirror."

"It's not every day an Amazon draped in a Tallchief tartan— or less—waltzes around my home." Nick couldn't resist. Silver looked so feminine, flustered but not about to leave the battleground. The view of a tall, well-stacked Venus, all soft and rippling female in the right places, had definitely launched a nettling, unwanted desire for her. Nick glanced at her tapping fingers. "Exactly why did you remove the mirror, Silver?"

Her snit expression changed, locked into a calm mask, shielding what ran deep inside her, but her fingertips continued tapping. "Vanity. Women don't like to age, you know, and mirrors show every pound."

Her answer was too ready and flip, as if she'd answered the question many times. Nick inhaled a curling wisp of her personal fragrance, that seductive light musk laced with a bite of citrus, and wished he hadn't. "You are a healthy eater."

She shrugged and ripped off a length of bacon with her teeth, following it with a healthy bite of biscuit. "I am an athlete, bub. Packing and dismantling the shop wasn't exactly easy. Now explain why this is your house and you are in it."

Nick didn't like pushy women or ready explanations. "There wasn't another place around and this one matched your requirements perfectly...right down to the lavender and herb garden."

She inhaled sharply, eyeing him. "You, of course, will be living here. You're not the kind to leave his home...to be a gentleman and gracefully recede into the shadows. You're committed to protecting the Tallchiefs, and I'll have to deal with you every inch of the way, won't I?"

"Yes. I'm certain we'll manage." Nick wanted to be very close to Silver after yesterday's escapade. "You know, my grandmother is fond of you—I have no idea why, but she is. Therefore, I'm doomed to baby-sit a spoiled—"

"I worked hard for my skills and my reputation. Nothing was

handed to me. I am a very talented 'Nose' and you're supposed to keep me happy, getting me every little thing I want…which isn't you. Your grandmother is very fond of me. I've made certain of it.''

"You're not on my menu, either, lady,'' Nick returned. She had just confirmed what he had suspicioned, that Silver played people, getting what she wanted—a calculating hunter. And she was good at it, because Mamie seldom let anyone too close to her but had immediately taken to Silver. She'd used her body to get what she wanted from De LaFleur, and now she sought something from the Tallchiefs.

Nick snorted quietly. Bouncing around the world, he hadn't made the effort to study a woman's complexities. That one gentle moment as she stood in the moonlight had scored a hit. He was as susceptible to a woman's tears and softer moods as any of his brothers or the Tallchiefs.

On the other hand, those smoky gray eyes strolling over his bare chest this morning slammed into him with enough sensual punch to instantly harden his body. Silver's seemingly innocent fascination did not equal the experienced women that Nick had known. However, life with De LaFleur would have taken her innocence; Silver knew how to get to a man, and that bothered Nick. She inhaled quickly and jerked her glare to him. "You cannot have your…your women stay here.''

She was territorial; Nick had studiously avoided possessive females. He reached to flick away the crumb on her bottom lip with his fingertip; the velvety contact burned. "They never have. On the other hand, I wouldn't appreciate Bill and Bob and Jack dropping in, either. Things could get crowded. Our relationship will be monogamous, at least while you're staying here…with me. That goes for De LaFleur, too.''

"Boring, boring… I'm used to a variety. We're going to be playing house—unless I can find a way out of this mess. Now doesn't that make me special? I mean, the only woman who has lived in the great Nick Palladin's home?'' she taunted.

Her glance took in his sparsely furnished home, the hardwood floors softened by woven rugs and sprawling wooden furniture in the living room. She peered into the laundry room, noted the washer and dryer humming, Nick's ironing board and steam iron. "According to Mamie, you're a great catch, though I doubt that with all your dark moods and glares—and what woman wants to be packed off like a sack of potatoes? Still, isn't that some sort of status ranking? Aren't I special, Nick?" she asked in a sultry tone, pushing him as she placed one slender fingertip on his bare chest to toy with the hair on it.

Nick caught her finger and a jolt of electricity skittered up his arm; his male alarms started clanging and the need to carry her back to bed startled him. Silver's eyes widened, her hand trembling in his. "Scowling won't scare me," she whispered, her bottom lip gleaming as it trembled. "I'll find another place."

Nick did not release the "You ungrateful little…" hovering on his tongue. He rummaged through the hours he'd wasted trying to wedge her away from his ranch; not another house matching her conditions was available in the small community. "Try to find something else, why don't you? Try to come up with another custom lab setup like the one I just had built for you on the north end of the house. But until you find your perfect Nick-free home, maybe you'd better think about closing your bedroom door at night, Silver."

She'd gotten to him again and, drawn from his customary easygoing cloak, Nick had struck back. "You cry and moan, and from the sounds, there is a real fight going on in that bed. Do you want to tell me about it? Or are you missing De LaFleur?"

She paled, straightened and reclaimed her hand to grip the plaid, her shields raised. "If I needed you to be my friend, I'd worry. I'm going to dress now."

Nick couldn't help grinning as Silver walked away. Her exposed lush backside was indeed very admirable and feminine. "Oh, Silver," he singsonged gently.

"What?" She turned, white-gold hair flying out and settling over her bare shoulders and flowing onto the tartan. The filtered sunlight slid across the delicate flex of her thigh muscles as she braced her legs, and a jolt of pure sensual awareness again slammed into him.

Nick rose slowly. He wanted no shadows between them when he made his point. He walked to her and noted that her eyes widened and she took a step back as he approached, looking up at him. He smoothed a strand of hair with his fingertip, letting it roam downward to her chest. He traced the taut, silky skin over her collarbone, and she shivered delicately. At least he wasn't the only one affected by this morning's encounter. "Let's get this straight. I like the predictable, and I can deal with your spoiled demands. Jumping out of the plane yesterday and showing off didn't exactly make you points with me. Mamie wouldn't want anything to happen to you, and I'm not about to play nurse."

Why did she seem so innocent and yet—

"You're very big…very…just *very*," she whispered unevenly as Nick took a step nearer, wanting to see what was happening inside those wide gray eyes.

He took his time studying the deep crevice between her breasts, and Silver jerked the plaid higher, allowing him a better view of her shapely knees. He'd kiss them one day, the fragrant backs, and take his time inspecting the rest of her, too. "The sight of a nude woman, one fully rounded and fresh from bed, could just set me off. But then, that's what you want, don't you? Me drooling after you? Just one more notch on your bedpost?"

Anger shot through the steel gray eyes locked with his, Silver's temper flashing. "You think I let you see my backside deliberately? Drool on someone else, Fido."

Nick slid his fingertip along her taut jawline, the silky flesh heating, flushing beneath his touch. "Can't take it, can you?"

"What?"

The rumpled bed behind her hiked his desire up into *sizzling*. "You're handing out plenty and waltzing around here in the morning in nothing, but bare skin isn't going to work. You stay on your side of the fence, and I'll stay on mine. This is strictly business."

Silver's head went back, sending a fresh wave of her scents to entrance him. "Threats?"

"Promises. You didn't know you cried in your sleep, did you? That must be hard on relationships…intimate ones. Did De LaFleur sleep through all that?"

The curtains dropped, her face impassive. "He was a gentleman. It was never a problem between us."

Nick had a big problem, his senses leaping to claim a woman who had slept her way into her skills. "A fifty-year-old man and a nineteen-year-old girl could have other problems."

Her smile was long and lazy and knowing. "Yes, well. We managed. Jacques always gave me what I wanted."

"I'll bet."

Her dark eyebrow hitched up. "I'm going to enjoy flattening you, Palladin."

"Just do the job you are paid to do."

Four

Nick ripped off his leather gloves and entered Tallchief House. He'd helped the men lay a new fence, while the Tallchief women visited with Silver. Leaving her amid the family he'd come to adore made him uneasy. Yet Nick needed the relief of hard, physical work, this morning's image of Silver's naked and well-endowed body still haunting him. Starting his day with the image of perfect uptilted breasts, silky skin and the intimate juncture of Silver's thighs, flowing into her long legs, had set his sensual clock ticking. He corrected the thought: Silver had set his senses racing.

He picked his relationships carefully and if he wanted to invite himself to disaster, he just might—

Silver. Hard, reckless, a natural temptress using her powers to get what she wanted. Gossip whispered that she was De La-Fleur's first mistress and protégée and he'd been devoted to her. The perfumer had hoarded his secrets, and only Silver had shared them, proving herself in the industry.

Inside Duncan Tallchief's home, scents of fresh bread and women and babies and love curled around Nick, stopping him in his tracks as they always did. He brought them into him, cherished them, for he was destined to live apart, alone.

This was a home for generations, all loving, and even the death of the Tallchief parents hadn't nicked that love. The legacy that Lloyd Palladin had given his sons hadn't stopped Joel and Rafe from finding happiness, but Nick doubted love was meant for him.

Every time he looked in the mirror, he was reminded that he was Lloyd Palladin's son—tough, cynical and big enough to hurt a woman if his passions ruled him. Living on the borders of his brothers and the Tallchief family, Nick had found a bit of peace and glimpsed how love could cherish and last.

Shadows and light and cooking scents danced through the huge living room, women talking quietly as they had for ages, a soothing sound. The woman dressed in the Tallchiefs' great-great-grandmother's doeskin bridal shift stood in the center of Tallchief House. Her pale hair contrasted with the Sioux warrior's shield on the rock wall, the arrows and bow used by Tallchief. Her fingers lovingly smoothed the old wood of a cradle carved by the warrior for his first child. Light flowed around her, upon her, settling upon the soft turn of her mouth, the vulnerable line of her throat.

The pose was timeless, effective—a bride wistfully touching a cradle that had held children, and longing for her own. The scene slammed into Nick with the force of a baseball bat. If he knew anything about himself at all, he knew that this woman was his.

He heard a soft chuckle and turned to the knowing grin of his brother Joel…but Nick had no time for guffawing, tormenting elder brothers, he only had time to study the woman surrounded by other women, his woman.

"Aye," he heard his brothers murmur behind him, but he had no time for Joel's and Rafe's taunting. He had to deal with the woman he had waited for all his life, bent over a cradle. The timeless tender scene squeezed his heart, slowing the furious flip-flops into an ache to take her into his arms, to shelter and protect her, to comfort and cherish—

For just a heartbeat, he caught Silver's wistful expression, and in the next heartbeat she straightened slowly, head high, single pale braid flowing down her chest across the blue beaded symbols of Tallchief Mountain. Body taut, her legs and feet braced apart in the leggings and moccasins, her stormy gray eyes locked with his.

She'd come for her quest and Nick realized that he wasn't letting her go. He fought the tenderness curling within him, the sight of Silver, dressed as a Tallchief bride, facing him as if they were alone in the room.

She's mine. That knowledge slammed into Nick, and there was nothing he could do but go to her.

"I didn't try on Una's bridal shift because it was lovely doeskin, weighted with pretty sky blue beads and fringes and memories of love. I didn't wear it because it was precious to the Tallchiefs, scented of romance and crushed lavender and kisses and dreams of babies to come. I tried it on because it brought me closer to their hearts, and I need them to think of me as one of their own. That way, I'll have what I want out of them. Then Nick had to ruin it all." Silver breathed in the sage-scented afternoon air carefully, lifting the weights she held in either hand. Dressed in a scooped-neck sleeveless cotton T-shirt and loose shorts, she was sweaty and mad, working off steam in Nick's home.

On her first day in Amen Flats, Nick Palladin had loomed behind her every step—quiet, lethal and putting a crimp in her efforts to get closer to the Tallchiefs. The guardian knight of the Tallchiefs didn't trust her. Fine. They were even.

She smiled tightly and lay down, hands behind her head, and tucked her gym shoes beneath a bar. Feet elevated on the workout bench, head on the floor mat, she began sit-ups. She forced herself to concentrate on her muscles, her breathing, and not the burn of Nick's hot gaze when he saw her in the dress. She touched her knees with opposite elbows before going down and back up, she cursed Nick's black heart for making her own leap and flip-flop at that look, the way he strolled toward her as if he were a hunter latched on to his prey.

"I make my own choices, not him. If I wanted to try on the

dress, it wasn't to please Nick Palladin.'' The sweatband on her forehead was wet, sweat pouring off her body like the temper Nick could raise with one dark, shielded look.

Clearly Nick was a fond member of the family, cuddling babies and kissing cousins' cheeks. Babies came to him for piggyback rides and to feed him bits of cake. He had no right to hold a black-haired, gray-eyed baby upon his lap, rocking her to sleep, nor to let them ride his hip easily, as though he were suited to the feel of a child draped around him. Nick, lying on the floor, buried beneath a flurry of giggling chubby little children and chuckling with delight, would stir any woman's heart.

Silver hurried through another set of elbow-knee exercises. Oh, Nick knew how to get to women. It was his gift. Women had drooled after him in the airport. More than one woman in Amen Flats had almost driven off the road staring at Nick this morning. Silver narrowed her eyes and hurried through another set, furious with Nick. He had a look that made a woman want to smooth back that wave from his forehead—

He was rotten to have the perfect house, a sprawling, warm, sparsely furnished home of wood and shadows, aching for light touches of plants and afghans and a loom by the window where a woman could pass hours dreaming.

As kitchens went, though Silver had cooked little more than sandwiches and frozen dinners in her lifetime, Nick's was big, neat and furnished with that gorgeous, long, sturdy pioneer table. The man liked to cook sturdy food, braids of chili peppers and garlic hung over pottery bowls, another bowl stuffed with cooking tools, green peppers on a wooden chopping board. A black skillet waited on the stove, a rack of evil-looking knives nearby.

The fireplace, taking up one wall, would be perfect in winter, blazing away and warming to the bones. The crock placed carelessly against the wall would be perfect for wildflowers and herbs.

His bedroom was as barren as the rest of the house, and Nick's high-tech black-and-chrome office, an extension of Palladin, Inc. in Amen Flats, had a view of nothing but fields and mountains and wide blue Wyoming sky.

But the laundry room, with its neat shelves and hangers and

worn ironing board and flashy steam iron had been well used, a small television propped upon a shelf, a fancy radio nearby. Nick had smelled like that this morning, of clothing detergent, of softeners and ironing.

Not that she was interested in home and families. Or marrying a potential partner and conceiving a baby—not even with those meadow green eyes and that cleft upon his chin. Silver pushed out the air in her lungs. Clearly she was physically attracted to Nick. All those muscles and cords and lovely tanned skin with the essence of how a man should smell—salty sweat, sage and leather, the hunger humming beneath— There was that lovely untamed tilt to his head, and danger in his dark eyes, like a warrior filled with arrogance and holy manhood, that just made her want to take him down. How he looked at her was enough to start her melting, heating, and she understood none of it. A part of her wanted to leap upon him and take—

There had been other men, interesting, gorgeous ones, but when Nick looked at her intently, he stood out from the pack, enough danger riding him to lift the hair on her nape.

She didn't have time for good-smelling, arrogant men...for big, wary, desirable men who could block her from reaching her goal.

Silver squeezed her lids closed and did a quick series of furious sit-ups. She couldn't afford to be one of his conquests— the message machine had several messages from women wanting more than they said. Mrs. Kelsey, a middle-aged sounding woman, wondered if he'd like to come over for her apple pie...and meet her daughter, Jennifer.

Nicholas Palladin wasn't sweet. When he'd returned from an afternoon of building fences, there was nothing friendly about the way his fiery green gaze immediately locked to her, his muscles taut and rippling beneath his worn shirt and jeans. He stood there, dappled with laughter and sunlight, a big cowboy dressed in long, lean faded jeans, who ripped off his leather gloves impatiently as he looked at her. "Prying out all the little secrets you came for?" he'd demanded softly.

How dare he start nettling her, when she had found the first peace in years?

Peace. Its name wasn't Nick Palladin.

His look had scraped at her, burning, possessive. "Lady," he'd said quietly, firmly, amid the children scrambling for attention, the men wanting food and the women hushing them. Nick's "Lady" had the sound of fascinating secrets left unsaid.

He'll be a fine beast of a man, haughty and proud and strong as a bear, gnawing at the maiden's shields, testing her, claiming her with wicked eyes....

Fantasy and moonlight had curled around the word, stunning her. She was almost afraid of him then, of what he could do, of how he could make her feel— He'd wrapped his hand in her single long braid and had tugged it lightly, playfully.

Silver finished a sit-up and slashed her terry-cloth wristband across her throat, her fingers staying to test her racing pulse. So she was a bleached blonde; so what? Did it matter? And why did the gentle flicker of his dark green eyes enchant her?

Flattening to her back, Silver used a nearby towel to wipe her damp face. She couldn't offend the Tallchiefs' favorite and spoiled bachelor. She'd play him; she'd destroy him.

She rolled her feet back over her head and leaped agilely to her feet. The previous hours' aerobic workout wasn't enough; weights and sit-ups weren't enough to drain the bristling energy in her.

She was so close to her goal, to Jasmine's goal.

She couldn't afford to make an enemy of Nick Palladin.

She hated him for coming to her in a moment when she recognized the depth of love, how it coursed through generations and how much the wedding ceremonies and tradition meant to the Tallchiefs. She hated him for seeing her wrapped in vulnerability, her hand upon the cradle, the startling, earthshaking desire to have a child nestling within her.

With an experienced movement, Silver dusted her palm across the white jasmine blooms on the potted plant and ran her hands over her sweaty arms and legs, keeping Jasmine and her goal close to her. She nipped a jasmine bud and placed it between her breasts, rubbing it gently to free the scent.

She glanced at the serene Tallchief Mountain shading the valley as jutting and hard as Nick Palladin. Outside in the yard, fragrant with wildflowers and meadows, cattle and sheep grazed peacefully. Nick's house…his rules… If she had to live in Nick's house, under his keeping, then she would. Silver quickly jerked on boxing gloves and attacked the punching bag, dancing around it, kicking and hitting it with all her strength.

"Aye!" she muttered, snatching a Tallchief word for a deep emotion, a pledge, and jabbed at the bag. "Here I was feeling sweet and feminine, and he swaggers in from the fields and stares at me as though I've committed a crime…oh, I'd like to—" She side-kicked the bag furiously. "I'd really like to take Nick Palladin's well-shaped backside and—"

Well, never mind what she wanted to do with his backside. Diving into that hard body wasn't on her list. *She didn't have the experience to do what she wanted with his backside.* He had no business looking so raw and primitive, challenging her and then delighted with the children scrambling upon him. The image was too appealing and one she couldn't afford. He had no business making her feel soft and feminine and yearning for love, a touch of a lover, those safe, strong arms encircling her. He had no right to call her "Lady" in that deep, raspy, uneven tone. She couldn't afford any of it.

She shot a furious one-two punch into the bag—it didn't move, Nick's hands holding it. He looked down at her as she wiped a sweaty forearm across her eyes. "Would you like to go a round with me? From the looks of it, you're not done with your snit."

Here he was again, barging in on her privacy when she wasn't prepared for that scent, her heart flip-flopping at the rugged look of him…for without his trappings of civilization, his suit and manners, and dressed in a cowboy's working clothes, Nick was devastating. "Snit? You wouldn't last five seconds. The big ones are easy to bring down…you start at the knees and—" And then she swung at him.

By the end of the week, June had arrived and Silver had not spoken to Nick. He had refused to obey Mamie's orders and apologize for dumping Silver in the horse-watering trough. It was either that or tossing her on the bed where nothing would be secret between them.

Nick's mandatory appearance before his employer and grand-mother, Mamie, cost him a day, flying to Denver and back. Silver's faked sneezes while she talked to Mamie had endangered "The Nose." Mamie had raised the three Palladin brothers, and she'd demanded perfect gentlemanly behavior from all of them. The twist of his ear accompanied Mamie's swift order—Nick was to treat The Nose as a lady, and to make up, he should give her a present. "Something romantic," Mamie had suggested briskly. "You know what women like. You've had enough of them hounding you for years."

"We're not a couple," he had returned, rubbing his ear and remembering Silver's too-sweet smile when she had replaced the phone earlier, ending the call to his grandmother.

On his return to Amen Flats, Nick glanced at the horses, noted the peaceful grazing of the cattle herd in the pasture and knew that Silver had wrecked his comfortable, predictable existence. The woman riding Montoya as though her life depended on the race, bent low in the saddle, was pure trouble, and he didn't want to admire how she handled the horse as though her Tallchief blood gave her that right. She rode the horse close to him, and Nick grabbed the reins. He couldn't resist mocking her, her furious expression pinning him. "Hello, sweetheart. I'm glad to see you, too."

"I'm stuck with *you*. There are three of you Palladins. You look just alike, and I have to be stuck with the contrary rottweiler," Silver stated in a disgusted tone. She swung down from the saddle, leaving him to take care of the Appaloosa gelding. The sweater tightened on her breasts as she placed her hands on her hips, sheathed in tight long jeans. "I am not a happy woman. I've asked the Tallchiefs to help me explore the countryside—to get a feel of the essence I want—and all I get is you. All very polite, of course. I don't want you and you don't want me, so let's do this the easy way. Leave me alone. Stop tagging after me."

"Lady, if I had a choice—"

"Good, we're agreed. You don't interfere with me, where I want to go, what I want to do. If you do, I can make life really rough for you."

Nick forgot his own dark mood and enjoyed the fascinating, furious woman in front of him. "You're good. Mamie bought your faked cold."

"You have no idea how inventive I can be." She breathed uneasily and smoothed Montoya's mottled flank. "Leave me alone, Palladin, or I'll take you out."

He wanted to pick her up, fuse his mouth with her saucy one and kiss her breathless. He'd never played with a woman, taunting her, half afraid he would hurt her with his strength, but with Silver the urge to tease her was too strong. "I love it when you talk dirty."

She stared blankly at him, then straightened immediately, in very proper, feminine outrage. "I have never spoken dirty in my life."

Nick released the grin inside him. "You know you want me."

The blank look slid into fury, her fists shooting to her waist, her legs braced and eyes all slashing hot steel. "I'll tell you what I'm going to do for you, ace—I'll develop a sweet little love potion for you. You wear it, collect a woman who can keep you off my back, and we'll both be happy."

Nick tugged on the long braid flowing over her chest, fingering the silky tip. "Lady, you're stuck with me. Whatever you're up to, I'll be right there."

"Someone should have taught you trust, Nick."

He let that remark slide—trust had been a scarce commodity in his life.

After cooling Montoya, Nick walked into his home, tossed his suitcase onto his favorite wood-and-cushion chair and went to deliver his required present.

Not that he enjoyed prowling through every quaint shop in Denver. Not that he'd ever spent time individualizing a gift for a woman. Not that the antique perfume bottle was romantic and perfect for a woman with iridescent silvery eyes and filled with secrets.

Nick glanced at the changes she'd made in his home, a row of ferns in the shadows, her antique perfume bottles and atomizers placed on a long shelf near the window, the glass sending a myriad of colors off into the shadows.

Nick frowned; he liked shadows. He liked his home uncluttered, just like his life.

The laundry room was a mess, his ironing board frothing with lacy underwear. He glanced at the low walnut coffee table at which he liked to work his puzzles. It was littered with herbs and florist boxes, and one glance at his antique maps, rolled and placed inside a small nail barrel, told him that she'd been prowling.

What was she hunting?

He found Silver, dressed in her lab coat in the new addition he'd had built for her, the view looking out across the meadows to the black waters of Tallchief Lake onto the jutting red cliffs and high meadows of Tallchief Mountain.

In contrast to her usual style, the laboratory was meticulously neat, filled with tubes and decanters and a sketching table near the window. The shelves were neatly lined with tight containers, each labeled in Silver's block business print. At her desk, a small laptop computer was closed and silent.

Nick stopped at the door, studying the woman bent over her craft. She sniffed delicately at a beaker of dark liquid and brushed the fragrance upward to encircle her. Eyes closed, she turned slowly, as through trapping the fragrance inside her, dissecting it. She opened her eyes and found him.

They stared at each other, the sultry scents snaring him delicately. The impact stopped Nick's heart. He wanted to take her in his arms and hold her, simply hold her close and safe, protecting her from whatever drove her to ride Montoya like a demon.

"For you." He tossed the small package to her and hooked his thumbs in his belt to keep from reaching for her to drag her lips to his.

Silver eyed him suspiciously and peeled away the plain brown paper, opening the box. She carefully eased away the tissue protecting the antique-cut glass perfume bottle and stopper.

Nick inhaled abruptly, realizing that he'd been holding his breath, waiting to see if she would take a gift from him.

Silver's pale hair gleamed, the dark roots noticeable as she turned the cut-glass bottle carefully, holding it up to the light and tracing it with her fingertips.

"This is very old and very nice. Thank you." The words, the tone, were proper and sincere, and just for a heartbeat, Nick glimpsed the intriguing feminine softness that ran inside Silver. Then she handed him a notebook and turned back to her work as if he didn't exist.

"These are good," Nick stated after scanning her layouts for advertising labels, marketing techniques and the spin-off soaps, salts and bath powders for the Palladin line. He wanted to prowl through her life, find the missing part and what she was seeking—

"I know. I am good. Now get out of my lab."

Nick settled back into the shadows of Maddy's Hot Spot, Amen Flats' local tavern. On a Saturday night and after a week of Silver, he felt bruised and abused. While the extended Tall-chief family circled the dance floor to country music, Nick leaned his chair back against the wall and brooded about the woman inhabiting his life.

She ate when she wanted—mostly peanut butter and jelly sandwiches—passing through the kitchen with a distracted expression, jerking open the refrigerator door to scan the contents. He doubted that she knew if she had eaten, or when. While she dropped her clothing throughout the house, her laboratory was spotless and ordered. Twice, the sound of Silver sniffing over old movies at midnight had cost Nick sleep. A woman working out frantically in a tiny, thin leotard, her body sweaty and taut as she concentrated, wasn't exactly calming, especially the rhythmic lifting of her hips from the floor. The sensual jolt had slammed into him, sucking his breath from a painfully hardened body.

Now, out on the Hot Spot's dance floor, sheathed in a loose chambray shirt, knotted at the waist, and tight blue jeans, pale hair fanning out as she danced, Palladin's "Nose" had gotten under his skin. Her written memo had reminded him that she required all windows to have a sheer or curtain covering. The lady did not like looking at her reflection; to his disgust, Nick enjoyed looking at her too much.

There were scents in his home, on his clothing, that no righteous man could ignore. He'd reached for the shampoo and found himself scrubbing a flowery scent into his hair. Montoya had tried to throw him; Rafe and Joel had smirked.

Finding a woman's lacy panties in his laundry basket could slam Nick's brain to a full stop. The silky tidbit had clung seductively to his freshly washed jeans and sent a flying punch into his lower belly.

Walking into the bathroom every morning was torture. The scents from her long, luxurious bath could drive a man over the edge. After taking his shower, he was certain that he wore her scent. For a confirmed bachelor, the mark of her possession was unsettling, as though she had claimed him and he was powerless. Nick didn't appreciate his brothers sniffing him and grinning. Nostrils flaring, Montoya had backed away from Nick.

Silver had allowed him a small shaving mirror and had removed the rest expertly, as though she'd done it many times. Her reflection in a glass window could startle her, pale her cheeks as she rubbed her hands lightly over the glass surface, as though wanting to plunge into the reflection and grasp it.

The professional woman beneath the huge glasses and the lab coat was one person—absentminded, leaving half-eaten sandwiches behind her, clothing on the bathroom floor—the sight of her lacy bra flung on top of the shower stall had stopped him in his tracks. When engrossed in her formulas, moving in and out of the laboratory, she'd wear whatever was at hand, including his white dress shirt, which reached past her thighs. Her safaris into his laundry room often produced the stunning picture of Silver wearing his overlarge T-shirts and shorts. The novelty of having a desirable woman wear his clothing had definitely poleaxed him.

The woman on the dance floor, laughing as she danced with any available male, had a secret that caused her to cry at night and drove her ruthlessly. For tonight, she'd given herself to release, enjoying the Tallchief outing at the local bar.

While Silver enjoyed herself, dancing a two-step with Maddy, the beefy bartender, Nick considered the woman who had just moved into Rafe's arms, laughing up at him. Rafe, a happily married man, shot a devilish grin at Nick, who scowled back.

"So how is it? Living with a woman after hoarding yourself for all these years? You're definitely smelling...seductive." Joel seated at the same table, flicked the price tag on a plastic rose, Maddy's concession to decor in the noisy bar.

"The whole house smells like a woman," Nick grumbled.

"Yeah. Life with a good smelling woman is hell all right. Especially one that looks like Silver. That cowboy dancing with her might like to take your place." Joel stood up and wrapped his arms around his wife, who kissed him long and hungrily.

Nick found Silver in the shadows, pasted to a tall cowboy who was tasting her ear. His hand slid low on Silver's lush behind, sheathed in jeans, and Nick tensed.

She was a desirable woman; he had no claim on her. Yet if that cowboy's hand moved a fraction lower—

The cowboy grimaced painfully and jerked away from Silver, who smiled coolly.

Nick settled back in his chair, startled that his muscles had tensed, ready to leap to Silver's defense. The lady could handle herself; she didn't need Nick's protection.

Nick settled back into the shadows, nursing his foamy draft brew. There wasn't one reason she should appeal to him...one reason he should want to knock that cowboy into the street...one reason he wanted to lay her down and claim her for his own.

Silver laughed up at Joel, who had just enclosed her in his arms, his wife flinging off to dance with her brother, Duncan. Under the barroom light, Silver swirled out from under Joel's arm, her hair fanning out pale and thick. Nick imagined her hair as black and glossy as a raven's wing, an inheritance from her Sioux chieftain ancestor. None of the images matched. The woman was pure trouble, and he wasn't getting involved.

Five

Silver laughed up at Joel, her arms around him as they danced to the country and western music. "You and Rafe look exactly like Nick, except you two are lots sweeter," she said. She didn't care one bit that Miss Tight Jeans and Nursing Mother Breasts had laminated herself to Nick's sizable, hard body. Silver had avoided coming close to him; she didn't care one bit that every woman in the room was angling to get close to Nick.

She didn't care that with other women, Nick Palladin was Mr. Charm and Seduction, his slow, easy smile causing them to melt and drool. If his devastating, slow, easy smile could be packaged, Palladin, Inc. wouldn't need to produce a male fragrance line. Men could just splash themselves with Nick's magnetic scent, and women would flock to them.

Mr. Charm sat in the shadows now, bracing his brew on his flat stomach and glowering at her. He disapproved of her, not that she was fond of him. "Your brother has primitive tendencies."

"He has a few rough edges when he's around you. We've

been tamed," Joel noted with a grin. "Nick still has to go through the process."

Silver glanced at Nick, sitting in the shadows, his legs propped on another chair as he glowered at her. "Now that's a thought. Why don't you find him some nice little sweet girl and settle his playboy bottom down? Then we can all have some peace."

"We're saving him. He's had women chasing him for years, and it's only fair that he find one he can chase."

"I'm not in the mood." After a full week of Nick looming near her, she enjoyed the release at the local bar, complete with nude paintings disguised temporarily with sheets. The pungent scents of beer, pretzels and peanuts, and laughter were easy, unlike the persistent taut fear that she could fail, and she flung herself into them.

Through the crowded room, Silver caught glances of Nick— surging from his chair, moving toward her like a stalking hunter. Though shadows obscured his face, she recognized the swagger, the broad shoulders blocking out the dim light. For once, she didn't have to pretend, to avoid mirrors, to try harder to be more…to push herself into exhaustion. Her body and senses lurched into alert, hungrily anticipating a raw, honest encounter with Nick.

Nick towered over her, his big hands reaching for her waist. His expression was grim, challenging and just what she wanted. She met his hard stare with her own and walked into the duel, senses quaking— She reached up with both arms to hold him, moving close to two-step with him—

She'd wanted to toss a flip challenge at him, but his arms enclosed her firmly, big hands flattening on her body, claiming her. He tugged her against him hard enough to push the air from her lungs—or was that the clamoring of her heart? She caught Nick's scent before he bent to place his mouth exactly on hers, slanting and taking the kiss deeper before she could push him away.

He caught her close and hard, his chest tight against her breasts, his arms pushing cords and muscles at her, his hands open and claiming. He wasn't leaving her, not when she had him in her grasp—Silver locked her arms around him and held on as the world spun around her....

He tasted of wild mountain storms, of devastating hunger, of souls flying through time, of a primitive beat that she had to catch. Silver dived deeper into his scents, wallowed in them, digging her fingers into his shoulders, sliding them through his hair. Thigh to thigh, stomach to stomach, heart to heart, nothing separated them but cloth. Here, now, everything was real... honest, his skin rough against hers, tantalizing...

Silver had to have more, reaching to cradle Nick's rugged face in her palms, keeping his lovely, tempting mouth close to hers, tracing the intriguing shape with her light kisses and waiting for his.

Tastes swirled around her, wonderful exciting tastes and scents and images of tenderness dappled with fire and strength.

She forgot everything but the delight, the tempting hunger of his mouth, lightly brushing hers, finding her ear, his uneven breath warm against her skin. She could float like this forever, moving gently, cradled by his body, secure, protected, wanted, needing—

In the midst of discovery, her professional mind clicked on for a millisecond and labeled Nick as an aphrodisiac, as sheer, undiluted pleasure; then she was spinning again, delighted by the power and the hunger of the man in her arms.

He shuddered, his skin warm against her palms, so roughly alive, textures dancing beneath her touch, waiting to be explored.

There was more, that soft melting that had come creeping upon her, winding magically inside her bones, creating a song that hummed in her veins.

There was no mistaking the hardened shape of his body, the way his open hand pressed into the shadows behind her, low and intimate, where no one could see and mock, binding her close to him.

Then, slowly, slowly, Nick eased from her, leaving her weak, his hands supporting her where before they had caressed. When she forced her lids to open, dazed by the emotions she had never felt, never wanted to pursue, Nick's jade gaze burned into her. "Stand and fight," he murmured.

Silver shook her head, clearing it, her lips still tasting the heated pulse of his mouth. "What?"

"The Tallchiefs have a saying—'Stand and fight.' Are you up to it? With me? You like kissing me, lady, and we've got a real problem."

Fury trembled, snapped, bit into her. Nick had taken his fill and stepped back from her, leaving her before she was finished dining upon him.

Silver fought her temper. "I like kissing, in general. You're not my first set of lips, you know," she managed to say as she moved away from him.

"Try again. You kiss like an innocent, sweetheart," Nick murmured huskily before he brushed her lips with his and she could taste his delight and his hunger.

In the next heartbeat, he had turned and was making his way out of Maddy's Hot Spot.

"You can't walk away from me like that, Palladin," Silver stated as Nick got into his pickup. Amen Flats' sheriff cruised by, his Italian tenor cassettes crooning to the moonlit night. Howling dogs accompanied the music, and in Maddy's Hot Spot, Patty Jo Black, a farmwife, began a throaty sexy song with Ed Rambo's heavy beat guitar.

"I just did walk away from you, and from a mountain of trouble neither one of us needs." Nick started the engine and placed the pickup in gear, needing to be alone with his thoughts. He left her standing alone, in the middle of the lamplit street, hands braced on her waist. The lady had tasted sweet and tender and hungry. His first taste of her slammed desire into Nick, and the need to possess her, to claim her. In that fierce heartbeat, he knew that she was his and that beneath the playgirl wrapper was an innocent. Another minute of that hungry petal-soft mouth beneath his, those fierce little gasps of pleasure as he tasted her, another second of her lush body pressing soft and warm against his, and Nick would have been unable to walk for a week.

He'd reached for an experienced woman and found an innocent, the discovery slamming into him, stunning him.

He glanced at the deer caught in his headlights, slowing for the passage of the small herd into the lush meadows high in the mountains.

Nick geared down to take the rough road leading to Tallchief Lake. Sex wasn't the real problem; he'd always been in control of his body, understanding its needs. With Silver, deeper emotions snagged at him, the protective ones, those tender little bites slamming him off balance when he didn't expect the punch. Joel and Rafe had settled their demons, but their women weren't Silver and he wasn't his brothers. He'd kept his emotions untapped, leashed, and while on the surface he cruised through life easily, Silver had reached her slender fingers into him and torn at the darkness prodding him. Tonight there was enough passion in him to hurt her—he opened his hands studying them. They were big hands, and he was a big man, with the same strength as his father. In passion, he could bruise Silver's smooth skin, and the thought frightened the hell out of him. He ran his shaking hands over his steering wheel and forced himself to breathe evenly. He wasn't affected one bit by Silver Tallchief.

The hard ache from his knees up to his scalp mocked him, pounded at him.

Nick rubbed his hand across his eyes. His father had raped a woman in front of Nick when he was just five, and now, the violent image slammed into him. With Silver, he could be just as forceful, as hungry and self-serving. He couldn't afford to do that to any woman, much less an innocent.

How the hell did a man, pushed by desire, take an innocent and walk away?

Nick settled into driving, listening to the purr of the engine and let the night enclose him. He'd kept his life on course—he inhaled shakily, remembering Silver's graceful body sheathed in Una's bridal shift.

"Stand and fight." What right did he have to enter the Tallchief family, suck mottoes from them and toss them at Silver? The only family he'd had was his brothers, and now they were happy with families; that should be enough. He could live on the borders of their lives—watching the love flow between them and their wives and children. But after one taste of Silver, Nick re-

alized that he wanted more than his mechanical life, living on
the fringes of other lives....

Headlights lasered into his rearview mirror, blinding him.
Whoever was driving behind him on the lonely winding road
down to Tallchief Lake was coming up fast, handling the road—
Nick narrowed his eyes, studying the headlamps of the vehicle
behind him—with the expertise of a race car driver. Smaller than
his pickup truck and probably faster on level, paved road, the
driver brought the vehicle to Nick's back bumper.

Nick smiled coolly at the expected jolt to his pickup. He
rubbed the scars across his knuckles, earned from when he and
his brothers brawled in alleys, fighting to survive. If that was a
drunken cowboy and his friends wanting to pick a fight, Nick
was up to the task. Tonight, he was in the mood for a refresher
course—anything to take his mind from the discovery that Silver
was an innocent, very likely a virgin. A woman's virginity—now
that was an unstable commodity that he had never wanted to
experience.

He eased onto a bumpy side road and, beneath the moonlit
pines, parked near the lake. He got out slowly, noted the owl
coursing high against the night sky, leaned against his pickup
and waited.

The headlamps blinded him slightly, and the outline of a long
legged, tall woman, packed with enough curves to send him aching again, stalked toward him. Her open hand slapped her thigh
rhythmically as though she'd like to apply it to his cheek.

The lady could drive; she dived into challenges like a woman
driven to win. Why did she live every day as though she had to
pack two lifetimes into it?

Silver shoved her finger into his chest, prodding him. "What's
the big idea? Just who do you think you are? What gives you
the right to kiss me like that?" Her voice raised, indignant fury
entering it as the night breeze brought her scent to him. "You
walked away."

"Why don't you pack that really nice rear end back in that
pickup and drive carefully the hell away from me?" Nick suggested in a cooler tone than he felt. In another minute, he'd be
reaching for her, and he didn't like the uncertainty of kissing a

volatile, hungry virgin. He rubbed his hand along his jaw and glared at her.

She folded her arms, braced her long legs apart and smirked. "We're monogamous, remember? I'll bet that's crimping your playboy style. Your dance card was pretty full at Maddy's."

Nick couldn't resist. He strolled his fingertip down her flushed cheek to her soft bottom lip; he tapped it lightly. "Why don't you just leave me alone?"

"My, my. Was that a big, daddy-bear growl I just heard? Do you really think I have a nice rear end?" she insisted in a flirtatious tone, leaning closer, and Nick groaned silently. She placed her hand along his cheek, and Nick caught her fragrance, his heartbeat kicking up.

Why had he just placed a kiss against that slender, delicate hand as if it was his right and his need? He jerked his head away from her touch.

Silver leaned closer, peering up at him. "I'm actually frightening you, aren't I? You've got that dark, closed look, your eyebrows drawn together in that fierce line—"

She smoothed his eyebrows, and Nick jerked his head back. "Wary of me, darling?" she crooned, and stood on tiptoe to nip his bottom lip.

She'd pushed through his defenses. Nick caught her close, unsettled by his emotions. He feared the strength in his hands, her slender body nestled next to his, the emotions slamming hot and fierce into him. Then, with a reluctant groan, he took her mouth as he wanted, opening himself to her, diving into the woman beneath the secrets and feeding upon her.

"Nick?" She tensed at the touch of his open hand easing onto her breast, cupping her lightly.

Did she want him to stop? Could he?

With one arm around her waist, Nick hiked her off the ground, nuzzled that fragrant softness and found the hardened mystery of the tip, suckling gently through her shirt.

Silver's hand held him close, her body trembling, the sounds coming from deep inside her, begging, startling him. Beneath his mouth her pulse kicked up, flames leaped between them and the urge to take her slammed into Nick painfully. "Is this what you want?" he asked, taking care to open her chambray shirt, button by button.

His throat dried at the sight of her breasts, lovely, cupped by lace and satin. There was a moment of protest, when Silver looked up at him helplessly, torn by her emotions.

"I have to—" She didn't need to finish the sentence and gasped when Nick's hand covered her breast. She went taut, sucking in air too rapidly, and panic flew across her face, sharpening it. Beneath his hand and the silky soft mound, her heart raced and a long shudder slid through her, an uneven sigh of pleasure. Her hands fluttered, then locked to him, fingertips digging in.

"At least this is honest," he murmured, trailing his fingertip across the lacy bra and finding, one by one, the twin peaks nestled in the satin.

Another ripple of her body told him that the stakes had just been raised. He'd barely touched her and she'd ignited. An experienced woman would have— Nick studied Silver's intent, flushed face, the quiver of her lips and the trembling of her body. Raw sexual need battled with something else Nick didn't trust and didn't like—the dark forces that could rule him. He glared at the woman who had torn him from the safety of his easy, practiced charm. He was angry at himself, at her— "You're a virgin, aren't you? You don't have the slightest idea of what to do next."

She stiffened, head jerking back, eyes flashing up at him. "I've got a good idea of the mechanics. I'm not asking you for a safari, Palladin."

"Then you'd better stop kissing me like that," he warned, and jerked the edges of her shirt together in his fist. He lowered her feet to the ground, jerked her to him and wished he weren't shaking with the need to take her. "Got it?"

"You're not very sweet," she said between her teeth, and sank her fingertips deeper into his shoulder.

The silent warning only set him off, made him want more. "Never have claimed to be, but I'm the man who is going to be in your bed, and you're going to tell me a few things before that happens. We'll take it from there."

"Sex on your terms? When you want? I could have you in one minute flat." She wasn't giving him anything, tossing back a challenge on a platter.

Nick smiled, feeling suddenly boyish. Silver did that, ripping off the scars and giving him a taste of delight, of youth and life. He let the light, easy laughter curl through him, warming him. He tugged her closer, his knuckles brushing those soft breasts, lingering against the hardened delicate peaks. "It takes longer than that, honey. I intend to be very careful with you. There's all that sweet kissing to get warmed up—and I do enjoy those hungry little noises you make."

"I make my own decisions, Palladin. You're trying to set up your own schedule, and I've never dealt well on someone else's terms. Now, let me think—duh—I think you're old-fashioned, the man setting the pace. Well, ace, times have changed."

He almost laughed aloud. "What are you going to do, sweetheart? Haul me to your cave and have me? This is a joint decision, Silver. There were two people in that kiss. You tried to suck my soul out of me. Maybe you did, for just that heartbeat."

He fought the need to kiss her and knew the disaster that waited for them— "I know who I am, where I come from...I don't believe in legends and bonding like the Tallchiefs. Aye," he said, reminding her of her Scots heritage, "you won't find me offering a bridal price for you. I'll wear the Tallchiefs' kilts and hold their babies, but dreams and legends aren't for me. I'm not your prince, fair lady."

The cold, bare truth of what he was, of what his heritage had made him, settled around Nick like a shroud. He allowed her to tug his hand away, her warmth lingering on his skin. "I haven't asked you to be my prince...you are a typical, thickheaded, arrogant, traditional male, packed with a hefty ego.... I am checking out," she said tightly, furiously, and turned to walk to her vehicle.

Oh, hell, Nick thought as Silver's four-wheeler barreled out of sight. He looked at the icy lake, measured the ache low in his body and began to strip.

Moments later, he furiously plowed through the icy water, arm over arm, grimly determined to freeze his need for Silver. The call from shore caused him to stop, treading the black, whitecapped water. Silver stepped from the shadows of the pines onto a moonlit rock and held his clothing up high. "Hey, Palladin. Be quiet when you come in tonight, will you? You won't be needing these—you've got all that lovely arrogance to keep you warm."

After an hour of reading Elizabeth's letters to Una once more, snuggling down with the latest issue of *Scents Magazine*, and eating a huge rewarmed cinnamon roll from Elspeth, Silver listened to Nick's pickup skid to a stop. He slammed into the house a moment later. While the shower ran, she smiled, nestled in her bed, glanced at the chair propped against the doorknob and smoothed the Tallchief plaid Elspeth had made for her.

She caressed Elizabeth's old letters, carefully wrapped in blue frayed ribbon and kept safely by the Tallchief family all these years. Added to the letters Silver already possessed, these letters told of Elizabeth's love, how it grew each day for Liam Tallchief. The carved cedar box containing the letters, preserved in a bed of wildflowers, rose petals and lavender, had been found by Sybil and returned to the Tallchiefs.

When Nick had kissed her tenderly, she hadn't expected the delight or the hunger, or the need to fling herself at him— She listened to Nick prowling through the kitchen—comfortable, friendly sounds. Not that Silver wanted to share her life with him; she couldn't. Peanut butter and jelly sandwiches had served her well enough through the years.

Nick's footsteps passed into his room, and Silver settled down, punching her pillow and hugging it close. A squeak at the door brought her sitting up in bed; Nick slowly pushed the door open, the chair skidding over the wood floor until it toppled.

The dim light from the moonlit window caught his cold smile, his shoulder gleamed, braced against the doorway. He placed his bare foot on the fallen chair and shoved it aside as if nothing could keep him from her. "Having fun, are we?"

"You really shouldn't go skinny-dipping, Mr. Palladin." Silver managed to keep her tone very, very prim.

"Uh-huh," he said tightly, a muscle tensing in his jaw.

He was so nettled, so tasty looking, dressed only in his jeans, that Silver couldn't help grinning at him. "Is our monogamous relationship over, dear?"

The light strolled down the triangle of hair on his chest to his flat stomach. "An experienced woman would know not to taunt a man she has just kissed the living daylights out of."

"Me? *I* kissed you?"

"That's how I see it, sweetheart. *You* kissed me," he murmured smugly. "*You* came to me. If we're having the relationship you want, it's one-to-one all the way and there are rules."

"You make me sound like I'm interested. Like I would actually let you set rules for me... I could put my hands around that big, thick, arrogant neck and squeeze slowly."

"There you are again, wanting to put your hands on my body. Please be gentle," he murmured before leaving her room and quietly closing the door behind him.

"Fiona will have Ian here at one o'clock for you to baby-sit.... Aye, you're in a mood, little brother." Joel slapped a paper-wrapped parcel down on the barn bench near Nick. The mid-June morning rang with meadowlarks and calves frisking in the fields, cows calling to them.

"Two weeks of Silver would do that to anyone, and if you tell her that she's getting to me, I won't baby-sit. You'll lose all those summer nights camping in that tepee with your wife." Nick, who was pounding nails into the corral fence, tossed the hammer aside and ripped off his leather gloves. He tossed Joel a piece of the Silver-puzzle. "The woman doesn't like mirrors."

"Or you?"

Nick eyed Joel's smirk; a man had to keep his pride with older brothers. "Women like me. I'm cute and lovable. I'm charming."

Joel chuckled and punched Nick's shoulder, a friendly blow, but with enough power to remind Nick that they were equally matched. "Baby brother, give it up. Make it easy on yourself. Apologize to her, do what you have to do to make her see that she's the only woman you've really wanted. Right now, she's in the lead and you're wearing big, bad bear signs. Mamie, by the way, is delighted with The Nose. Grandmother said she knew she'd saved you for some reason, and now she knows why. She'd really like you to—''

"Say it and die,'' Nick warned darkly, too aware of Mamie's shielded matchmaking comments.

Joel smirked and looked at Silver walking toward the house, dressed in a cotton T-shirt and long, tight jeans, her arms filled with a wildflower and lavender bouquet. "Now *that* is a woman. Got to be going. Married life, you know. That's a copy of my favorite cookbook. Women require more than steak and potatoes and chili. I saw The Nose working out on the high school's gymnastic equipment, and from her skill, flipping over bars and flinging through the air, I'd say she hasn't spent much time in the kitchen. You'll have to learn. Feeding women helps the taming process—yours.''

He ducked the bucket Nick tossed at him.

Silver returned from her long, lonely walk from Elspeth's and a lovely afternoon poring over Una's journals. Just as they had for the two and a half weeks of her visit, the flock of sheep scattered, flowing over the peaceful green meadows. Amen Flats and the Tallchief families were timeless, a Camelot that slid lovingly from generation to generation. And somewhere in the lime green meadows high on Tallchief Mountain, or in the jutting rocks, or in Tallchief Lake, Elizabeth's gray pearls waited—

Silver swept out a hand and ripped a tall stalk of buffalo grass from its mooring, crushing it. The Tallchiefs cared too easily, and enjoyed her prowling through their legends, their inheritance. They weren't making it easy, claiming her for their own when she had just escaped her own family. She'd had enough layers of guilt to last a lifetime.

Why did Elspeth have to show Silver how to sit at the loom, thought to be Una's, to weave the timeless patterns? Why did Elspeth tell her to feel the wool, listen to what her heart tells her to do and to follow it? Elspeth saw too much, with her Celtic seer and Native American shaman gifts.

Silver couldn't afford to be in any pattern again in her lifetime—the loss when the family came unraveled had hurt too much. With Jasmine, they'd been happy, complete— Silver turned to study the mountain range, the high meadows and jutting rocks that had reminded her great-great-grandmother of Scotland.

Sybil, Duncan Tallchief's wife and an expert genealogist, was searching for more of the Tallchief legacy. She knew that Elizabeth had written many letters to her friends and family in England, and yet only a few had survived. Those that had were in Silver's keeping, and she didn't intend to share.

She would mislead the Tallchiefs into sharing everything, and yet she wouldn't give them honesty. She couldn't bear to let them know about Jasmine, about the dreams they'd shared, their lives twined together so closely they were of one mind, one heart. She'd come for a purpose, to wrest information and the pearls from the Tallchiefs' keeping; now guilt clenched her, so heavy with selfish greed and fear that it took away her breath.

Another predator, Nick sensed that she moved toward her goal, and she could not forgive him for that.

Those dark green eyes traced her movements in the lab, mocked her, until she wanted to pounce upon him, feed upon him.

How dare he reach into her and tug at dreams she'd killed long ago?

How dare he make her want him, challenge her, when he knew that she rose to challenges too easily?

How dare he touch her, kiss her, look at her body, her breasts and place his lovely mouth upon her? How could she know that exquisite beauty of his mouth could tug so violently at her needs?

How dare he place his kiss into the very center of her palm for safekeeping? Silver scrubbed her palms against her jeaned thighs, and yet the tenderness of the light kiss remained. She couldn't have him interfering with the path she had chosen.

And he would, for he was the hunter now, watching her.

She pushed thoughts of Nick away, not an easy task when her body was humming with the need of his. *I'm the man who is going to be in your bed....* After the brief shudder, a sudden sensual awakening escaped her, Silver refocused on her goal— The pearls waited for her and she would have them and then Jasmine could rest.

In her letters, Elizabeth had written, "I've flung my pearls into the black abyss, for I would easily sacrifice jewels and riches so that my fine, tall and dark lord, Liam Tallchief, can keep his pride. The villains had torn them from me that day we met, and Liam returned them to me, circled them around my throat with his own hands. It was then I knew the magic of the man and of the pearls, and with that gesture, he placed himself within my heart. May the pearls rest in the gloomy shadows until another woman's heart reaches out for love and comes searching for them."

The "gloomy shadows" could have been any of the caves on Tallchief Mountain, or resting in its shadow, flowing over the meadows. Silver bent to touch a thornbush budding with pink wild roses. "This is not moving fast enough, Jasmine. Nick is at my every turn. He isn't a man who can be misled...well, there was that virgin thing. No gentleman would say something like that, but he isn't nice. He knows I want something, the problem is— Aye, I do want him. He's like a volatile, wary, untested scent that fascinates me. The mix of base, middle and top notes is too intriguing. He's cocky, arrogant, and not malleable at all. Then he's boyish, and devastating, and tormenting and—he's so vulnerable to his past, fearing it, fearing himself. I understand him on that level—"

She opened the door to scents of baking and casseroles, the sounds of washer and dryer humming and the sight of a tall, powerfully built cowboy balancing a toddler on his hip and chuckling. Half pulled free from the rod, the sheer panel swathed the man and child, the toddler's chubby hand locked to the fabric. When he saw Silver, little Ian Palladin held up the panel to play a gurgling peekaboo.

Nick's smile died slowly. He stood holding the green-eyed toddler, who looked just like him. Silver's heart stopped as Nick's gaze locked with hers, the toddler investigating his ear with a chubby finger.

Silver panicked; she had to escape the softness of the scene curling around her heart. Locked to the floor and tangled in dreams and tenderness, her booted feet refused to move.

"Come here," Nick ordered quietly over the loud flip-flop of her heart.

Silver shivered. This was the dream she'd shared with Jasmine long ago—a home, complete with a man holding a baby and—

"Come here, sweetheart," Nick repeated more softly.

Sweetheart. Her? Stripped of challenges, the word vibrated inside her, thrilled her, blanketed her with dreams gone long ago.

Silver locked her icy hand on the doorknob. "Home" wasn't for her, or green-eyed warlords with babies on their hips. She had pearls to find, and then she would be free—

She backed against the door, flattening to it, trying to suck air into her lungs. Children and husbands and homes...

Nick walked slowly to her. He snapped a stalk of jasmine on the way, tucking it over her ear. His kiss was too light, too sweet, too tender, brushing her parted lips. "Tell me what you want," he said simply.

She wanted Jasmine alive and laughing; she wanted her family happy and complete, she wanted the huge Montclair pearls and not the baby who had squealed and leaped into her arms, all chubby, fragrant and soft. She wanted freedom from the shadows, not the green-eyed man who saw too much as the baby toyed with her hair and claimed her heart.

The telephone's ring tore her from the moment, and she hurried for freedom, away from Nick. She reached for the telephone, her hand shaking, and her brother's voice slid through the miles to her. "Glynis?"

Glynis. The name shattered her, shredding the previous moment. It had been "Glynis and Jasmine" for the first seventeen years of her life. Now Jasmine was gone and Silver had emerged, terrified that she had survived, that she had sinned by simply living.

"Don't call me again," Silver said quietly, the icy shroud, her desperation folding around her once more. Fearing that Nick would see her tears, she pushed the baby at him.

In the morning he was gone, soaring off into the sky and leaving her free.

A day without Nick Palladin looming behind her was enough, and she'd set the stage for freedom with a scribbled note—*Visiting a friend for a week*—and set off to explore Tallchief Mountain. She'd had one good day upon the mountain, following the trail the Tallchiefs had for generations, upward to the meadows and the jutting rocks and caves; an experienced horsewoman, she handled Montoya easily. In the evening, after harvesting a bouquet of mountain wildflowers, Silver banked the campfire, placing ashes over the coals, ready to be scraped back in the morning. She crouched beside the fire and listened to Tallchief Mountain settling for the night, coyotes howling at the moon, birds roosting, rustling the limbs, owls on high branches, watching for prey—

The night breeze riffled through Silver's short-cropped hair, the bleached strands cut before leaving Nick's ranch. She'd hurried to dress, to saddle Montoya, to meet her fate. She wanted to hunt on the mountain like a Tallchief, her Sioux blood rising, eager for the search. Her climbing gear was safely tucked in the Palladin, Inc. tent, borrowed from Nick, and tomorrow she would climb the jutting cliffs. Tethered for night, Montoya nickered, lifting his head, hooves stamping uneasily and then he settled, staring into the forest's shadows.

Sprawled before the campfire, Silver inhaled the fresh scents of pine and earth and studied the meadow, the stream rippling quietly. A peanut butter and jelly sandwich would serve as her meal, but for now she wanted to enjoy the night without Nick and the emotions that he aroused. He'd tossed her young dreams at her feet, offering no bridal price, no prince, no legends, no bonding—

She ran her hands through her hair, the short spiky feel of the natural glossy black strands almost sensuous against her palms. The new cropped length was easier to manage, taking less time, and Silver needed time to hunt— Elizabeth's "gloomy shadows" could be a small canyon, not a moonlit lush meadow that had reminded Una of Scotland. To find the pearls, Silver needed her inheritance of a Sioux shaman and a Celtic seer. She listened to the night, and it gave her nothing but delicious, dark scents.

She scanned the stars and wallowed in her freedom, a day pried away from Nick's watchful eyes. She couldn't afford the panic and the painful tenderness that lurched, alive and vibrating, when she saw him, or the sheer, throbbing hunger.

She folded her arms across her knees and rested her forehead on them, the Tallchief tartan draped around her shoulders. She was too tired to fight away dreams of Nick holding her, that sweet kiss and the dark, passionate hunger.

"He'll be a fine beast of a man, haughty and proud and strong as a bear, gnawing at the maiden's shields, testing her, claiming her with wicked eyes and the pearls nestled in his hand. If he places them upon her, warmed by his flesh, and gives her a sweet kiss, the pearls will be her undoing. Then their hearts will join forever."

Silver scrubbed her face with her hands, willing herself not to think of Nick. She wrapped her arms around her bent knees and rocked herself. She had to find—

A stick cracked behind Silver, just as the back of her denim jacket was gripped and used to haul her to her feet, spinning her around. A man's big, leather encased fist gripped the front of her jacket.

Six

In the firelight, the man towering over her was unshaven and there wasn't a friendly, forgiving thing about his scowl. She should have been frightened; she wasn't. At the sight of him, a tiny thrill of pleasure swept over her. Nick's fist remained clamped on the front of her jacket, and he shook her once, hard. "Visiting a friend, are you? Isn't that what you wrote in your note, to keep me from finding you? Didn't you think I'd notice my missing camping gear? Exactly who were you planning to visit? A bear? Or a mountain lion?" he flung at her.

That surprising warm glow of pleasure surrounding Silver's heart shriveled.

He dodged the swing she took at him, and sidestepped the kick. He shook her again, and hitched her up a notch until her toes barely touched the ground. Nick's narrowed, accusing glare was waiting, level with hers. "Do you have any idea what could have happened to you on this featherbrained escapade?"

It was difficult to threaten him when she was hanging from his fist, but she managed. She slapped the Tallchief tartan over her shoulder with as much dignity as she could manage. "Let me go, Palladin. I've had enough of your bullying."

"Bullying? Me?" he roared loud enough to wake those dangerous mountain animals. For an instant, Nick's expression went blank as though he had stunned himself. Then he glared at her, nostrils flaring and jaw set as the echo shot off the mountain and curled around them. Then he said too quietly and between his teeth, "I...never...yell."

"You just did. Don't blame it on me." Because she couldn't let him push her around, terrorize her, without returning the favor, Silver grabbed fistfuls of his jacket and shook.

While the night breeze danced in his longer hair, tangling the waving strands up and into the night, Nick didn't budge; he peered at her. "What are you doing?"

"Shaking you. Darn you—shake." The powerful muscles and bone remained solid and unmoving, but Nick lowered her feet to the ground. If she'd had bones and flesh that obeyed, she'd be off and running. Instead, she murdered him with her stare. Slayed him and made him crawl. His devastating, delighted grin said she had truly terrified him.

"Why?" he asked curiously, tilting her head to study her cropped hair with interest, while he held her imprisoned in one arm.

She ducked and swatted at the big hand skimming across her head, rubbing and exploring her short hair. "I'm furious, that's why. You've just scared the life out of me, you jerk."

She must have imagined he'd chuckled just then, because didn't he know that she was furious with him?

He crushed her to him, grinning. He bit her chin lightly, startling her, and moved to nibble on her ear. "Aye, you're frightened—monogamy with me terrifies you...admit it. Now give me a kiss and tell me you're glad to see me."

Toes off the ground again, arms pinned at her sides, Silver opened her mouth to tell him where he could go and found his mouth fused to hers. Oh, he was an arrogant savage all right, she thought dizzily, before sinking deeper into the kiss and giving it back with the hunger that had leaped out of her.

She could have twisted her mouth away. She could have bit

that tormenting, tantalizing tongue that sought and claimed bold entrance to her. Instead, she met him in battle, pushed her mouth against his and slayed him with greed and hunger, drinking in the taste of him, the unique scents of Nick Palladin. *Nick. Real...raw...solid...*

His hands opened upon her, then caressed, circling her nape. He eased her head back, allowing him to trail kisses along her throat.

Silver latched her hands to his hair, fisting the heavy waves, keeping him close, devouring him, until they were both panting, glittering hot-eyed at each other and hearts pounding for another round.

Lips swollen, tasting of him, she managed to pant, "I got to you, didn't I, Palladin?"

"I'm not so far gone that I won't recover. But the next time you feed upon me, you're staying for dinner," he snapped back unevenly, glaring at her.

"Dessert." She upped the ante with a grin, magic singing through her veins, carrying her inches above the ground.

His eyes scalded down the length of her body, draped in the tartan, and back up, heating her skin despite the cold mountain air. They were equal now, each hungry for the other; predators, standing toe-to-toe, pretenses ripped away and not willing to give the other an inch. "On your terms?"

"Always." She shrugged, too tense to be casual. She wanted to haul him into her tent and ravish him. She studied him as she slowly circled him, appraising his nice backside and broad shoulders. Ravishing a man Nick's size could take—she had no idea how long or the method of seduction. She patted his tense jaw, and stayed to stroke the stubble beneath her palm. "A gentleman would make this easy for me."

"Saving time and avoiding complications, you mean." His hand swept over her cropped hair, rubbing it as if he were a friendly brother. His palm met her nose and he pushed her back a step, setting his own rules and distance between them. "You've left your mane on the bathroom floor."

She wanted the heat back, not the control or the tenderness in his expression. "Scared you, didn't it?"

His low whistle brought an Appaloosa mare to him, and Nick began unsaddling her. "If I didn't know how contrary you could be, I might have worried."

"I did make you worry, didn't I?" she persisted, anxious to have him admit her victory, to wrench it away from his grasp.

"My only worry was how you would sit in the saddle on the way down after I finished the spanking you deserve.... I'm hungry. Feed me, will you?" he asked, as though they'd shared a lifetime together and he expected her to have his supper ready.

His request and his arrogance took her back a step. Nick braced his legs and looked down at her, eyes flickering beneath his lashes, testing her. When her tongue unlocked, she managed to say, "I don't cook and you know it."

He crouched to forage in her backpack and groaned when lace panties caught on his glove. He stared at them as if they were ready to bite him, then impatiently jammed them back into the tangled pack. He stood, muttering, "Peanut butter and jam... instant coffee and snack crackers. Figures. That's why I'm here, darling. To feed you and to keep your precious hide safe. You at least should have packed a trail mix of nuts and dehydrated fruits."

Until she'd met Nick, she had been safe, wrapped in her drive to set Jasmine free— "Do I look in need of a keeper? You're baby-sitting me because I'm an asset to Palladin, Inc. Because Mamie would fire you if anything happened to me, Palladin's little moneymaker," she snapped at him.

"No," he answered thoughtfully, his eyes softening upon her as he reached out to rub her short hair. In no mood for friendly play, she dodged his hand. He reached to tug her earlobe gently and let his hand be swatted away. He shoved his hands into his back pockets. "I came because I wanted to be with you. I missed you. I missed your hot, sassy mouth and dark, witching looks."

Silver tried to ignore the zinging, heady warmth, the enchantment his words brought her. She braced herself against his charm, unwilling to fall to him as other women had. "You've decided to oblige Mamie. I could have you and waltz away quite free. Not a bit of guilt on my part."

"There would be on mine. I'd want more, and Mamie has

nothing to do with this," Nick murmured after a long look up into the stars.

More. She'd been through enough emotions to last her lifetime. The thought sent Silver reeling into reality, knocking the breath out of her. "I can't afford this," she admitted unwillingly, feet braced against the ground, fear pumping wildly through her. She followed him as he led the mare to Montoya, tethering her. He ran his hand over the Appaloosa's flank, patting the mottled hide, before he turned to Silver.

He was taking his time, darn him, setting his logic in place and fitting puzzle pieces together, while her emotions were in shreds. "I can't afford you," she repeated, challenging his grip on her passions. "You've changed the rules of play to suit you. I'm not made for what you want. I can't."

"You suit me," he said quietly.

Passion, she told herself wildly, desperately. That was all she felt for Nick, heat and storms, and when she had feasted her fill, the world would stop tumbling....

He tossed her a small package from his pocket. "You've been collecting Elizabeth's letters, and you might want this. It was supposed to have been hers."

Silver stared at the small, light package in her hand; it could be an emotional bomb. She'd liked the last gift far too much and had given nothing back. She'd planned to return it but couldn't. Greed and curiosity drove her, and she didn't hide her excitement as she dashed away the wrappers, then slowly peeled away the layers of tissue to reveal an exquisite cut-glass antique perfume bottle. The delicate scent of English roses curled into the night air, as though Elizabeth called out to her from another time. Elizabeth had loved Liam desperately, and he returned that trust. Silver had come to the Tallchiefs falsely, tearing at their legends, betraying them, and she wasn't worthy of the beauty—and Nick was in the mix, wanting truth and more from her.

The cut-glass stopper caught the firelight and shot it at Silver in tiny, colored, slicing swords.

The first tear burned down Silver's cheek, the tug too deep and painful in her heart and raw to conceal. Her legs quivered and weakened, sending her down to her knees, her arms curling protectively around her. "Oh, Nick..."

Through the smoke curling from the fire, Nick watched Silver pace back and forth. When he'd reached for her, she'd pushed him away with a snarl. He wasn't experienced with comforting, but he knew that he could use a kind word and encouragement when dealing with Silver's volatile emotions. He'd pushed down his frustration and knew that she'd fight him, fight the softness he didn't know how to give. Brooding by the fire, she had refused the meal he'd cooked, tearing furiously at her peanut butter and jelly sandwich and glaring at him.

In his mind, Nick saw another Silver, dressed in a treasured doeskin shift, her eyes soft upon a cradle made long ago. The softness within her frightened him; her fingertips flowing lightly against his face had taken something from him and placed it into her keeping. The way her silvery eyes locked upon him, sometimes flaming, sometimes soft— The woman within her beckoned to Nick on a level that was primitive, yet almost quiveringly soft, an element that he'd known little about.

She'd left him. Left the nest he had provided for her and had come to find her destiny without him. A man with a scarred past, Nick wasn't expecting to feel as if his heart were gripped in a steel fist. The empty house and the terse note had frightened him. Then a call to Duncan proved Nick's fears to be right—Silver had ridden Montoya up Tallchief Mountain. Cold terror drove Nick every step up Tallchief Mountain...anything could have happened to her—

Along the way, swearing as night draped the mountain and his progress slowed, Nick realized that when he found Silver, he'd find the only woman who could complete him. Along the way, terrified that he might find her body torn apart, broken, at the bottom of a ravine, Nick had decided to marry her. It was just a matter of getting Silver's full attention and presenting himself to appeal to her. Nick wanted her to be just as desperate for him. For her to come after him, giving him a small dab of comfort, needing him—

Nick spread his fingers, studying the scarred, tanned skin. The son of Lloyd Palladin knew how to reach out and take. To claim. Silver, a woman bred of magic and moonbeams and legends, needed a gentler man, one who knew how to play nicely and give her dreams. Nick inhaled abruptly, uncomfortable with his vulnerability. He would give her what he could and more.

Now he sat admiring the angry, brooding female wrapped in the Tallchief tartan, fringes flying as she stalked back and forth. He noted with satisfaction that her grip on Elizabeth's bottle was firm, clutched in her fist, just as he wanted her to want him. With cropped black hair, her graceful body taut with anger, she stopped pacing, long legs braced apart on the ground as she faced him. "A man whose hobbies are laundry and ironing is too complicated. That iron has enough gizmos on it to fly. You iron everything, even your shorts and T-shirts. That laundry room is overneat, the softeners and detergents lined up like soldiers. I do not like a crease in my jeans. You wear a crease in your jeans that could cut bread. And you…"

She struggled to list his faults, no easy task when she wanted to leap upon him and change that shielded expression to one of passion and one to take her breath away. "You cook with a flourish. Laundry and cooking—the refrigerator is always filled, the cupboards are chock-full—all methodically arranged, of course—and you approach a puzzle as though games are a luxury. I do not understand any of that. You come after me—fine. I understand that. I am an asset to Palladin, Inc. You are protecting the company's investment and potential earnings. I've known you two and a half weeks, and none of it has been sweet. Now, you're shoving something else on the desktop—you say you want to be with me, that you missed me. What does that mean?"

Nick nudged a rock with his boot. Fear, frustration and anger had ridden him since Duncan's call informing him that Silver had ridden up the Tallchief trail. Her first reaction—that expression of sheer pleasure—had startled, then pleased him. Now, he was as welcome as yesterday's cold french fries. What had he expected? Loving, open arms, sweet kisses? Her statement had hurled, like a spear thrown down between them, a challenge that covered something deeper—at least she'd noticed him.

"You figure it out," he said, settling back to watch her storms through the smoke and the sparks drifting between them.

He glanced at his hands, spread them, studying their strength and the scars. She couldn't know how, as a child, Nick had lived in filthy clothes, his father too busy pulling scams and wrapped in his own selfish passions to care for his children. A washing machine, when they could find it, had been a luxury to them, and a dryer, pure heaven. They had hoarded bars of soap and took showers in freezing rain to keep clean, to keep the other children from taunting them. Regular and healthy food was a luxury, and the need to fit puzzle pieces together, make one composite, streamlined picture, arose from his haphazard, painful youth.

She shot out a hand as if to cut him from her life. "You look like your brothers, but you're not at all easygoing like they are. You're in my way, Nick Palladin. I've got things to do. You're complicating my life."

"Okay." Nick intended his relationship with Silver to get very complicated. The image of her dressed in Una's shift and touching the baby cradle swept through him again, leaving a poignant ache.

Silver eyed him and ran her hand over the new short length of her hair, riffling it. "If you're worried about a claim of sexual harassment—don't. I can take care of myself. I don't understand you. Why are you afraid of me? Of having me?" In an afterthought, she restated, "Why are you afraid of me having you?"

"Ah. Equality. *You* having *me*." The image shot down his body, hardening it.

She took a step closer, watching him. She nudged his laced hiking boot with hers. "Get out of my way, or I'll go right over you."

Along with his anger and frustration and fear upon finding that Silver had flown his keeping, Nick had placed his thoughts in meticulous order and knew what he wanted. "You can try. I'll want children when we're married, but those terms are negotiable. I'll never stray. I'll never hurt you. I'll be there when you need me. I'll help you find what you're looking for. I'll give you what you need."

Need. The need for Silver frightened him. Yet it was there, not to be ignored—for she was fiery and bold and yet soft and quivering and beautiful. Nick rose to his feet and walked to her. When her scent snared him, caused his senses to leap, Nick pushed his hands into his back pockets to keep from reaching for her. Silver stared at him blankly, her lips parted. Though her expression wasn't of a joyous woman in love, the frustration coming upon it pleased Nick immensely.

Standing draped in her Tallchief tartan, legs braced in her tight jeans and staring up at him, the cut-glass bottle clutched in her hand, Silver was exactly perfect. Not exactly sweet, but a woman of heart, a fighter, and a woman who fascinated him, who made his senses leap and his heart race. If she wanted a seduction, he'd give her a permanent one. Nick bent to kiss one corner of her mouth and then the other. "Good night."

All she had to do was to drag his two-hundred-plus-pounds-and-six-foot-four, very delectable body, into her tent. Nick lay outside, close and protective, in his sleeping bag. To a woman who made her living by sampling, by taking chances, the challenge and curiosity were irresistible. He'd handed her an invitation to marriage as though he expected her to comply. He'd made promises without asking for them in return. He'd laid out his terms.

The man was old-fashioned, layered by man-woman rules and scarred edges from his past.

Marriage to Nick Palladin would be a disaster...impossible. She tossed the offer aside. She had her goals; she'd worked a lifetime to achieve her independence, her life apart from family ties and the twisting pain they could bring—

If he came into her tent...if he came into her tent, she would have him without commitment.

The Tallchief tartan ran smooth beneath her hand, as she thought of how to skip the preliminaries, take what she wanted and be on her way. She trailed a finger down the exquisite sharp edges of Elizabeth's perfume bottle and lifted the stopper to sniff the elegant rose fragrance. He found her attractive, didn't he? she thought as she lightly touched the tiny glass rod between her breasts. She replaced the stopper to the bottle. The gift was romantic, not a box of chocolates, but meant for her alone. He'd taken the time to search out a part of her heritage. He'd been vulnerable then, a big man standing with the small package in his work-roughened hand, as though he feared she would not take his gift.

She would take his gift and more.

And more. Nick wanted more....

There was no mistaking that dark glow of his green eyes tonight, or the tenderness and those heated and whimsical kisses. He could be her companion, her lover, but not her confidant. Her beautiful, exciting, warm, cuddly accessory. She even liked his ill-temper at times; it provided a release valve for her own. At the moment, he was a headache to be handled delicately, for Nick Palladin was a sensitive, old-fashioned and definitely caring man. His fear for her had been honest; and he'd come after her. He'd spoken plainly, each word a promise. She wanted more from him, more delight, more words to treasure, more enchanting kisses—

After an hour of restraining herself and the realization that Nick was not making himself available easily, Silver drew the Tallchief plaid around her flannel pajamas and went to attack Nick.

He lay near the small fire, his back to her, his shoulder gleaming above the sleeping bag. Silver sat down behind him, studying her prey, who slept quietly, without her restless needs, without the need to challenge or seduce her—

She touched his shoulder and found it hard, immovable and cold. Unable to resist, she bent to place her lips on that expanse of tanned skin over cords and powerful muscle. She smoothed his hair, thick, warm waves flowing through her fingers, releasing more of his intoxicating scent. She drew it into her, placing her nose close to his skin, just there behind his ear, where the scent lurked true and dark and mysterious. She skimmed her nose across his shoulder and down his arm where there was power and sniffed lightly at his hand, where there was gentleness and pleasure. She drew back, studying him. Asleep, Nick seemed younger, the harsh lines gentling on his face. She couldn't bear to think of him struggling to survive with his brothers, their rough, unstable life.

She lightly prodded the strand of hair that lay across the jacket he'd rolled and used as a pillow. Crisp and waving, his hair ran smooth beneath her touch. The Palladins were wrapped in pride, trying their best to right their father's wrongs, to live honorable lives.

Unable to resist, she placed her cheek along his, nuzzling him as she inhaled his scent. Tempted by his hard lips, she eased to trace them with her own.

Wrapped in sleep, Nick shifted slightly, answering her kiss gently. She braced her hands beside him, leaning to savor the light kisses she needed. She sniffed again lightly, taking in the essence of the man—dark, heady, dangerous and real—the smoke, horse and leather. He'd held a baby during the day, the scent stronger along his throat. There on his new beard was the fragrance of soap and magic and lime. She traced his bottom lip with her tongue, tasting him, enjoying Nick at her leisure. She gently traced his ear with her parted lips, the texture delighting her.

Nick shivered and groaned, his breath ragged, and Silver sat up behind him, studying him as the firelight played upon his rugged face, his rumpled hair. She smoothed the waves, let them flow beneath her palm, and then her fingers found that beautiful, bare, powerful shoulder.

She opened her hands on his bare cool back, studying the contrast of her pale skin against his, the muscles rippling slightly as he adjusted to her touch. She traced a cord, bent to kiss it. She had to claim Nick, taste him, have him. She had to take what was hers and her right to take. Aye, she would take him— She was on her ancestors' land and he was hers to claim. She smiled softly, mocking herself, her pride in her Sioux and Scots heritage, her will to have what belonged to her. She was the hunter now, strong and with just that bit of savagery that she knew Nick could match. Honest and raw, pretenses swept aside, Nick equaled her, completed her, fascinated her. Silver closed her eyes; Nick was hers...now...here. She didn't have to worry about Jasmine, or her shattered family…she only had to please herself. Nick, she sensed, could please her thoroughly.

Silver undressed slowly, moving carefully through her thoughts. Nick would treat her gently; she trusted him on that level. In the morning, she'd be sleeping in her tent, having taken him and enough beautiful memories to last her lifetime. She glanced up at the stars, treasured them on this night with Nick, before the past caught up with her in the morning—

Silver eased the zipper downward and slid into the sleeping bag against Nick's back. She sucked in her breath, the length of naked and powerful man shocking her. She blinked and jerked her fingers from his naked hip. Of course, Nick would sleep naked; she should have known. She closed her eyes; he fit perfectly, all that warm lovely back against her bare breasts, that hard taut bottom spooned to her lap—she eased her arm over his, smiled as his muscles flexed and leaped, her fingers smoothing the hair on his chest.

Nick groaned unevenly and Silver held her breath while he turned to her, drawing her close to him. His cheek, rough with stubble against hers, nuzzled her gently, his lips finding her ear to whisper drowsily, "Is it yes?"

"Yes." He was sleeping, of course, dreaming, and she had him in her power, here in the night where all that mattered was here and now, the rest of life pushed away. Nick's big hand slid to caress her back, from shoulder to hip, and lower, cupping her bottom, drawing her close to him.

The bold hardened length against her stomach momentarily frightened Silver, and she braced herself against the surprise, the intimate male form new and dangerous.

"Yes?" he asked again, and though he was sleeping, Silver knew that Nick would never force himself upon her.

She whispered "Yes" against his lips, the gentle, seeking kiss, his hands opening, smoothing her. His tongue tasted her lips and Silver parted them for him, for the daring heated play she had to have. Then he kissed her ear, roamed to her jaw and bit her gently as she arched toward him.

Nick moved over her, eased his face against her throat and caressed her breast, cupping her gently.

When his lips touched her breasts, found the aching tips and suckled gently, one by one, Silver found and matched the rhythm with her hips, easing up against him, aching. Heavy against her, his face warm, his lips tugging at her breasts, Nick's fingers slid downward, between their bodies, to stroke her intimately.

The gentle intrusion surprised and delighted her, and Silver locked her arms around him, bit his ear and found a desperate, aching, melting rhythm that took her inside herself. The intimate delight poured over her gently, and the taut muscles in her body slid into silk.

"Yes," she whispered, giving herself into Nick's care as he moved closer, safely, heavily upon her. The heavy pressure was familiar and new, opening her to him, flowing gently—

"Silver?" he murmured unevenly, his body trembling over her, taut and hard and burning.

Whatever he wanted, she wanted equally, the need flowing just beyond her reach and she locked her body against his, fierce with the need to have everything, to capture this man, to free herself—

She hadn't expected the sharp pain as he came into her, tightening against him. She panted, focusing on the intrusion, the mystery of man joining with woman, giving her his trust. He stopped and she protested, drawing him nearer, and then he began again, filling her. She didn't know that a man could be so gentle, painstakingly soothing her with wonderful, dark, intimate words, which she would hoard and treasure. She'd given him beauty and pleasure and delight, she heard him whisper distantly, his hands warm and gentle upon her. He told her how he felt inside her, warm and tight and as if she were the other part of him. Magic curled through her, the pain easing as Nick came fully, gently, into her, giving her time to adjust, whispering to her.

Magic, she thought again, as he moved upon her just once, locked within her keeping. Warm and bold and hers. *Nick. Nick.* His hands moved beneath her, helped her flow into the magic, his body blending with hers like silk upon warm waves. Textures, heat, throbbing… Fire. Storms. Need. Every scent, every touch, real…stark…truthful…releasing her—

The shattering of her body sent her soaring, the rhythm so fast

WELCOME TO THE
CASINO!

Try your luck at the Roulette Wheel ...
Play a hand of Twenty-One!

How to play:

1. Play the Roulette and Twenty-One scratch-off games, as instructed on the opposite page, to see that you are eligible for FREE BOOKS and a FREE GIFT!

2. Send back the card and you'll receive TWO brand-new Silhouette Desire® novels. These books have a cover price of $4.25 each, but they are yours to keep absolutely free.

3. There's no catch. You're under no obligation to buy anything. We charge nothing — ZERO — for your first shipment. And you don't have to make any minimum number of purchases — not even one!

4. The fact is, thousands of readers enjoy receiving books by mail from the Silhouette Reader Service™ before they're available in stores. They like the convenience of home delivery, and they love our discount prices!

5. We hope that after receiving your free books you'll want to remain a subscriber. But the choice is yours—to continue or cancel, any time at all! So why not take us up on our invitation, with no risk of any kind. You'll be glad you did!

Play Twenty-One For This Exquisite Free Gift!

THIS SURPRISE
MYSTERY GIFT
COULD BE
YOURS FREE WHEN
YOU PLAY
TWENTY-ONE

It's fun, and we're giving away **FREE GIFTS** to all players!

PLAY **ROULETTE!**

Scratch the silver to see where the ball has landed—7 RED or 11 BLACK makes you eligible for TWO FREE romance novels!

PLAY **TWENTY-ONE!**

Scratch the silver to reveal a winning hand! Congratulations, you have Twenty-One. Return this card promptly and you'll receive a fabulous free mystery gift, along with your free books!

YES!

Please send me all the free Silhouette Desire® books and the gift for which I qualify! I understand that I am under no obligation to purchase any books, as explained on the back of this card.

Name (please print clearly)

Address   Apt.#

City   Prov.   Postal Code

Offer limited to one per household and not valid to current Silhouette Desire® subscribers. All orders subject to approval.   PRINTED IN U.S.A.

(C-SIL-D-12/98)   **326 SDL CKFT**

The Silhouette Reader Service™ — Here's how it works:

Accepting free books places you under no obligation to buy anything. You may keep the books and gift and return the shipping statement marked "cancel." If you do not cancel, about a month later we'll send you 6 additional novels, and bill you just $3.49 each, plus 25¢ delivery per book and GST.* That's the complete price — and compared to cover prices of $4.25 each — quite a bargain! You may cancel at any time, but if you choose to continue, every month we'll send you 6 more books, which you may either purchase at the discount price...or return to us and cancel your subscription.

*Terms and prices subject to change without notice.
Canadian residents will be charged applicable provincial taxes and GST.

If offer card is missing write to: Silhouette Reader Service, P.O. Box 609, Fort Erie, Ontario L2A 5X3

019561919-L2A5X3-BR01

SILHOUETTE READER SERVICE
PO BOX 609
FORT ERIE ONT
L2A 9Z9

CDMA

Canada Post Corporation/ Société canadienne des postes

MAIL ⟩ POSTE

Postage paid   Port payé
If mailed in Canada   si posté au Canada

Business   Réponse
Reply   d'affaires

0 1 9 5 6 1 9 1 9 9   01

she couldn't catch her breath, command her senses, restrain them—she could only pour herself against Nick, meeting him, floating gently back into herself.

She kept him close, his cheek resting on her breasts, his taut body easing up on her, his hands stroking her luxuriously.

She drifted, giving herself to his warmth, the pulse running through him, and once awoke as Nick's hands gently moved upon her, cleansing her with a warm, damp cloth. Certain that she was dreaming, yet unfamiliar with a man's intimate touch, she gripped his wrist and Nick whispered, "Go back to sleep, sweetheart. I'll take care of you."

Why did she believe him, even in her dreams? Silver wondered distantly as she slid into sleep, welcomed it and the man who came back into her arms....

Silver awoke to the scents of smoke and coffee and Nick's essence, blended with her own. She sniffed delicately and the scent of their lovemaking curled around her. Sunshine stabbed at her lids and she squeezed them shut. She sniffed lightly, catching sunflowers and sunlight. She lay still, absorbing the different essences—pine, cedar, juniper, rich earth, grasses.

She stretched delicately, her body aching slightly. The male chuckle caused her eyes to open and she flattened as she looked up at Nick, crouching beside her. A sunflower spilled from her hair to her nose and tumbled down her cheek. Nick caught it and dusted it across her nose.

"You were smiling in your sleep. You seemed quite pleased with yourself," he said as she jerked the sleeping bag up to her chin.

"Now, look, Nick—" she began, unable to collect just exactly what she could say...she'd planned on returning to her bedroll and she was in his. She took a second look at Nick-in-the-morning: bare chest, droplets of water gleaming on his shoulders, wide red suspenders striping his dark skin, jeans opened at the snap—

The narrowed, hungry look in his eyes stopped her from speaking. His hand wrapped around her nape and he bent to kiss her shockingly, hungrily, fully, and when he released her, the

heat and possession in his brilliant jade eyes took her breath
away. He half lifted her and the sleeping bag until her back was
braced against a log. "Stop sulking, sweetheart. You had me last
night. My honor has been compromised. You've seduced me,
quite nicely."

She looked at the coffee cup he'd just placed into her hand
and the freshly baked biscuits, buttered and jammed, on her lap.
There was no retreating…she gathered the sleeping bag against
her body—and since she was naked, she couldn't deny she'd
come to him. Nick's cocky, devastating grin nettled her. She bit
into the fluffy biscuit, damned it for being delicious, just like the
man who looked extremely pleased with himself. She downed
the hot coffee, burned her lip and damned him for looking so
appealing, her body quivering with the sight of all that tanned
chest beneath his opened shirt. "You were having a nightmare.
I merely comforted you."

He laughed outright, the sound rich and carefree and enchanting. "Try again. You wanted me. Admit it."

She eyed him, nettled that he'd cut straight to the truth that
she'd wanted him. "Is this going to be a dissection the morning
after? How boring."

"Ah! The jaded approach. That's very good, but predictable.
Don't forget I've seen you at your best, that first day we met—
the cranberry silk witch, furious and impatient." He skimmed his
hand over her hair, grinned as though delighted, then sipped his
coffee. "What are we hunting today?"

"We?"

"You're after something. I said I'd help."

"Fragrances. Mountain violets. Wildflowers," she lied airily.
"Nothing that would interest you. You may leave."

There was nothing friendly about Nick's shielded glance at
her. "Not a chance. I came to get you…to be with you."

"Get you…" The phrase sent an icy chill skidding around her
warm body, her senses prickling. She decided to attack, get his
temper hiking, and he'd leave soon enough. "You realize that
I'm uncomfortable with this conversation."

He grinned again, the boyish, playful look stunning and delighting her. His hand ran across her head again, the gesture friendly and almost brotherly.

In the next instant, he reached for the plate and cup, setting them aside. One tug took the zipper down an inch, and Nick whispered, "Let me look at you."

She launched herself at him, protecting her life, her dreams, her goals, and Nick easily captured her wrists, his gaze locked with hers. He carefully examined her wrists, arms and shoulders. "I won't look at you, unless you want me to. Do you?"

Wary of him, she sensed his fear and disgust and knew her fear of sharing anything with him. "Why?"

"Bruises. Because I'm afraid I hurt you, past what was necessary your first time," he said too rawly, as if the pain had been locked inside him for years. "Will you let me look at you?"

Silver's hot flush moved from her toes up to her head. Once again Nick was asking her for more than she'd given anyone. He'd had his share of bruises and pain, and she couldn't let him think he'd hurt her. Slowly, one by one, she eased her wrists from his hands and lowered the zipper. "I'm fine. Look."

It was no easy matter, exposing her body, but to reassure Nick, she would. Silver fought the quick heat rising up her throat to her cheeks.

Nick stroked her hot cheeks and she looked away, shy of him, as he eased away the flannel-lined sleeping bag. He looked slowly down her body, his open hand skimming her shoulders, her breasts, her stomach and thighs, her legs down to her feet. "Turn."

She obeyed and cold air met her backside, Nick's hand warm, cruising down her back, her bottom, her thighs and calves. She turned again and found his frown. "I'm fine, Nick."

"I'm sorry I hurt you, sweetheart." Satisfied, he shuddered, folding the cloth over her body again, and closed his eyes, a muscle contracting in his cheek.

Too vulnerable now, appearing lonely, his past wrapped around him, Nick needed warmth and— Silver's hand stretched out to lie along his jaw. She ached for the pain in his expression, for the brutal past that haunted him. "Nick, you didn't hurt me."

"It was more than I expected, making love with you," he

admitted, pressing his face into her palm, his vulnerable shudder flowing into her keeping. "More. I'm a controlled man.... I've been very careful with women, with how I felt, even during sex, and I hadn't expected—what you gave me. Thank you."

"You're not like your father, Nick." She couldn't bear to have him ache because of the beauty they'd shared.

"Aren't I?" he asked dryly, sadly. "With you, I wonder."

"If I knew what the hell we were looking for, it would help." The man hanging from a climbing rope beside Silver as they rappelled down the face of a red stone cliff wasn't in a good mood.

"Daisies," she muttered, and wondered how a man who could be so sweet the morning after, who could make her stir to magic with lovemaking and tender words, could be so ill-tempered now.

He caught her ankle, planted her boot on a safe ledge and snarled up at her. "Get up on that ledge. We've been down two cliffs today. You've got skinned knees and hands and you need food, and if you kill us, I'm really going to raise hell. Mamie will do that twisting ear thing and make me feel lower than mud. Rafe and Joel will invite me into a brawl—they're nasty in a fight, and as the youngest, I always got the worst of it. On top of that, I don't feel much like a groom right now."

She grasped a root, tested it and swung onto a sizable rock ledge and stared at Nick as he laboriously made his way up to her. Heavier than she, he had to test each outcropping carefully. Silver studied Nick's scowl. "What are you muttering about?"

"My honor, lady." With a powerful movement, Nick hitched himself up onto the ledge. He calmly opened a canteen of water and drizzled it upon her head. She swatted the sunlit droplets away and Nick grinned down at her. His kiss, quick, hot and hungry, stunned her. While she was floundering, he ripped a scarlet flower from its rock-bound stalk and tucked it into the front of her shirt. His thumb ran down her breast, brushed the peak of her nipple, and his look changed into wicked, sultry, tropical heat. "You've got beautiful breasts, sweetheart."

His familiarity with her body caused Silver to flatten against the stone wall behind her, her knees weakened at the look in

Nick's eyes as he flipped open one button of her shirt. "Blushes become you. You've got that wild and smoky look, desperate and frustrated. I like it, because I know I'm in there somewhere, revving you up. Let me look at you."

She scanned the jutting rocks above them, and the depth of the canyon below, and tried to stop her heart from racing, her body from melting. "Nick?"

One quick look down his body told her that Nick wanted her. She fought the hot blush rising to her cheeks, the way her skin ignited when he looked at her. His scent curled around her, familiar but wary, clanging, exotic, dangerous and very hungry.

Nick glared at her. "I wasn't sleeping. You said yes and I've been looking forward to the excited bride-to-be chitchat. You know…the wedding date, arrangements, that sort of thing—"

"Let's talk about this," she began when she could start thinking again. She backed away from him, trying to find safety when one look at Nick took her breath away. "First of all, I admit to nothing. We only met two and a half weeks ago—"

He lifted a dark eyebrow, mocking her. "I will not offend my grandmother by seducing a Tallchief woman. We're getting married. There was that 'yes.' Several of them."

Silver stared at him, recognizing the hard negotiator in Nick. "You were keeping a checklist?"

"I wanted to make certain that you knew exactly what you were committing to. You had every chance to back out. I wouldn't have forced you."

"What do you mean, it was a first for you?"

Nick scanned the clear blue Wyoming sky, the jutting red cliffs dotted with white bighorn sheep, and the valley below, the tiny herd of deer grazing on the rich grass. "I think I'm feeling fragile today, thanks to you. I've never come close to an innocent— which you were—and I've never stayed the night. Until you, I was beginning to think that my sex drive—it's been over five years since I've been with a woman, Silver, and a virgin in my sleeping bag assured me that all my equipment knew exactly what you were designed for…for loving. You slept very well, by the way. No tossing and turning and crying. You're a cuddler, all arms and legs tangling with mine. I didn't appreciate the sharp knee jabs, but I'll get used to protecting myself."

She could have pushed him over the cliff. "I am experimenting with my sexuality. The scents of lovemaking. I may duplicate them. You were there, I took you. Think of it this way—I'm a Tallchief, you were on my land and I took you."

"This experiment is feeling delicate. I'm not a trophy and you're not a female knight with sexual rights to men on your ancestral property. Try again." He narrowed his eyes and wrapped his hand around her wrist. "You trusted me with your body, but not your dreams. What are you looking for?"

"Peace," she returned simply, truthfully, as memories of Jasmine came hurling at her. "And you're not it."

"He'll be a fine beast of a man, haughty and proud and strong as a bear, gnawing at the maiden's shields, testing her, claiming her with wicked eyes...

She wrapped her arms around herself, scanning the small canyon nearby. She'd find the pearls and she'd be free— *Jasmine...*

Nick slowly lifted the canteen to pour a stream of cold water over her head. Ripped from her dark thoughts by the tall intruder next to her, Silver licked a drop from her upper lip and steamed, wondering where she should hit him first. Then calmly, glaring at her, Nick poured the cold water over his own head. When he looked so fierce, the droplets clung to his head and eyebrows, dripping from his nose, Silver found herself laughing.

Slowly Nick's expression changed into a devastating grin and sunlight danced around them like magic. "I like it when you laugh," he murmured, tipping up her chin with his finger to give her a light, lovely, enchanting kiss.

With her lips against his, Silver asked, "Did you mean everything you said last night?"

"Every word."

"Tell me again." She had to know if the magic had happened.

Instead, Nick slowly unbuttoned her shirt, eased her T-shirt above her breasts. He cupped the softness of one in his hand, treasuring her and then slowly bent to take the hardened tip into his lips—

The image of his dark skin against her pale softness, his lashes closed and brushing her skin, his hair waving upon her body, matched the aching pleasure his mouth gave her.

Seven

Nick fought the groan curling out of him as he sat by the campfire. He ached from his head to his toes, every muscle locked in pain. He glanced at the woman devouring the meal he'd cooked, busily licking her fingers as butter dripped from the hot camp biscuits. Butter glistened on her chin as she reached for another quail roasting on the spit, tearing into it with an appreciative "Mmm. This is great. Yum. Baked potatoes and corn on the cob. I'll get fat."

Nick almost groaned again when her agile little tongue flicked away a crumb on her bottom lip. She'd never get fat, not at the pace she'd moved today. Silver had scaled the cliffs of Tallchief Mountain effortlessly, leaping over rocks and tumbling streams, and peering into caves. She'd gathered wildflowers from the meadows, enchanting him as she studied the petals, bruising them. Once he'd lost her, and the branches of a cedar had moved as she burst from them, exclaiming about the beautiful scents as she wrapped her arms around the branches. She smelled everything from flowers to grasses to trees.

A woman moving with feline grace while every muscle in his

body felt like a rock grating on pain was annoying. The pleasure of watching her wallow in the scents of Tallchief Mountain had stunned him. The deer and animals of the mountain had fascinated her, and she had wept at the Tallchiefs' family cemetery, a meadow studded with Scottish heather.

While Nick fought another groan as he reached for the coffeepot, his muscles protesting, Silver rose easily to her feet and stretched her arms out to the night sky. She jogged in place and spun around, arms lifted again. "This is wonderful. Beautiful. I could stay here forever. The scents are fabulous. Let's build a sweat lodge. We can use sagebrush for scent in the smoke and— Nick, there is no reason to glare at me. You may leave at any time."

"Wouldn't think of it." He attempted a cold, calculating smile, baring his teeth. He should have come up with a romantic reason why he stayed with her. The image of Silver swinging from an aspen limb and agilely hefting herself up to a branch to get a better view caused him to shudder. Even his butt hurt. Nick considered Silver's shapely backside, almost felt it undulating in his palms...and he went hard.

He was in good shape, a man built for strength and endurance, not aerobic, agile exercise. Women usually took him very seriously. He ticked off his pluses: he was appealing, charming...a perfect catch...and in pretty good shape. He wanted to be the object of Silver's predatory instincts.

She peered across the campfire's drifting smoke. "You've been in a snit all day. You've been glowering at me for the past hour. You are a very good cook, Nick. Thank you. You are appreciated. I'll do the dishes."

Nick stealthily, slowly, rubbed his hot coffee cup up and down his aching thighs. Pleasantries wouldn't soothe his bruised ego. He settled down for an unfamiliar but necessary sulk, nettled by the woman he wanted to capture and marry. Last night had proven that Silver was his alone, and he'd wanted to comfort her today. He'd had visions of lying her down in the mountain meadows and telling her more of his heart—those delicate little moments a man wanted from his love.

Instead, she felt "wonderful," fully charged and ready to build a sweat lodge. Nick leaned back onto Montoya's saddle, sipping his coffee and wondered how to take off his boots for the night. His legs felt like logs, unable to bend. He slid a cautious glance at the woman effortlessly crouching and washing the cookware, leaving it to dry. The haphazard tumble of dishes resembled what Silver had done to his intentions to move deeper into their relationship and the commitment he wanted. Then there was that missing bridal chitchat that he had looked forward to hearing. He'd known he wanted to claim Silver, and he hadn't moved too quickly. Silver was an impulsive woman and would know what she wanted—she hadn't given him a "no way, José." But she wasn't exactly bubbling with the idea of being his wife. Instead, she "appreciated" his cooking. As one would "appreciate" an appliance, a dishwasher.

Silver glanced at him and smiled tenuously. She knelt at his feet, unlacing his boots and drawing them off, tending Nick, who couldn't bend his legs without groaning. He who wanted to take Silver in his arms and make love to her. He doubted that possibility existed tonight. "I can do that myself."

"Stop growling." Her cropped hair gleamed coal black in the firelight, her breasts flowing softly beneath his borrowed T-shirt and worn flannel shirt. She arched and stretched, slid away the flannel shirt to replace it with the Tallchief tartan, smoothing it against her as she looked up into the stars. He wanted to place his lips on that smooth length of throat and— "Nick, do you really think the Tallchief legends are true?"

Shielded uncertainty and fear lurked in her question, and Nick studied her intently. Her reason for coming to Amen Flats and Tallchief Mountain was never far away. Whatever secret she hoarded was too painful to share with him. A man who had crawled his way out of filth and hunger, Nick did not believe in dreams and whims, he gave her what he could— "They have come true for the Tallchiefs and my brothers, who married Tallchief women."

"I am a Tallchief woman. I've never felt so alive as today, seeing the crystal cave where Liam collected the crystals for Elizabeth.... I feel deeply that what I want is here. Sometimes the feelings are so strong that I know if I reach out, I can claim my ancestors' talents, the seer and the shaman blood in me. In my heart, I know that every word written in Una's journals and in Elizabeth's are absolutely true.''

She glanced at Nick, then down at her hands, running her fingers over her palms as if tracing her thoughts. "I won't hurt the Tallchiefs, Nick. But I can't be a part of them. I don't want to be a part of any family again, including my own. I do not intend to have children."

She glanced at him again. "You're angry, aren't you? You're an old-fashioned, macho male and— Nick, I think your biological clock is ticking. You're surrounded by families and babies, and then Mamie is definitely pushing you to acquire me. You love her and you want to please her. You want the ones you love to be happy, even if it costs you your own happiness."

"I told you that Mamie doesn't have anything to do with us."

She tilted her head again and placed her hands on his tense shoulders, massaging them gently. "You need to relax. I know you weren't expecting last night…with me. I should have been more gentle with you. I have no idea, but you could be hurting now—from our intimacy. You seemed to walk rather painfully, and you have groaned. I've failed to be sensitive to your needs, to cuddle you and give you that morning-after confidence that men like you require. I've read articles. I know that men of your species—delicate and gentle—need pampering and care. If you'd stop scowling, you'd feel better."

"I've got a headache," Nick managed to say, nettled by her attempt to placate him. "You're it."

She smiled gently and ran her fingers over the line between his brows, then across his lashes. "You're a survivor, Nick. Just like me. I respect your predatory instincts. We're alike. Tell me what you need, what you need to be told to comfort you, and I'll try."

She tilted her head to peer at him curiously. "I didn't know that you could be so—delicate."

"*Delicate?*" The word lifted the hair on Nick's nape. He had the quick image of Joel and Rafe, who were seasoned fighters, sneering at their baby brother—he wasn't up to the brawl. He stared at the object of his discomfort, the woman peering at him curiously, her lashes long and matching the blue-black sheen of her cropped hair. Her fingers fluttered along his neck and taut shoulders and Nick forced himself not to wince. Wincing wouldn't do. "You need a massage, Nick. Your muscles are like stone. Let me get my oil."

He needed to hold her, to be inside the one woman he had ever wanted to claim, to give her what she needed. His gaze locked to her backside, the jeans taut against her curves as she pilfered through her saddlebags. Moments later, Nick groaned as she lowered his suspenders, stripped away his shirt and began massaging the aromatic oil into his neck and shoulders.

"You're so tense. You really need a nice long soak in a chamomile bath. This is only an almond oil base with bergamot, juniper, rosemary and a few other essential oils." She moved to sit behind him and her kiss on his nape caused electricity to jolt through Nick's body. "There. Feeling better?"

He wasn't relaxed; Silver's light kiss and delicate touch had shaken him. The aromatic oil reminded him of the fragrance of their lovemaking....

"You're still tense, and brooding." Silver hesitated, then slid her arms around his chest and massaged oil onto the tense muscles on his chest, and her legs around his hips. She rocked him gently, making him very aware of her breasts pressed to his back. She pressed her cheek to his back, and Nick held very still while she attempted to comfort him. "I know you're worried about being like your father, but you aren't. Oh, you may yell and act like a bear sometimes, but you're just being honest. I prefer that honesty."

"Is this a normal conversation that you might be having with Joe or Jack or Billy Bob?" Nick asked unevenly. "That is, if you had made love with them last night?"

"But I didn't. I made love with you, because you're sweet."

"I was on your land and you felt the need to rise to your Sioux and Scots blood—"

She kissed his ear and Nick shivered. "Absolutely true. Can't deny that. The moment was at hand and I seized it."

"Don't tell me that you decided to dispense with your virginity and—"

"Of course not. I like you, Nick. We might even be friends…maybe. You're real and raw."

"*Raw*…thanks."

She kissed his shoulder again, nuzzled it with her cheek, as her hands smoothed his bare chest, the aromatic scents rising to him. Her fingers toyed with his nipples and Nick's entire body tightened painfully. "My friends enjoy the same pleasures— Nick, you just tensed again. They don't need soothing and comforting. You do. You've got all those prickly edges, but you're sensitive and sweet, a romantic at heart. I should have done more this morning to make you feel better. I'm just not that experienced with delicate, sensitive men."

"Is this supposed to be therapy?" Nick asked cautiously, placing his hand over hers on his stomach, too aware that his body had hardened at her first touch.

Her hands slid upward, massaging his nipples delicately, and Nick's body reacted painfully as Silver said, "I'm trying. You shouted last night and shuddered so long and hard and wilted that I know the exercise caused you pain."

"Exercise? Like a rowing machine? Is that what you think happened?" Nick forced himself to speak quietly, to fight his rising temper. The tug of her inquiring fingers upon his nipples had sent white-hot cords contracting in his lower body. "There was that one little delighted cry from you and those purrs."

The slender hand wandering across his chest, toying with his nipples, stopped. "I'm trying to comfort you, Nick. It's obvious to me that you're in a bad mood—"

He sensed her preparing to leave him alone and desperately launched a capture technique. Silver wasn't escaping, waltzing easily from him. "Why don't you sit on my lap? That would help. Just a perfect little therapy touch."

Silver hesitated, then moved around beside him. Her hands cradled his jaw. "You're so tense. Warm. I hope you don't— after—*that* doesn't cause a fever, does it? You're bristling, sparks jumping off you. You do need cuddling, don't you?"

He eased her thigh across his, eased her curved bottom upon him, straddling his legs. "It would help."

* * *

Nick Palladin was really sweet beneath all his hard exterior. And tastable. Silver couldn't resist placing just one small kiss in the center of his chin, just where that enticing little cleft nestled in his tanned and slightly rough skin. She rubbed her cheek against his, enticed by the stubble there and slid her hands behind his neck, to pull herself closer.

With oiled hands, she rubbed the curling, crisp hair on his chest, studying the rich gleam between her pilfering fingers.

"Let me get this straight," he said slowly as though wading through his thoughts. "You're feeling sorry for me—"

"I'm sympathetic. I know what last night cost you and that you've needed time to recover."

"'Time to recover,'" he repeated slowly, darkly. "So this has nothing to do with my past. That you might be afraid of me."

"Heavens, no. Why would I be? You offer no threat at all." She spoke carefully, not wanting to wound him more. "Nick, you've overcome tremendous problems. Mamie, while she was doing her sell of you, told me the whole heartbreaking story...poor little Nick.... Your brothers love you, your grandmother cares enough to advertise your nonmarried state and that she wants grandchildren from you. Plus you're the pet of the entire Tallchief family. I've seen you cuddle their babies, and you'll make a wonderful father for those children you want." She patted his chest and traced the intriguing muscles beneath his dark skin. "Someday, you'll find a nice sweet girl and you'll get married and everyone will be happy."

"I don't offer a threat?" he repeated slowly, thoughtfully. "Not a serious threat? You see me as a kindly, brotherly type?"

"You're not that bad. After our business is complete, we may even be friends. I'll make you that love potion. I've made it for other guys." She wiggled a bit on his lap, adjusting to the thrusting hardness and Nick's big hands clamped down on her hips.

"Hold still. 'A guy.' You see me as a guy...someone to jog with, to share that friendly cup of cappuccino at a sidewalk café, to share an umbrella with in a rainstorm, a 'let's do lunch' sort of guy?" A small pulse began pounding beneath the tanned skin on his temple.

She patted his cheek and smoothed that thick wave of hair

back from his lined and scowling forehead. She kissed his throbbing temple, the muscle clenching in his jaw. She smiled and traced his tightly pressed lips, the grim lines bracketing them. He'd told her he'd missed her and to be fair— "I missed you, too. Why don't you get some rest, and everything will be better in the morning. Now that our…basic attraction has been settled, we can develop an easier relationship—one in which you are more relaxed and you go about your business, and I can focus on what I came for—"

"'Basic attraction,'" he repeated darkly, scowling at her.

She ran her finger down the line between his eyebrows. "You're repeating what I say. You're under stress. You don't want to disappoint your grandmother, and your biological clock is ticking. You've been influenced by all the scents of the Tallchiefs, all that baby powder and love and—"

"Any more featherbrained theories about me and why I might want a relationship—a very intimate relationship with you?" he asked, the sound grating ominously in the night air.

"I've built a business from scratch. I have a small, but good reputation as a perfumer. I am not featherbrained, and you know it. Now you're angry…I can smell a regular hot froth pouring off you." She sniffed delicately in the area of his tense jaw. "Bergamot, ambergris, clary sage, cedar and a mulling, dark scent that is definitely unique to you. I'd like to bottle that— tempering it, of course. The essence is too raw and primitive, too bold and almost quivering with tropical heat…. I was only trying to help. You're clearly under pressure to perform."

"'Perform'?" The word sounded like a rottweiler crunching a bone.

"Don't get upset. You're delicate now. Sensitive. You've never had to commit to a relationship and you're afraid. The playboy types always are. You've been footloose and fancy-free, and now you feel like running away from what your grandmother and your brothers and the Tallchiefs want. The weight is too much, the strain is showing. Once you find a nice girl to settle down with, to marry, the tension will ease."

"Are you quite finished with your 'let's keep this light and

easy,' analytical, screwball kiss-off, sweetheart?'' Nick asked too
quietly, his hands easing up to her shoulders.

The next afternoon, while she gathered larkspur, daisies and
sunflowers, Silver studied Nick, who was standing by the stream,
watering the horses. He stood, legs braced apart, shoulders wide
and taut beneath those magnificent red suspenders. Looking at
him now, she almost forgave him for mashing her to the ground
last night and kissing her until she couldn't breathe, until she
ached, until— There was a certain intriguing violence, tempered
with control, as Nick fed upon her mouth, her skin, her breasts.
She could have pushed him away at any time, but he'd placed
the choice in her hands, and her hands wanted him. His touch
was far too knowing, sliding along the elastic trim of her panties
and one touch in a very intimate part of her body had sent her
over the perfect, shattering edge. Then he had retreated with a
dark, satisfied look, eyes glittering as she tried to find her melted
bones and stuff them back into her. She had managed one hand
flop.

"Let's go make that sweat lodge now, Miss Tallchief," he'd
said in a satisfied, low growl before pushing himself to his feet
and stalking off toward the moonlit lake.

She tore a sunflower from its stalk as Nick turned to study
her. Lying in her sleeping bag just inches from the man who had
pushed her away, who had torn off his clothes and dived into a
tiny icy lake, hadn't been easy. His naked body running through
the moonlit meadow was enough to keep her awake. She'd never
thought about stark male beauty, strong bulky lines, flowing toward her. Intriguing glimpses of his thrusting arousal reminded
her that Nick hadn't been satisfied. That he had merely acted to
point out her need of him. If she could have moved, she would
have run him down and made him pay. Instead, she fell into a
beautiful, deep sleep and dreamed of Nick curled close to her,
the friendly, safe, brotherly Nick—the tastable, sweet Nick.

The last week of June, Nick had picked his battleground, his
office at Palladin, Inc.'s Denver skyscraper. Silver had not yet
entered the serious bridal chitchat mode, and he sensed that she

prepared to treat him like a friend, a brother, an appliance, another cappuccino guy. She'd avoided any personal conversations with him, while spending hours in her laboratory or with the Tallchiefs.

Nick wanted the woman he was about to acquire to realize that he was checking out of the friendly-guy-buddy business with her and entering a new and committed relationship. He was stepping out of the guy chorus line to lead position. Nick tapped his fingers on his desk at Palladin, Inc. headquarters, and studied the woman across the gleaming walnut expanse. Dressed in a smart black sheath that showed her long legs to perfection, and suited the dinner meeting with Mamie, Silver had been shown the offices that would deal with marketing the signature fragrance she created. Silver looked crisp and ready to present her ideas to Mamie, all business and ice. Nick wondered how she would look, a few moments later, after he'd presented to her the real mission of their flight to Denver. He sucked back that tiny tinge of guilt. Prices had to be paid for moving out of the ranks of the doo-wop boys and into the featured-player role.

"Very impressive," Silver murmured as Nick finished scrawling his signature on necessary papers, dictating orders to the company secretary and arranging flight plans back to Amen Flats in the morning.

Nick moved around the desk, wanting nothing to clutter his advance on Silver Tallchief, negotiating her into the marriage he wanted. He leaned his hips on the desk and offered her a glass of champagne from the bottle chilling in ice. "I want to get a matter cleared between us, before we dine with my grandmother. She's elderly and I don't want a scene in front of her."

Silver sipped the champagne and lifted a sleek black eyebrow. Nick noted again the beautiful slant of her cheekbones, the glossy raven cropped haircut that spoke of her Sioux heritage and the smoky gray eyes of her Scots great-great-grandmother. She was perfect for him, fitting his hands, his body and his heart; in his lifetime, no other woman had attracted him like Silver. Nick had never felt the tenderness he had discovered with her. With the sheer joy of acquiring Silver as his wife went a few difficulties, and he had prepared to take action. He eagerly anticipated her reaction to his next move. He reached into an ornate box and withdrew a smaller velvet one. "I want you to wear this to dinner. It's an engagement ring," he said, defining the unusual Celtic design.

A standard solitaire diamond wouldn't have suited Silver's carefully disguised passions. But Nick had stepped inside her boundaries, and tasted the woman beneath the puzzle. On one level, he knew her very well. She was predatory, feminine, delightful, tender, and she was his.

He opened the box and waited for the explosion as Silver stared at the huge bloodred ruby engagement ring, smaller rubies clustering around the huge center stone. The bold, almost primitive new setting made the statement Nick wanted. To have the woman he wanted wear the mark of his possession was a primitive instinct, a claiming. With Silver, he was very possessive.

She choked on her last swallow of champagne, and Nick patted her on the back. She recovered and glared at him. Nick reached to tip her glass up to her lips, satisfied when she took another sip. After effectively completing his opening attack, placing his offer on the bargaining table, Nick placed the open box aside. He sipped his champagne and studied the woman he intended to marry.

"I won't do this to Mamie," Silver managed to say shakily, paling beneath her light tan.

"What do you think you'd be doing to my grandmother?" Nick asked, prepared to spend as much time at crafting this bargain, as much patience as he needed to secure Silver Tallchief as his wife, his lover, the mother of his children.

The light of his dreams scowled at him and rose to stalk back and forth across the lush carpeting of his office. Denver's evening lights twinkled in the background, outlining her taut and very feminine body. Nick could feel his body harden, her silky skin moving beneath his hands. He pushed down his desire and waited.

Silver stood in front of him and the deep breath she took allowed Nick to appreciate the crevice between her breasts. "You want to fake an engagement for your grandmother's benefit, and I will not be a part of deceiving her."

Nick launched his second attack. "There's a wedding ring that goes with the engagement ring. I thought you would appreciate the Celtic design, a tribute to Una. The rings can easily be exchanged to something you'd like better."

The wide ornate ring glittered richly against the black velvet of the box. Nick pictured it on her slender finger, the only item she would wear in his bed. He'd given women presents before—but it was very important to him that Silver like what he had chosen. He shifted restlessly as he realized exactly how fragile he was where she was concerned.

His sweet bride-to-be had paled, staring blankly at him and then at the ring, as though it were a stake, ready to drive through her heart. "You're on overload. We've known each other just one month."

"We've made love. You trusted me. You gave me something you've never shared before. It's clear that I'm not just one of the guys, someone to share that umbrella and that cup of cappuccino," he returned easily, offering her a smile. The past week of aching to have Silver, of planning this moment, was almost worth it. While waiting for bridal chitchat, Nick had been on edge, a first in his business dealings. He regretted snapping at Rawlins in bookkeeping, and the manager of a Palladin-owned sporting goods store. He must have said something too sharp and impatient to several women who had called him on insignificant matters, who stopped him, chatting away about daughters and home-cooked meals and batting their lashes at him. He'd been a bit kinder in his single days, looking for the right woman beneath all that eye-batting and crooning, but now he hoped they took care of their eye problems and left him alone to pursue Silver.

No other woman could make him come alive as Silver could, every moment explosive and packed with curiosity at how she would react next. He smiled as he remembered how she had absently taken the strip of bacon he'd fed her this morning, how her teeth had closed over the meat, sending a sensual jolt into him. How she'd walked to his laundry room, pilfered through his ironed stacks of shorts and T-shirts, selected what she wanted and dressed in them. He liked taking care of Silver, of her feeling comfortable with him.

All he had to do was make her comfortable with this new level of their relationship and take himself out of the buddy chorus line.

"When you show your teeth, in what you think is a friendly smile, I don't trust you," Silver noted warily. "You've been too quiet. Too…brooding, and now this. I have no intention of marrying you, Nick."

He ran his finger over the button at her throat and down the opened circle of fabric that modestly exposed her chest. Nick allowed his hand to be swatted away…for the moment. "I'm committed to making this relationship work. You should know that. I've already told Mamie that you've agreed to marry me—"

"You what?"

After one look at Silver's growing outrage and her taut body, Nick decided to place the desk between them. Leaving Silver melted and hot and fragrant with musk in that moonlit meadow had caused him to lose sleep. Her aching purrs had shattered any possibility of sleep until she was tucked safely in his bed, wearing his wedding ring.

"It's now the third week of June. We can be married before the Fourth of July. You did say yes."

"Huh?"

Eight

"Huh?" wasn't a term Silver had ever used, even when she was distracted in her lab. It was a sign that Nick had her wavering; he advanced carefully. "That night on the mountain, when I came to you, I asked you several times to marry me and I clearly defined what I wanted before we made love."

"Yes…smesh…I meant yes, I would— Yes…you were— We must have been talking about two different things." She waved her hand airily, dismissing the fact he had just placed in front of her. "I did not agree to marry you."

"I'm a very serious man. I'm good at details. I told you exactly how I felt. I'm committed now and there's no turning back. You've compromised me, and now you'll wear my ring. You will marry me."

After a full five seconds of staring at Nick, Silver collapsed gracefully into a chair. Nick refilled her glass and handed it to her. "Thanks," she muttered automatically and drank, emptying the glass.

He refilled her champagne glass again and watched with interest as Silver eyed him. "That's what this is, isn't it? An engagement dinner? You had this all planned."

"I'm good at planning and reducing things to basics." Nick hoped he wouldn't have to use his backup plan to secure Silver. Acquiring Silver by today's politically correct methods wouldn't be possible, and every molecule in his body told him that his troubleshooting background had brought him here, to this moment, facing Silver with an established, ring-certified marriage proposal.

He wanted his marriage in place before she discovered that he'd chatted with her parents and brother.

She downed the champagne and reached for the bottle, sloshing more liquid into her glass. She lifted the glass and eyed him. "You will go in there and straighten this out. I won't be responsible for misleading your grandmother. I respect her. We've grown very close."

"You're hunting something in Amen Flats, and it's related to the Tallchiefs and their legends. I will secure it for you. You have my promise. As my wife, you will have my full dedication and my protection. I want you to be happy." Nick watched Silver filter through her emotions, shielding them quickly. He ached to hold her, to share the pain within her. He could not do that with Silver holding him at a distance, offering to help him with love potions and regarding him as "one of the guys."

He was putting himself on the marital platter and praying that he wouldn't fall into the reject pile, not with Silver.

"I don't think I like this side of you," she muttered as she glared at him. "I liked you when you were sweet and vulnerable."

When I was the appliance, one of the doo-wop boys... "I do have a nasty streak, when I want something. And I want you. I'm hoping we can move into our alliance easily and make everyone happy—"

"No...way...in...hell." Silver poured another glass of champagne, drinking it quickly.

Nick didn't like his momentary bounce into the reject "guy" pile. An experienced troubleshooter knew when to gamble and when to tighten the noose. He wanted Silver's very desirable neck within his reach and moved to close the gap. "The alternative isn't pleasant. There's that breach of promise thing."

"You're breaking my heart. Your pride wouldn't let you—"

"Yes is a word that goes very deep with me. I didn't force you then, and you agreed." Nick pushed his temper and his uncertainty down. Silver was a strong woman, determined to flow her own way, and he intended to be included in her life. "You're not receptive to my invitation?"

"Listen, you—"

Nick didn't give Silver a chance to storm at him. "You could be pregnant."

When the idea first hit him, as he was sprawled over her, trying to pull his brain back into his body and unmelt his bones, Nick had floated, almost hoping that she would carry his child. Now, he desperately wanted her as his wife and he wanted a family; he didn't want to be an outsider to life. He wanted a home, not a camping house, where every day he woke up to Silver and went to bed with her every night—and several times during the day. He watched awakening emotions zipping across her face, ranging from shock to wary admission of the potential, and then to furious denial. "One time," she snapped back at him, defensively.

"We both know our biology, sweetheart. I was there, remember? And you took me by surprise...ambushed me in my sleep. However, I was fully awake when I asked you to marry me." Nick watched Silver's shaking hands reach for the champagne bottle and pour another glass. "You don't drink. Take it easy."

"I'm trying to empty this bottle, so I can smash it over your thick head. I thought you were easygoing...you're not. You're doing the suit thing. You're almost cute when you're concentrating on cooking or ironing, but—" Her gaze took in his suit. "Black, formal, tie, shoes polished so bright you can see lights in them. That gangster-pirate look. That showing your teeth thing, like a wolf getting ready to feed. You're enjoying this, aren't you? You've set the stage for tonight. This isn't a business dinner...you're out to satisfy your family."

She eyed him carefully, and Nick wanted to run his hand along that long, smooth line of her thigh— "What was that again about your protection? Why would I need your protection?" she asked.

"My family has nothing to do with this. I want you for myself. I want to make a life with you. I want to court and romance you and help you find whatever it is you want in Amen Flats. Marriage is just clearing away the debris and moving into a different stage of our relationship."

Silver's gray eyes flashed at him beneath her long, straight, glossy lashes, her lips tightening. "I can't settle for that. I manage my own life. I won't be placed on a bargaining table, Nick."

Then as she stood and prepared to leave, Nick plopped Plan B on the discussion table. "Then there's my obligation to Palladin, Inc. I can't let you bamboozle my grandmother. That is why you need my protection. If you betray Mamie, then I'll see to it that you lose everything. As my wife, you would be protected from the excellent legal muscle of Palladin, Inc."

They were on his ancestral territory now, and Nick was claiming Silver—permanently.

"Did you say bamboozled, my dear?" Mamie asked at the head of the dinner table. "What was that about a gangster, suit-predator, a pirate boarding your ship?"

On the elegant tablecloth, Nick's ruby engagement ring glittered on Silver's third finger, left hand. Her other hand was enclosed in his big one as they sat close together. He frowned as Silver tried to withdraw her numbed, cold fingers from his clasp, holding her easily. She settled for placing her sharp heel over the toe of his gleaming big shoe and pushing down hard.

In the elegant candlelight, his green eyes narrowed and he showed his teeth in one of his icy smiles. "She's an impatient woman. Eager for our wedding. Silver said she's very happy, but she's tired. Too much excitement...the wedding preparations..."

He'd plopped a threat in her lap and walked out of his office, leaving her to follow. She couldn't leave the beautiful ring unattended, and had jammed it on her finger as she'd run after him. Before she'd had time to launch an attack, he was introducing her to Mamie—

"The Tallchiefs will take care of arrangements. Their weddings are unusual and wonderful. Rafe and Demi have that fabulous castle—they were married there."

"No castle." Silver fought to keep afloat in a fast-moving current called Nick Palladin. She was a little fuzzy on the details right now, but she'd untangle the mess at any minute.

While Nick and Mamie dropped into the warmth of the Tallchief family and Rafe's and Joel's new families, Silver studied the ring—the rubies were huge, glittering, bloodred against her lightly tanned skin. The gold Celtic setting intertwined the heavy stones, creating a rich, opulent, yet savage design. Just exactly the style a pirate would place on his captive princess's finger before he swept her away. Just exactly what she and Jasmine had dreamed about with their princes— "Oh!"

Mamie peered at her sharply. "You look close to tears. Is anything wrong, my dear?"

"She's emotional now," Nick explained smoothly, and raised Silver's hand to kiss her palm. "We're hoping for a girl just like her." He bit gently and heat skittered through her body. She wondered if she could skip dessert and take Nick on the huge table.

Of course she couldn't. There was that little girl to consider, one with laughing green eyes and a dimple in her chin. Then Silver would have to worry about protecting her innocence from great big wolves, younger versions of her father.

She was angry at his gangster-pirate technique in his office. Nick had carefully outlined just how she had defaulted on the contract: The "liquor" for Palladin's new scent was to be developed after months of research—on site. Nick had a file of hard evidence sucked from her notes, sketches and her computer. The liquor formula, the marketing campaign, the sketches for the crystal perfume bottles, packages for the soap and bath products, had all been developed *prior* to her arrival in Amen Flats. She had worked quickly since he'd first contacted her, and though the essential scent-liquor was good, the ideas strong, they were not her best. They did not convey the unique setting Palladin, Inc. had chosen to duplicate in scent. The word "fraud" lurked in every fact Nick had neatly placed in front of her.

"Fraud" and contract default could ruin her career as a perfumer. She wouldn't be trusted again. Nick could methodically tear apart everything—

A master puzzle-solver, Nick had effectively closed all protests to what he wanted: marriage to him.

The ring glittered ominously on her finger and Silver drank another glass of champagne, meeting Nick's forbidding frown with her own.

"I'm going to finally see my great-grandchild from Nick—the last Palladin desperado and the great-great-granddaughter of Una and Tallchief. You'll make a marvelous mother, Silver, and I couldn't be happier about you coming into our little family. Nick needs you to keep him in line, from running off with the ball, so to speak. He gets a little heavy-handed, and moves quickly when he thinks takeover is necessary. I'm glad you liked the ring, dear. Nick wanted your Tallchief heritage to be included in the design he created for you, and the jeweler worked overtime creating it. Nick has told you, of course, that the stones are from my own wedding ring, from my dear husband. I took the reins of this business after he died, and through the worst of financial times, I saved that ring for Nick, the youngest of my grandsons and the last to marry."

Mamie lifted her glass in a toast. "Now that Joel and Rafe are happily married into the Tallchief family, and Nick is about to complete the circle, I couldn't bear to have my ring sitting cold and alone in a bank's safety box. Years of hopes and dreams and happiness are in those stones. They belong where life and love and excitement fairly burst from the bride—"

Mamie's eyes shimmered with tears, her well-preserved beauty visible as she traced the ring with her finger, then took Silver's hand. "You've made me very happy, dear. I have worried about all of my grandsons. They've overcome much of what my son did to them. Now, with Nick so happy and a baby on the way so quickly, I am relieved. A child would not be an accident between you two strong-minded young people. You both know exactly what you want and how to get it, and you must have instantly wanted each other, aware of your destiny. I knew that once the two of you met, Nick's life would change. He's always been a lone wolf, avoiding entanglements, flying all over the place, and now he's found you. From what I know of you, you've traveled extensively yourself. Two like people finding each other. You'll do perfectly.''

Silver stiffened under the weight of Nick's warm hand on her nape, a reminder of his intended possession. His warm thumb cruised along her ear. "She's a little nervous. I didn't give her very much time to decide.''

Mamie laughed with delight. "He's been running from women for years, my dear. I'm glad you've caught him. I'm looking forward to a profitable alliance—'' She winked at Nick. "And more great-grandchildren.''

"Not if I can help it," Silver muttered.

"What was that, dear?'' Mamie asked. She quickly frowned at Nick. "He's not being a bully, is he, Silver? I will not have my boys bullying women into marrying them.''

"As a matter of fact—'' Silver began slowly, preparing to appeal to the older woman.

Mamie's eyes narrowed at Nick, who smiled blandly. The silent battle waged past Silver, who was fascinated by the exchange. Petite and agile, eighty-plus-year-old Mamie pushed away from the table. She plucked the bottle of champagne from the iced silver bucket. "Silver, you look to be in good shape. Let's adjourn to my exercise room for a girl talk. Bring the glasses. Nick, you are not invited.''

Nick rose to his feet, carefully pulling out Silver's chair as she rose. She smiled up at him, aware of the old-fashioned gentlemanly manners petite Mamie demanded from her towering grandsons. She winked at Nick's glare as she followed Mamie.

A half hour later, draped in a lamé stole, seated on her Exercycle and pedaling slowly, thoughtfully, Mamie studied Silver. She lay on the workout bench, her head very light and her body very heavy, a champagne flute balanced on her flat stomach. Mamie's discussion about Silver's progress with Palladin's new scent line slid slowly into— "He wants you desperately, you know. Nick hasn't had to pull out his charm to acquire women, they've simply tumbled into his life, and frankly he hasn't been that interested. Until now. Perhaps you could forgive him if he is a little arrogant and remember that I haven't long to live now—with my heart acting up—and if only I could see Nick happy for a small time before I passed on, that is all I could ask of you. I'm really looking forward to the wedding. If anything happened to prevent it, I don't know how my heart would react—are you groaning, my dear?''

Silver struggled to present her case logically. "I might not be pregnant. Chances are that I am not.''

"Nick is hopeful. He's positively beaming. If there is anything that would rev up my poor old heart, make me want to live at least another few months, it would be to see Nick happily married, child on the way or not. Did you groan again, dear?''

Nick let himself into the penthouse. At three o'clock in the morning, he badly needed a shower, sleep and a reassuring taste of Silver's soft lips, her scent curling pleasantly around him. A drunken driver had forced a Palladin eighteen-wheeler off the highway, sending the truck down a mountain ravine. The truck had come to rest on the edge of a cliff, the driver bruised and frightened. One wrong move could have sent the truck into a gorge, and with expert direction, Nick had set the weight of his helicopter on the rear of the truck. In a driving, icy rain, he'd secured the cables from the team of wreckers, attaching them to the truck. After helping the driver safely out of the truck, Nick had climbed back up onto the helicopter and signaled the truck to be hauled back from danger.

"Blasted cameras and newswoman cluttering up the job—what made that woman think I needed her hug?'' After a five-hour fight to unload the truck and drag it back up the incline, the driver and the shipment to Palladin's Department Store were safe.

A battered, grim man returned Nick's look in Mamie's ornate gilt mirror. He smelled like diesel fuel—the fuel tanks had to be emptied before hauling the truck up the incline. A metallic spark could have started a forest fire. He smelled like sweat and curses and loneliness.

In the midst of the danger and icy rain, Nick had thought of

Silver. Blackmailing her into marriage was typical of his trouble-shooting technique—if the bargain wouldn't budge, apply force.

Nick studied his tired reflection. His father's hard features stared back at him. A man set on serving himself, Lloyd would have used blackmail to get a woman he wanted.

Nick tiredly rubbed his rope-burned hands across his jaw. They stung a bit and he stared at them, remembering the slight bruises he'd given her during their lovemaking. With Silver, he hadn't been charming.

He'd wanted her…had to claim her. The need was raw, prim-itive, essential…more than sex—he'd taken her virginity, prized it. A shudder skidded through Nick. He was like his father on that level, too.…

A woman like Silver needed to be approached like a fine puz-zle, the player taking time to fit the pieces together. He'd lacked that patience, but he had made a trip to her parents, and now he better understood what drove her.

In the mirror, his father's hard eyes glittered at Nick. A woman like Silver couldn't be forced into marriage—shouldn't be ac-quired by blackmail. Nick was a predator, like his father, taking a woman whom he wanted with an intensity that terrified him. Nick sucked diesel-scented air into his lungs, forcing himself to breathe. He didn't expect Silver to be waiting for him. The best thing he could do for Silver was to step out of her life. He'd crawled from a gutter, done things he shouldn't have, and he'd survived with the memory of his father's backhand slamming into his face.

In his darkened room, Nick stripped away his clothing and stepped into the shower, letting the water sluice over him, praying that it would take away his need to hold Silver. Drying quickly and wrapping a towel around his hips, Nick braced himself for a long, lonely remainder of the night and his grandmother's tongue-lashing in the morning. He took one last look in the steamy bathroom mirror and shook his head. Nick recognized his father's ability to charm, and beneath it all a savage, raw power to possess.

Every year of his life lodged wearily in his bones, every dirty deal his father had committed, including the murder of the Tallchief parents, and the filth that he and his brothers had crawled from, fought to escape. He knew how to survive; he was a predator. Silver deserved—

Silver flung open his bedroom door, eyed him and stepped into the room, slamming the door behind her. Covered by his dress shirt and nothing else, she braced her fists on her waist, tightening the material around her body. "Finally. You've come home."

Nick locked his body, forbidding it to reach out and take her into his arms. He forced himself not to look at her long legs, outlined in the dim light, the thrust of her breasts against the material, that dark band of her briefs. Tired and vulnerable to this woman, he jerked up his defenses.

She sniffed delicately, then stalked across the room to sniff his jaw and throat. "You showered, but it's still there."

"What is?" His need of her? His past? Nick's mouth dried as he caught her scent, the quiver of her breasts beneath the light fabric. He wanted to—hell, no, he wasn't grabbing for her. His body had hardened immediately at the first sight of her, and her breath upon his skin had caused his entire system to hike into "Alert."

"That newscaster-woman kissed you."

"She'd gotten a good story. She was thanking me." He placed his hand on her chest, fought the need to lower it to her breast and held her away from him. He needed time—

"She was trying to suck you— Nick, you're hurt." Silver blinked up at him, her eyes widening as her finger traced the scratch along his jaw. She looked down at her hand, the smear of blood on her skin, and suddenly hurled herself into his arms.

Reeling back from the impact of her body, Nick realized that Silver's long legs gripped his waist. Clutching his hair in her fists, she covered his face with kisses. Just when Nick had adjusted to the happy-dizzy grin that began inside him and spread to other parts of his body, and his hands began lowering to cup her bottom, Silver dropped away lightly, agilely from him.

She scanned his body, eyes widening at the purple bruise along his side, caused by an unfriendly rock. "Oh! Oh!"

She hurried to kiss the bruise, and when Nick sucked in his

breath, his body hard and aching, his limbs shaking, Silver tugged his hands toward her. She turned up his palms where rope burns formed thick pink stripes across his skin. "Oh, Nick..."

The tenderness with which she drew his palms to her lips, kissing them, frightened him. He stood very still, heart racing, aware that no one had ever tended him so earnestly.

"Don't you move. Stand right there." Silver hurried to the bathroom, retrieving an ointment tube and a roll of gauze. She smeared the salve gently onto his palms and smoothed it with her fingertip. "I wish I had time to mix an herbal salve for you, but this commercial brand will do for now."

She glanced up at him. "You're shaking, Nick. You're uncertain and vulnerable now, just because I'm caring for you. I know that you were never touched like this, that your mother died when you were very young. When you three were struggling to survive, Rafe and Joel did what they could, but you don't know how to take tenderness when it is meant just for you. I like tending you, putting my hands on you. I'd like to cut your hair—it's gotten too long and you're looking as if no one cares about you. Well, I do. I care very much what happens to you, apart from Palladin, Inc.'s investment in me."

She leaned to kiss his chest lightly, then continued her ministrations to his hands. "You jumped, just then, shocked by affection. You act so surprised and unworthy, so humble. It's part of your appeal, that helpless little boy beneath all that grim, macho aura. I almost wish I were pregnant with a little boy like you— You've got to clear that with Mamie— Though I doubt I'd have any resistance at all to him, just like I don't have when you— Never mind about that now."

She capped the ointment bottle briskly and began rolling gauze around his hands, taping them securely. "That should do for now.... On the other hand, I'm very angry with you. I know where you've been—" The flat of her hands hit him on the chest, hard; the back of his knees hit the bed and Nick went sprawling over it.

He lurched to his feet, a little mortified that a woman had unbalanced him, and found Silver's shaking finger beneath his nose. "You've been out there—flinging yourself around a rock bluff, having a magnificent time while I worried about you. Oh, no, not a word to me about leaving—oh, you're really in for it now. There you were on television, swinging from your helicopter on the truck, to the ground. You're not agile, Nick. You're built for power and endurance, not for swinging from limbs. I could have helped you, you jerk. You made my nose stuff up when I cried. A 'Nose' can't afford that. You could ruin my career, but most of all you stopped my heart—the sight of you all muddy and clothing ripped. You protect everyone but yourself, Nick."

She wove slightly to the left, blinked and frowned at him. "You can't put me under your wing, Nick. I know what I want, and I'm going to get it. You are not stuffing up my nose again, got it?"

A delicate hiccup preceded her nose nuzzling his damp chest. She swayed backward and lifted her hand to run it through his wet hair, fisting it. "All this honor stuff, Nick...it's really outdated. Not that I don't appreciate the effort, but I'm certain that I'm not a fallen woman, just because you and I made love. I wanted you. I took you. It was as simple as that. You are not obligated to marry me."

Nick was too tired and vulnerable to match wits with the woman he wanted to hold in his arms. The idea that she could knock him off balance still nettled him. The concept that she wasn't exactly welcoming his first foray into marriage irritated him. Tempers and emotions at a bargaining table were useless.... Nick inhaled abruptly. The image of himself as the bargain spread on the negotiating table was a little humiliating. "We'll talk about this in the morning."

But Silver was gaping at his lower body. "You're naked. All of you." She took in his body from feet to head, running her fingertip downward until Nick eased it away. "You're magnificent...a gangster, a pirate. You can't have my ship, and Mamie is going to be very disappointed when her great-grandchild isn't on the way."

She held her head in her hands. "It's all so sad. Poor Mamie."

"Are you going to be sick?" Nick asked cautiously as she fumbled with the button at her throat.

"No, but Mamie's heart could give out at any minute. She doesn't qualify for a transplant, and the doctor said that the slightest upheaval could be fatal. Don't tell her about the non-baby, Nick."

Nick frowned and helped Silver ease the shirt from her. His mouth dried at the sight of her curved, warm body, the delicate flow of her rounded hips into the V of her thighs. He closed his eyes, sniffing delicately at Silver's scent. There were advantages in developing his sense of smell. He remembered the scent of their lovemaking, of her arousal, and shuddered. "Mamie told you that?"

His eyes opened when she pushed her nose into the hollow of his throat, looped her arms around his neck and nuzzled him. "Poor sweet Nick. Just trying to make his grandmother's last days happy. I would have understood that, Nick."

"I think my grandmother will be fine, sweetheart," Nick said above her head as the enticing scent took her nose lower. He sucked in his stomach as she nuzzled his navel, sniffing his wonderful scent.

His hands clamped on her shoulders, stilling her. "Take it easy with that nose."

"I like her. We're not going to let anything happen to her, are we, Nick? She's raised you and your brothers, struggled with you—" Silver raised to tap Nick on the nose with her finger. "You were always in trouble, Nick, and she worried most about you. She's delicate, you know. Always has been. You were a burden, but her son—your father—that must have been awful."

"It was. Nothing is going to happen to Mamie, sweetheart." Nick lifted Silver to pour her into his bed. He stretched out beside her, and before he could escape, Silver wiggled upon him, getting more comfortable.

"I like you trapped where I can know that you are safe. The newscaster said that one spark could set off a fire and you'd be— Your grandmother was worried, watching the broadcast with me, and we shared a bit more champagne. She said you were a fierce little boy, stubborn and contrary, and leaping in to defend your brothers. When arguing with her wouldn't work, you used your charm, that whimsical little-boy smile. It still works.... Don't rock the boat,'' Silver muttered as Nick pulled the black satin sheet over her back. She caught his hands, ached at the sight of the bandages, kissing them. Nick cared so much about other people, and little for his own needs. ''I was so worried about you.''

Nick's voice was very deep and uneven. ''I'm safe. Go to sleep. We'll talk in the morning.''

His hands slid up and down her back, the caress comforting, and Silver snuggled upon him. There was one need she knew that Nick took very seriously, greedily—his need of her. She tapped his nose lightly. ''You need me, don't you, Nick?''

His heart thudded heavily beneath her breast and when he spoke, it was very carefully. ''Very much. You complete me.''

''Likewise. But you can be irritating, and I didn't like being dumped in that horse watering trough. A nose has to be very careful, and a cold can ruin a reputation.'' She sniffed lightly at his ear and he inhaled sharply as she tasted the contour with a flick of her tongue.

She dragged her breasts across his chest experimentally and Nick shuddered, his hands opening and closing on her bottom. Silver lifted to study him. ''Nick, you're flushed and warm. We'll have to do the best we can without those pearls, Nick.''

Nick tensed, his expression grim. ''If you want pearls instead of the rubies—''

She waved her hand high in the air, studying the glittering bloodred rubies. ''Nah. I love them. I love you. You need me.''

''I really think we should get some sleep.'' Nick couldn't move, stunned by Silver's admission. He decided to be gallant and not pursue a commitment she might regret. An athletic, health-conscious woman, a nondrinker, Silver was likely influenced by the champagne.

Still. Nick gathered the precious words into him, hoarded them. He'd never been told he was loved, not even casually. Mamie had looked at him with tenderness, but in her hurried struggle to maintain a corporation and to raise the unruly youths, she had not voiced her affection. Silver had just provided him with a unique, somewhat shattering, woozy emotion.

He struggled to collect himself as Silver braced her arms on his chest and toyed with his hair, combing it through her fingers. "I would really like to trim this—"

She kissed his lips lightly, ran her open mouth along the hard bottom contour and across the top one. "You've heard that before, haven't you? Those three little words."

"No, but I like the sound of it," he said warily. Strange what those words could do to a man, almost disabling every logical thinking process. He focused on logic—waiting until the morning, having a logical discussion with Silver about their relationship, making himself appealing to her— Nick sucked in his breath and stared at the woman rubbing her nose against the hair on his chest.

Silver inhaled his fragrance, bringing it into her. Perfect. Masculine, yet vulnerable. A gallant man struggling with his emotions. Nick was perfect, sweet, shy, adorable. He could look so boyish, but right now he looked like a big, dangerous challenge, a very fit, tanned playground. He loved his grandmother. He was gentle. Love burst out of Silver like flowers and sunshine. "I love you, I love you, I love you...."

She glanced downward, found him hard and thrusting against her stomach. She stared, fascinated, at the difference between them and touched him lightly with her fingertip. He groaned unsteadily, as though the sound was torn from him. She was just moving down to explore him further when Nick shuddered again and eased her upward and to his side. He turned to her, covered her shoulder with the satin sheet. After a lengthy pause, Nick said, "I'm glad you came to me tonight."

Silver smiled softly. She realized that Nick was uneasy with sharing his emotions and that he wanted to say exactly the right thing. She snuggled against him. "You need me. On the television, I saw the desperation on your face, those haunting eyes, and I knew that you needed me.... Nick, I think I may have inherited a little of my ancestors' seer and shaman talents."

"You may have, but I've needed you all my life. I've waited for you."

His admission came slowly, as if the words were rusty and uncared for, afraid of light and tenderness. She'd had a family who loved easily, sharing it, but Nick's life had been cold— She caressed his chest and allowed her hand to wander downward. Nick sucked in his breath and caught her hand, drawing it up to his lips.

"We'll work out our relationship, Silver," he began carefully. "I know this is too soon for you—"

"Stop troubleshooting and negotiating. You smell quivery...unstable, your basic notes are trembling like tiny antennae. The top, distinctive note is your insecurity about me. The middle note is that you're feeling guilty. You want to apologize for your gangster-pirate act, your attempt at takeover. You're sorry. How sweet."

He glowered at her, a male who had always concealed his more tender emotions, suddenly exposed as sweet. "I am not insecure, and the attempt was successful. I am rarely called sweet."

"You are uncertain and shy. Nick, don't be afraid to show your feminine side with me...don't act prickly and wary and arrogant, because I know it's all a cover-up. Tough-guy time is over, Nicholas Palladin. You are shy of me." She grinned at him, suddenly outrageously happy. Nick wanted her desperately and she was flying, powerful, filled with awe. "Are too."

"Am not."

Then he grinned slowly, magnificently confident, and Silver couldn't resist. She slid her hand downward, curled her fingers and captured him. Nick sucked air, his body stiffening immediately. He shuddered. "Careful."

Silver laughed with delight, her emotions tumbling into desire. "I want you," she cried out fiercely, and launched herself against him, locking her arms around his shoulders and her legs across his, her face mashed to his.

Nine

"Silver, wait—" Nick wanted to reassure Silver that he wouldn't hurt her. He wondered then if the son of Lloyd Palladin could make that promise—

Then Silver placed him inside her, that moist, clinging, tight sheath, and her tiny constrictions took him deeper. The fantastic sounds of her arousal shook him. She was already flowing, heating over him, her breasts dragging erotically against his chest—

In an effort to slow her, to control his almost bursting body, Nick reached for her wrists and she pushed against him, her hips thrusting against his. Turning her, Nick realized too late that they were on the edge of the bed. He twisted his body as they slid down the satin sheets onto the lush carpeting. He turned again, protecting Silver, covering her with his body, as he deflected the lamp that had been caught by Silver's flaying hand. It crashed a distance away from them.

"Make me hear bagpipes, Nick," Silver whispered desperately.

Nick shook his head, trying to understand. He'd heard his heart thunder when he made love to Silver, he'd heard the music of her sighs, but— "What?"

"Bagpipes. Mamie said you played them. Oh, Nick. I'd love to hear you play—"

"Mamie talks too much," he managed to say before Silver's tongue slid across his lips, and he plunged into the hot, hungry kiss, meeting her.

A heartbeat later, as Silver's agile body recaptured his, her arms locked around his neck and her legs drew him up tight inside her, a soft but persistent knock sounded on Nick's door. He groaned, passion racking him as Silver's body went taut beneath him— "Yes?"

"Nick?" Silver whispered desperately, her expression a mix of panic, frustration and desire. Her nails lightly raked down his back, and instinctively Nick found her breast, gently biting it— with a cry, she bolted high against him, arms flying over her head to latch onto the nightstand. He deflected the champagne glass tumbling toward them, and it crashed against the door.

The knock sounded again, louder this time.

In an attempt to soothe Silver, who was racing on without him, Nick placed his hand on her breast, caressing the softness. She groaned shakily, and he knew that for the moment, the doo-wop boys were far behind his lead. Her body tightened again, tiny constrictions enveloping him, and Silver reached for a pillow, jamming it over her face. Her muffled, frustrated cry delighted him.

"Are you all right, sir?" Mamie's elderly butler asked on the other side of the bedroom door.

Nick couldn't be finer, buried deep inside Silver's thrashing, hot body, her frantic muffled sounds exciting him. In an effort he considered heroic, as her tiny muscles began to squeeze him again, Nick managed to say unevenly, "I'm fine."

"Very well, sir. Breakfast at six, as you asked."

"Make that, ah, later."

Nick tugged the pillow away from Silver's flushed face and found her mouth, taking it with a hungry desperation he couldn't stop. *Silver loved him. Everything was going to be just fine.*

* * *

In the morning, her finger wore his ring; her wrist wore his bruise. The dark mark on her fragile skin sickened Nick. He hadn't been able to control himself, plunging into Silver, swept away by passion, until he collapsed, melted on her. With her scent around him, her hands gently smoothing his hair and back, he'd tumbled into sleep.

When his passions were aroused, his dark legacy had slid free; his father had hurt women, and now Nick realized his full potential for harming the woman he wanted. Silver hadn't spoken to him all day, unable to look at him, her silvery eyes avoiding his. She'd slid into her laboratory the instant they'd arrived at his ranch, closing the door against him.

Hours later, she'd showered and shut her bedroom door behind her, a fortress wall. At three o'clock in the morning, Nick hadn't slept, uneasy with the darkness inside him. Drawn to the woman he had hurt, Nick had to see her. He eased open the door to her darkened room, caught her scent and moved silently to stand over her bed.

He'd hurt her. Pain knifed into Nick, the realization that he had inherited his father's ability to wound. He eased down onto her bed, took her hand gently in his and brought it to his mouth, placing his face in her palm.

"Nick?" Silver's uneven whisper curled around him. "Why can't you stand to look at me?"

"I've hurt you. I'm sorry."

"What do you see when you look at me?"

Nick took her face within his hands, cradling it, running his thumbs lightly across her cheekbones, the gentle sweep down to her lips. "I see you. The woman who completes me. I've been alone for so long, and now there is you."

Her fingers moved across his cheek, tested the moisture on his lashes. "You're terrified you're like your father, aren't you? You aren't. Not a bit. You take care of those you love, you are a gentle man, Nick."

"You have bruises on your wrist. I put them there. This is the second time." He shuddered, remembering the bruises his father had given other women, and his brothers.

"Is that why you can't look at me, because you feel guilty?

There were two people in that room last night, Nick, and I wanted you just as desperately. I saw the marks my nails made on your back. I wasn't exactly sweet. I can be…very determined, single-minded, and right then—''

"You were perfect." He lifted her wrist to kiss the slight bruise and fitted his finger to it. "I should have controlled myself."

"I want you to make love to me now."

"There's something I have to tell you—''

"Tell me tomorrow."

Silver struggled out of the tangled sheets, inhaled the fresh sage-scented air from the open bedroom window and caught Nick's wonderful scent. She crushed the pillow against her, wallowing her nose in it. In her mind, she saw him rising above her, his features honed, savage, eyes brilliant as he plunged into her—resting so deep and full within her that nothing could tear them apart—giving her what she wanted—giving her everything….

The male voices in the kitchen rumbled pleasantly as Silver eased from the bed and took her shower. Rafe and Joel were probably discussing business.

Nick hadn't said he loved her. She could deal with that. Nick was a cautious man and uneasy with his emotions. Fine. She didn't need an undying admission; it was enough that he needed her. She wasn't certain if she could handle his love…that knowledge could be a commitment, and that frightened her.

Nick was right. She hadn't met the contract; she'd betrayed a legendary inheritance and Mamie's trust. As she dressed, scents from the mountain stirred in her, and she methodically separated the base notes, the middle notes and the top notes. The rich fabric of the Tallchief family had been missing, a smooth, constant note, which would call for adjustment in her liquor formula. The dawn glittering on the mountain dew, Nick's gleaming meadow green eyes, the amber tones of his skin, stirred an image of a tiny, fluted opalescent bottle filled with light amber liquor. Amber and green shades curled across the marketing packages, a bold green striking across the box.

Once she found the pearls, she could concentrate on untangling her formula and deliver a better product.

She studied the Celtic design of the ruby ring on her finger. The bold claim made a statement. Nick could be difficult, but she trusted him on a level she hadn't shared with anyone since Jasmine. She studied the bloodred rubies. Nick had wanted her, and he'd set about securing her. While his methods of acquiring her were bold, predatory and instinctive, she could trust him. She could understand wanting something so badly—

One glance in the mirror, her Tallchief features standing out starkly in the bathroom's shadows, and Silver closed her eyes as that familiar pain swept through her. She tossed the towel over the mirror and braced herself, preparing to meet the men in the other room, and caught the delightful scent of coffee and breakfast—bacon, biscuits and—Silver sniffed delicately—grapefruit, broiled with a topping of brown sugar. He'd already started laundry, the machines humming pleasantly. She smiled whimsically. There were advantages to living with Nick.

The intimate twinges in her body told her that she had enjoyed more than Nick's food. She had reveled in the heat of his lovemaking, his desperate hunger for her…as though no one else had passed before him, as though no one else could ever— They were equal in their fiery desire. Silver trusted that raw sense of her power, of his raw desire to taste her, to fit himself within her body, to draw her into him. His flickering heated look down the length of their joined bodies had taken her breath away.

Both men looked up from the kitchen table as she entered the room. Nick, dressed in jeans and nothing else, studied her quietly, the other tall, slender man with black glossy hair and smoky eyes stood slowly to face her. "Hello, Glynis. You're looking…well tended."

Silver's fist rose to her chest, locked there to protect it, pain searing her. "John!"

"I invited your brother here," Nick said quietly, rising to his feet. Dressed only in his jeans, his muscles tensed, his body braced as though preparing for a blow.

"I'm working to create a signature scent for Palladin, Inc., John. This is business. I don't have time to—" she began, and an image of her younger brother playing with her and Jasmine hit her. They'd served him tiny teacups and cookies and he'd tossed a worm onto the table, making Jasmine scream— There was that angle to his head, that sweep of cheek shared by all the Tallchiefs—by Jasmine...

Nick moved toward her, his face grim, and she stopped him with a cutting motion of her hand. She'd trusted him and he'd betrayed her— Nick's outstretched hand came down slowly to his side, forming a fist.

"It's not his fault. I wanted to see you, and I called Nick when you wouldn't answer my calls or letters," her brother stated warily. "Mom and Dad are worried, Glynis. When Nick visited last week, he invited me to come here when I could. I had to see you. Because of him, I think Mom and Dad understand better. I do." There was that quick searching look for the sister who wasn't there; Silver's features reminding John of her identical twin—*Jasmine.*

Silver swallowed; she could feel the tugging, tangling emotions dragging her down, choking her. She gripped the back of the chair to prevent sinking into the icy bog of pain at her feet. "Last week?"

Nick's quiet tone hit Silver like a spear, thrust into her heart. "I know about Jasmine."

"You knew about Jasmine before we—" As a teenager, she'd trusted Jasmine to recover from the illness. As a woman, she'd trusted Nick.

John had left immediately, sadly, and she'd been unable to look at him. Now, standing beside Tallchief Lake, the brewing storm whipping at Nick's clothing, plastering it to his powerful body, she glanced at the ring she'd discarded. A mix of Celtic curves and rich rubies, it lay upon lush, dewy grass as green as Nick's eyes. "You had no right to enter, to open my life, Nick."

He was pushing, prying, opening wounds she'd fought for years— "The mirrors you didn't want, the lack of contact with a family that clearly loves you...the pieces didn't fit. But that isn't why I went—"

Outraged, she flung at him, "You thought you could make

my life *fit?* Fit? Like a puzzle? You intruded into my family and dug out what you needed to know about me because I'm a puzzle to you?''

Pain tore at her, brought her curling to her knees, her arms around herself, rocking her body. She closed her eyes, keeping in the pain. *Jasmine…as pale as the hospital sheets, sliding into death despite whatever Silver tried desperately to say, to do—*

Nick started toward her, hesitated and braced his boot on a fallen log. ''I saw the pictures of you and Jasmine together. No wonder you don't like mirrors.''

She fought the icy chill shrouding her, the memory of Jasmine's pale, thin face. ''You wouldn't understand.''

''I know what looking like someone can do to you. How it can eat and twist inside you.''

Despite her own pain, a flicker of Nick's sliced through her. ''You're nothing like your father. Jasmine and I were not only twins, we were…one. We knew what each other would say before it was said. We were not only sisters, we were friends. We had dreams, Nick. We dreamed of Elizabeth's legend, of finding her pearls and meeting our true loves.''

''You watched her die and you came apart.'' He understood now how deeply Silver's emotions ran, the fear of failure and loyalty to her sister's memory driving her to find Elizabeth's pearls. As a Tallchief, Silver's instincts ran to finishing promises and completing life circles; for her sister, Silver would try to complete the quest and dreams began as girls, and in doing so, she would find peace.

''I watched my entire family die, day by day, shattering apart when she was gone. One essential piece of the whole beautiful picture could not be replaced, and I was only a reminder of the half that was missing. A well-tuned, loving family slid into a dysfunctional one. She was just seventeen, Nick. Just a girl who hadn't lived her dreams. I tried so hard—I tried so hard to make her live—and every hour, she slid away from me. I was so angry at her for not living. My parents can't bear to look at me, either. I see it in their faces every time, before they shield it. They're looking for Jasmine in me…in me…and I can never replace her.

The only way I could survive was to make a new me, to change my hair, my clothes, to make a new life away from them.''

He placed his hands on her shoulders, shaking her gently. He was grateful to De LaFleur for helping Silver survive. "You're trying to live for two people. Let go, sweetheart. Let them love you. You can't feel guilty for living—"

She tore free, facing him, braced against the storm and her furious pain. "I do, damn it. Don't you see? *I* lived. I lived and Jasmine died." She hated him, glaring at him as she pushed herself to her feet, shaking with anger. His ring gleamed in the midst of the summer rain, and she scooped it up, hurling it out into the dark, fierce waves of Tallchief Lake. It could rest at the bottom with any trust she had placed in Nick. "How could you know anything?" she asked bitterly.

He looked out at the white, frothy waves, the tiny splash caused by his ring. "I know what it's like to look in a mirror and be reminded of another person…one who had an impact on your life."

Silver swiped away the hot tears on her face, torn by the vulnerability in Nick's expression, the shadows written on his face. "You're Nick, guardian of the Tallchiefs. You're brave and you're strong and you care about those you love. But you don't know about this— Why did you go to my parents?"

The wind lifted his hair away from his face, honing his angular features as he looked out at the lake where her ring had fallen. "I asked your parents for permission to marry you."

"You what? Nick, you can't arrange someone else's life. I couldn't make Jasmine live—" She was crying now, silvery eyes lashing at him, her body shaking, pain tearing at her.

He'd done that to her…torn the trusting heart right out of her. The son of Lloyd Palladin was bred to hurt. In the mist and slashing rain, the wind beating the cattails at the shoreline, Nick stuck his hands into his pockets. If he took Silver in his arms, she'd fight him and he'd hurt her.

Nick felt twice his age and twice as worn. He'd hurt Silver, who'd had enough pain. He'd wanted to help her, to understand her desperation to succeed, to take every challenge, to smooth

those rough edges, never too far from the surface. He'd wanted
to protect her, to marry her, to love her—

At an unexpected break in the coming storm, the misty summer air curled seductively around him, tormenting him with
dreams that could never come true.

"If the Montclair pearls are anywhere, they are at the bottom
of Tallchief Lake," he said quietly, giving her what he could.

Silver braced herself against the impulse to turn into Nick's
strong body, to let him comfort and shelter her. He'd said the
Montclair pearls— "What do you mean, Nick?"

With a long, defeated sigh, he reached out to sweep his finger
across her damp cheek. "It's just a theory, but where you threw
your ring is exactly where I think the pearls might be resting."

Silver turned to the storm-tossed black waters, the white waves
whipping across the lake. A lifetime of dreaming, of planning,
had come to this one moment, and she prayed that finally Jasmine
and she would be free.... She reached out to take his hand, needing the anchor of his strength. "Nick?"

He moved behind her, sheltering her from the wind, and ran
his hands down her arms to circle her wrists. "Feel it, Silver.
Put out your hands and close your eyes. Focus on what is beneath
the water and what waits for you—"

"I don't know if I— Nick? Would you pinch my nose?"

"Right. Have to take care of the nose. Scents would distract
you." She felt him shaking his head as he grumbled, one hand
lifting to pinch her nostrils.

"Only your scent can do that."

"Thanks," he muttered flatly. "Ready?"

"Ready." She wondered instantly if she was always ready
when Nick was concerned, her senses leaping at the scent, or the
sight of him.

He lifted her arm, and slowly Silver reached the free one,
spreading her fingers, letting the scents and the rain flow between
them. "You think I have Elspeth's powers to sense things, that
I've inherited seer and shaman talents—"

The mist tingled on her skin, much as it would have done on
Elizabeth's all those years ago—

"You're a Tallchief. You stand and fight for what you want. There's that predatory, hunting instinct and ties to the past, to your legacy. It's worth a try. Let everything go, and try to feel what is out there—"

"I'm afraid I'll fail. I'm afraid, Nick—" She'd always been alone, and now, suddenly, with Nick standing warm and alive behind her, his arm running along hers, his hand circling her wrist, closing her nose, she believed in her own strength, apart from anyone—alone and without Jasmine.... "Tell me what you know, talk to me."

His cheek was rough against hers, damp with rain and her tears. He kissed her lashes. "You smell like sunshine. My sunshine."

She shook her head, then rested it back against his chest. "I can't be too close again, Nick."

"Don't think about that now," he murmured slowly, his thumb caressing her wrist. "You're trembling. What do you feel?"

She reached inside herself, rummaged through her senses. "You're frustrated, but you're tethering yourself and it's difficult for you. You don't want anything for yourself—"

Nick inhaled abruptly, and his hand tightened briefly around her wrist as he muttered, "Oh, I truly do."

"You like holding my nose. It's not a gift like a marble, Nick. You don't have to be so delighted."

"Why don't you just get on with business?" he grumbled.

Sensations trembled along her fingers, her palm. She reached for them, spreading her fingers. "There's more. It's on my fingertips...like gold dust, shimmering. Scents. Essences. Moondrops flipping on lily pads. Silver fish gliding through green silk—dark satin, swords of light, a rock castle, a tunnel... Nick? What's the base note?"

"I've learned to translate that perfumer's jargon—the foundation upon which I base my theory. What holds it all together? I compared two maps—one created during Elizabeth's lifetime and the other is current. The contours are different and the lake surface is much larger today. Years ago, an avalanche opened the entrance of an underwater stream, causing it to flow into

Tallchief Lake. It raised the water level. Elizabeth's pearls could be resting in an underwater cave, or on one of the rocky ledges.''

"*An underwater cave. A tunnel. They could be the same.*" Silver leaned against him, needing his support as she realized how close she could be to discovering Elizabeth's pearls. "I don't know what to say. I've been so thorough. I didn't think to examine changes in geography."

"Let me help you find what you need." Their fingers laced, his arms folded around her, his kiss warming her cheek.

"You already have. I would never had tried sniffing with my fingers, I mean feeling. I really felt all those things, Nick, and I would never have tried without you." Silver found herself turning, meeting his gentle, seeking kiss. "I adore you, Nicholas Palladin."

"Adoring is okay," Nick whispered unsteadily. "Can I unpinch your nose? Nasal tones from you are fine, but—"

Silver felt like laughing, like crying, like loving Nick. "If I told you that I wanted you now…here, in the rain…what would you say?"

His words came slowly, firmly, as he released her nose and drew her to him. "I would be honored."

Between them, the mist shifted and Silver found herself lost in Nick's jade green eyes. "I'm sorry about Mamie's rubies."

"We'll find them," he said, his hands smoothing her waist and pressing possessively into her denim-covered hips. "We'll find what you need. Now what was that about making love?"

He'd come to retrieve her from the depths of Tallchief Lake, and Nick's scowl behind the diving mask said he wasn't in the mood to argue. His finger pointed to his diving watch, then his thumb jerked upward, signaling their necessary ascent to the surface of Tallchief Lake.

After three solid days of diving, Silver began to doubt her vision of the watery tunnel. She took one last survey of the murky rubble of fallen trees and boulders at one end of Tallchief Lake, then began to make her way upward. Already in the large fully equipped boat that Nick had commandeered from a friend, he reached to haul her over the side. He grimly took off her mask, stripped away her tank and began unzipping her wet suit. Before he turned away to strip his own wet suit, the look he shot down her bikini-clad body was hungry, hot and frustrated. "You've been diving for three days and working all night on the signature scent. You need rest and food. You're stopping for the day, and I'm telling Mamie that the conference with Marketing next week is canceled. There's no way you can keep up this pace."

"I'll meet that contract and every meeting it takes to put Silver's Signature Fragrances into Palladin's marketing machine. But right now, I'm going back down—"

Nick's narrowed eyes flashed at her, his open hand slamming against the side of the boat. "The hell you are. I was out of my mind to agree to let you dive alone. That lake is reputedly bottomless with a strong current— You were supposed to keep that rope tied to you and you were supposed to tug it every five minutes. Instead, I pulled the rope, and you weren't on the other end."

Her muscles ached; she was drained, tired and too frightened to stop. "So you came after me. I don't like being kept on a leash, Nick. I'm an experienced diver and I do not like heavy-handed men. You like to push…you've been using your trouble-shooting abilities on me. I'm a woman, Nick. Not an acquisition."

Nick glared at her for a solid minute before speaking, a muscle clenching in his jaw, darkened with a day's growth of stubble. He looked raw, sexy and frustrated, shoving his hand back through his hair. It had grown long, waving down the back of his taut neck. "Handling difficult women and mules has been easy, until you. Be sensible. You work all night, moving around your beakers and scents and your notebooks, sketching and—"

"You mean you can't charm me into having your way. Carrying me into your bed wasn't my idea. I was perfectly happy—"

"Sleeping with your head on the laboratory countertop. I wanted it on my shoulder. Your sketches for the new designer bottle are good, by the way. The swirl is a clean, elegant design. That little gold Celtic medallion tied to the top provides a whimsical touch. We can use that coin image in other marketing ideas.

Let me know when you want a primary consultation with our marketing department."

"The glass should be iridescent, pale blues and greens. Like sky at the beginning and the end of the day, like meadows shimmering with dew." Silver scanned the lake. "I want to go down just one more time.... How would you like it if I pushed you into a shower at two o'clock in the morning, soaped you down—muttering about contrary women—and hauled you off to *my* bed?"

"You smelled like sex. Not a delicate scent, but powerful enough to rack a man's nerves. If one whiff of that caught on the wind, I'd be called out by all the bachelors in the area and probably a few married men," Nick returned darkly.

"I was testing a scent liquor in massage oil. I got a little carried away with the keynote scents, and fouled the dilution ratio of the carrier mix. Jojoba oil has a way of slipping away from you, you know," she muttered. One sight of Nick strolling by her laboratory door, dressed only in his boxer shorts, and her hand had automatically reached for the sensual scents.

Nick could be distracting, especially when he laughed aloud while playing with one of the Tallchiefs' children. Awakening this morning, curled next to his body, she could have almost forgotten what drove her, what she had to find. Almost. She looked out onto the lake, shadowed by the rugged mountain where her ancestors had lived and loved. Other women had sought and found peace; Silver had to do the same. "I want to finish this, Nick. I have to."

"You will."

July's heat spread upon the dark surface of Tallchief Lake, the temperatures icy at the bottom. At dusk, the scent of sun warmed pine and the lush reeds bordering the lake curled around her, the light summer wind bringing her other scents, those of pungent sage and softer sweetgrass, and—Silver lifted her head slightly, taking in the scent of the Tallchiefs' meadow, filled with grazing sheep.

She studied the rippling water, trying to see to the murky depths, and another darker, immediate scent slid around her—Nick's. She turned to him as he crouched to put away their diving gear. Clad in loose bathing shorts, Nick's muscles and cords rippled beneath his tanned skin, his hair gleaming richly in the sunlight. His head turned slowly, his eyes lasering across the slight distance to her. His large hands gripped the air tank tightly. "Do you have any idea what it does to a man to have his woman downwind and sniffing him?" he asked in an uneven, deep, raw tone.

Nick studied the woman who had turned from him, her eyes closed as she reached out both hands, opening her fingers to the sensations as she did often now. The dying sunlight pooled around her bikini-clad body, and his throat tightened almost painfully, his body needing hers. There hadn't been time to court her as he wanted; instead, the hard need to claim Silver had shot out of him like a bullet. The phrase "his woman" smacked of a traditional, possessive male, who knew he had bonded forever with one woman...a haunted woman who hadn't given herself fully to their relationship. Maybe his need to help her was selfish, to free her for himself. Maybe it was because he knew the fear of failure, knew how it felt to be the mirror image of someone else.

He ran his hand along his jaw, the sound as raw as his emotions. He feared for Silver's safety, and that once Silver had the object of her quest, Elizabeth's pearls, she'd leave him. Patience had always been his, an easy charm for the women who circled him. But with Silver, he'd reached out and taken.

Nick realized the fine edge of fear, dissecting it. As a child, he both loved his father and hated him. And Lloyd had never been there, always running off without a word. For Nick, adult insecurity was new. The lush pleasure of making love to Silver, of needing her in his life, had startled him. A man in command of his passions and his life, avoiding entanglements and pursuing his goal of serving the Tallchiefs and his brothers, he'd been hit like an avalanche by Silver. Greed was new in the life of Nick Palladin, but he'd fight to keep this woman.

The image of her dressed in Una's bridal shift and touching the Tallchief cradle was enough to begin the search for another cradle, handmade and sold by Tallchief to provide for his family.

In Denver, after he'd returned from salvaging a Palladin's transport truck, she'd said she loved him. Though drizzled in champagne, the words meant no less to him. He'd felt a little weak then, humbled, and had hoarded the memory inside him. Silver was a woman with enough strength to deny her needs, to protect herself—and to turn her back on love.

Silver turned suddenly to him, her face flushed, eyes flashing with excitement. She spoke quickly as though leaving him a goodbye note before she hurried on with her life. "You've got that dark and broody look. I keep forgetting how sensitive you are, and I'm really sorry about yelling at you the other day about using garlic. The odor stopped any progress on my work. But, Nick, I really think I'm getting the hang of this sensory business. I felt a tingle just now, and there was the tiniest bit of sun ray spearing down into the water. I saw a glimmer of gold. It has to be your ring... Your grandmother's rubies are down there, and I'm getting them. Nick...if your theory is right, Elizabeth's pearls could be—"

With that, she dived neatly over the side of the boat and into the water. Nick blinked at the sight of the black water splashing around her bare soles and cursed. The woman he loved wouldn't be predictable, or easy, but— Then he grabbed an underwater light and followed her into the cold, dark water.

Underwater, swimming desperately through the icy water without her wet suit, Silver smiled tightly as Nick's hand wrapped around her ankle. She paused, felt his hand glide upward on her body. He tugged lightly, signaling that he wanted her to swim to the surface, but Silver turned to him and shook her head.

In the shadowy water, Nick grimly agreed and Silver blew him an underwater bubble-kiss, before jackknifing her body and swimming toward her goal.

The ring lay on a rock ledge just ten feet below the surface, glowing in the light Nick had directed toward it. Nick reached for it, placing it on her finger, before diving deeper.

Beneath the rock ledge was a small opening, too small for Nick, and Silver immediately made for it. Again, Nick grabbed her ankle, tugging her back to him. He shoved the lantern into her hand and, nodding, held her ankle again as she eased into the narrow opening. She understood that he would draw her to safety, that the fear in his expression was for her.

A school of small silvery fish swooshed by her, roots of fallen trees tangled the entrance, and just there— The lantern's light caught a dull gleam. Silver placed the lantern on a rock, focused on the gleam and with both hands, reached for it.

She furiously tugged away the feathery roots, which had held the chest safe for years beneath the water. The small wooden chest, banded by brass and studded with buttons, came into her keeping as though waiting for her.

Outside the small cave, Nick took the chest and they hurried to the surface, bursting through and gasping for air.

Nick carefully eased the chest over the side of the boat, placing it on the deck. He turned to Silver, who was clinging, exhausted and gasping, to the small ladder. He cupped her face between his hands, wiped away the droplets on her skin and studied her closely. "Tell me you're—"

She sucked air into her lungs and managed to say, "I'm fine."

"Thank God." He looped an arm around her waist and hauled them both upward into the boat, where they sprawled side by side in the dying light, the chest between them.

Silver placed her hand over the aged, water-soaked wood, Nick's hand covering hers. She had just enough strength to run her fingers across a brass band and in the dying sunlight, the dark metal gleamed. The chest, which had been her quest for years, was not at that moment as important as the man who believed in her, who supported her. Their gazes locked, the world stilling, spinning beyond the boat, the waves gently lapping at the sides.

He'll be a fine beast of a man, haughty and proud and strong as a bear, gnawing at the maiden's shields, testing her, claiming her with wicked eyes...

She had the object of the quest that had driven her for years, haunted her, the chest wet and real beneath her hand. The pearls could rest inside it, or was it a myth? For now, she had to rest, to force herself to breathe and think and push away everything that had burdened her for years. She'd run so hard, living for two women, pushing for the moment, and now Jasmine seemed so far away, and the tall man watching her with green eyes, so near, almost a part of her. Silver closed her eyes and let the gentle rocking motion of the boat, the sound of water lapping at the sides, take her into sleep.

She awoke to find Nick wrapping a blanket around her, drawing her onto his lap against the lake's chill, though it was a warm July night. On the shore, frogs signaled to their mates, an owl soared in the night sky and deer drank from the lake. A fish leaped from the murky water, a silver, moonlit flip, a light splash and only ripples marked his foraging for night insects. Silver placed her opened hand upon Nick's chest, feeling his heart beat, needing him with her. "I don't want to open it, Nick. Not now. I couldn't bear to find that everything was a lie, not now. The moment should be special, and I'm—"

He eased her head into the safe cove of his throat and shoulder. "It's enough for now, isn't it? Just looking at the chest and knowing that you've gotten it?"

The chest was a small dark lump on the moonlit deck, its brass dark with age. "It shouldn't be opened quickly, rather at the right moment. It has waited this long."

He stroked the long line of her back, soothing her. "You want to savor your booty."

"It came too quickly, the end of the search."

"Yes, sometimes the perfect thing you want comes so quickly, you can't believe it's happened, and then you know," he agreed slowly, firmly. "And then you just know."

Nick's big warm hand laced with hers, and Silver settled back against him, content for the first time in years. His heartbeat was solid beneath her hand, the textures of skin and hair on his chest familiar to her cheek, his thighs hard beneath hers. Nick was right; for now, the chest within her grasp, Silver knew that it was enough. She'd finally found a measure of peace, and Nick had helped her.

She curled more deeply against him, too content and weary to think of anything but rest, and Nick holding her safely.

Ten

On her way to Nick's office, Silver stopped, caught by Elizabeth's chest. For years, it had cast its web around her life, and now she could actually see it, touch it. After four days in the shadowy air of his living room, the chest's outer wood had dried and split, the contents unknown. In the midmorning light, lying on Nick's walnut coffee table, the chest's brass bands and studs gleamed warmly, invitingly. Silver couldn't bear to open the chest, not just yet. The moment had to be perfect, a tribute to Elizabeth and to Jasmine…to the Tallchiefs. To rip open the chest did not acknowledge the magic of the legends, of Elizabeth's love for Liam, of Una's for Tallchief. When the moment was ripe, Silver would know—

With one hand, Silver held the large art presentation pad against her and with her other, pushed her fingers through her hair. The chest had been found too quickly after years of preparing, searching. She'd come to the Tallchiefs on false pretenses, moving into their family to enable her to hunt the chest, and now it was here…to open it could end everything, the reason for her staying in Amen Flats… And then there was Nick—powerful, tender, needing her. He was delicate in his way, uncertain of her, his scarred past always lurking nearby. Silver smiled softly. Every time she touched him, Nick was too quiet, tense—as if he treasured each caress, longed for it, took it inside him to hoard.

Or were the pearls the most important element in her life? She had to decide the value, and the costs of her dreams, her life, and she had to be truthful with Nick....

Nick's deep voice came from his office, impatience ringing through it. Silver gathered her large presentation pad closer to her body and turned Nick's ring on her finger. Since recovering the ring and the chest, Palladin's towering guardian had insisted on feeding her nourishing meals; he'd dressed her in his T-shirts after her showers, deflected any calls for her and had asked nothing of her. He'd let her set her own pace—sleeping for three days, the nights spent curled safely against him.

She was pushing now, aware that out there on the lake, Nick had opened a secret within her, that her shaman and seer blood had given her abilities, other than her keen sense of smell. She couldn't give Palladin anything but her best, and on the fourth day, at dawn, she'd lurched out of Nick's arms and hurried to his laundry room. She'd grabbed an apple along the way, munching it as ideas flowed through her mind. Dressed in his T-shirt and boxer shorts, she'd hurried to her laboratory, her scents, her work. Her nose itched, ready to work, her mind keen. She was a Tallchief, given talents that she could not use improperly, not here, not on Tallchief land. She would give her best.

Nick, arms crossed over his bare chest, had followed, leaning against the laboratory doorway. Then he'd left her alone. For the next four days, she'd buried herself in her work, and a week had passed since the chest had come into her keeping. Nick seemed to know when she'd burst out of her lab, driven by hunger. More than once she'd clasped his face in her hands, pushed her lips against his and devoured him, before hurrying on. Though his expression was steamy, his hands tightening on her, he'd never tried to keep her from her work. At night, exhausted, she'd showered and come to his bed and his arms. There in the night, curled against Nick, her Tallchief tartan over the sheet, gripped possessively in her hand, she forgot everything—except the lovely fragrance of the herbs and lavender and wildflower bouquets that he had waiting. The man knew how to make a woman feel welcome.

Silver glanced at her workout equipment, covered with a fine layer of dust. If she hadn't been so tired, the impulse to take Nick, to make love to him, would have suited her better than the equipment. She had to resolve what she had begun and then she could deal with Nicholas Palladin, guardian of the Tallchiefs.

She considered Elizabeth's chest; fear kept her from opening it. The pearls, if they were inside, would end a quest that had taken Silver thirteen years to complete. The moment of opening the box had to be just right—

"Hell, no, you aren't saving Palladin, Inc. money by delivering a second-class product. You can either have a sample replacement of that insulation material for the jackets on my desk in Denver, or you can overnight it to me here at the Amen Flats office. The alternative is no more business with Palladin, Inc. at any time.... I've talked to our quality-control engineer. He's handed the matter to me, and I am not debating—" Nick, dressed in jeans and a black short-sleeve T-shirt, glanced at Silver as he stalked across his ultramodern office, looking like the bold, powerful, hard knight that he was, ready to fight, ready to serve Palladin, Inc.

He'll be a fine beast of a man, haughty and proud and strong as a bear, gnawing at the maiden's shields...

Who tended Nick? Silver wondered. Intrigued by the frustrated male in his lair, she wandered into his sunlit office. His scent tore through her—urgent, hot, impatient, wood and leather, soap and that underlying darker scent that caused something to quiver inside her. Packaging Nick into a scent could be profitable—if she wanted to share.

He rammed a hand through his hair, pushed the overlong length back impatiently. His green eyes ripped down her body, clad in his T-shirt, boxer shorts and socks, flopping slightly at her toes and ending at her calves. His leaping sexual need skittered like a lightning bolt across the room to her, pounded in her, heat awakening at the sight of him. His eyes narrowed, his muscles tensing beneath the black T-shirt, Nick continued his business conversation. He walked to her, wiped away the peanut butter and jelly smear on her cheek with his thumb, licked it and bent to kiss her briskly. He ran his hand over her hair, a familiar movement, and cupped her nape, running his thumb along her jaw, a movement born more of fondness than of heat. He cupped her chin, tilting her face up for his inspection, studying her intently. Then, satisfied, he continued to rip Jameson-someone apart. "Palladin, Inc. will not sacrifice quality because you've made a bargain with a subquality producer."

Nick watched Silver place her sketchbook on his desk. He sprawled in his chair and braced a boot on a filing cabinet. With the July sunlight pouring through his window, the lush Tallchief fields behind him, Nick looked tough, a man who knew his power. "This conversation is finished. Our legal and contracts branch will take care of final measures to see that our negotiations are finished. Do not bother to send your sales people to Palladin, Inc.— What? Oh, I'm certain that our attorney would love to hear from you... Fire me? Tell him what? Go ahead, he's my brother."

His cold laughter sent a shiver up Silver's spine. Nick could be tough; he could be gentle. But for her, he was fascinating, almost an addiction, she mused as she studied the man who had entered her life. Silver ran her fingers through his long shaggy waves, lifting it to study the lights—intriguing reds and lush browns tangling in the sunlight. She noted that Nick sat very still, tensing at her touch. He smelled of ironing, carefully putting creases in his jeans, setting his world right with detergents, spray starches and softeners. The ultraexpensive washer and dryer weren't common, but trophies of a man who had lived in the streets, in filth and hunger.

Nick scraped his hand across his jaw, the raw sound of his stubble meeting his callused palm, reminding Silver of how he had dedicated his time to her. He'd placed balanced, appealing meals in front of her, some of which came from the brand-new pasta maker on his gizmo-filled kitchen counter. He'd watched her carefully, noting how much she'd eaten. She noted that Nick did not use garlic or onions in his sauces, taking care of her nose. He'd acted as if her nose was a treasure, pinching it for her out there in the lake, with the storm approaching. A man who knew exactly how to block her sniffing senses was a true find.

At times, after finding the chest, he'd smelled of livestock and leather, of lavender and wildflowers, of need and passion and tenderness. She studied him now, that lovely sleek skin shifting over those powerful muscles, his green eyes narrowed upon her, the hard set of his mouth and the adorable cleft in his chin.

Nick continued the conversation with Jameson, who had by now agreed to amend his poor-quality goods and deliver a proper product for down jackets. On impulse and with Nick diverted, Silver picked up a pair of scissors that were on his desk and hurried to the laundry room to recover a neatly folded towel. She hurried back to his office, and adjusted the towel around his shoulders.

Wary of being tended, Nick shot her a warning glance, which she ignored, drawing a comb through his thick hair, sectioning it into one layer. She traced the deep *V* of his hairline, an intriguing new discovery about him. Nick's eyes followed her warily, then he abruptly finished the conversation and sat very still. "What's this?"

"You can't go to the business meeting this afternoon looking as though no one cared for you. What would your grandmother think? She still thinks we're engaged, doesn't she? That there's a little green-eyed Palladin baby on the way?"

"I've been busy," Nick stated in a grumbling tone that said he hadn't corrected his takeover move on her life. "What do you mean, 'this afternoon'?"

She snipped another layer, loving the crisp texture of his hair in her fingers. "You're flying me to Denver. I've already called Mamie. She's setting up a presentation meeting of marketing, production, and your brothers. I'm ready to present the new Palladin's Silver's Signature Fragrance campaign. Ah…!"

She tapped Nick's arm as he reached for the sketchbook. "You'll have to wait."

"I have a barber," he grumbled as she combed his hair, smoothing the curls at his nape. "I didn't ask you to cut my hair. I won't have you waiting on me—"

"You'll have to suffer, because that is just what I'm doing. I like touching you. Aye, I do.'' Silver concentrated on cutting his hair, aware of his hands locked to her hips, to her thighs, as she moved around his chair. He tensed, sucking in his breath when her breasts touched him. Nick was so responsive, absolutely delightful, fascinating. When she was finished, she tilted her head to study her work and drew the towel away.

She eased to straddle his lap, her hands on his shoulders. "I've missed you, Nick.''

His lips answered her light kiss warily, yet his hands tightened on her waist, sliding lower to cup her bottom. "I've missed you, too.''

"How much?'' Silver whispered, and Nick's shoulder muscles tensed beneath her fingers.

"Enough.'' A cautious man with a scarred heart, he wasn't giving her more.

Her fingertips traced his mouth. "What did you say to my parents? When you asked to marry me?''

Heat rushed up into Nick's dark cheeks, and he shot her a sidelong, hot look. "That I— I said what I told you up on the mountain, when you took that featherbrained notion to—''

She leaned forward to kiss him, to taste his hard lips with her tongue. She nipped his lip and smiled as his breath hissed by her cheek. Silver slipped her hands to his T-shirt, tugging it free from his jeans, drawing it up over his head. She could barely breathe, the need to love him coursing through her like wildfire. Her fingertips smoothing his bare chest, prowling through the hair there, Silver studied him. "You know that gangster act in Denver was—''

"Out-of-date,'' Nick muttered impatiently, his expression reminding her of a little boy whose hand was caught in the cookie jar. Yet his big hands slid upward, resting just beneath her breasts. He stared at her body hungrily, and Silver's body lurched warmly, damply, softly upon his hardened one. Nick inhaled sharply, skimming one hand lower and smoothing her bare flesh.

"Very old-fashioned, but determined. Like you. You act decisively when you undertake to resolve your needs. I like that. A wishy-washy man wouldn't do for me at all. I can count on you to react in a certain way. It's quite comforting.'' She grinned as his hand stopped exploring her body. The sudden flaring of his nostrils, the sharpened, narrowed drop of his eyes to her braless breasts, gleaming in the light, were all so beautifully predictable. "I left my undies in the laundry room," she whispered, batting her lashes flirtatiously at him.

"Oh, Lord," Nick murmured in a helpless tone before Silver ripped away her borrowed T-shirt and fused her lips to his.

He caught the edge of the desk as they began to tumble, half shifted her, and eased her to the floor beneath him. Nick's body reacted perfectly, humming with sensual need, thrusting against her. Nick hurriedly slid out of his jeans and briefs, his mouth open and hot upon Silver's breast, drawing those heated cords taut, pushing her into heat and rhythm and hunger. The intense pleasure his suckling brought her caused her to throw away all caution, crying out wildly, her arms and legs locked around him.

Nick reached into his desk drawer and lifted slightly away from her for a moment. Then he was in her, safe, hot, hard, pulsing so deep, the lock complete. She answered his kiss with her hunger, meeting him out there on that burst of pleasure on equal terms. The rhythm ran wild, flowing, pulsing, tossing her higher as Nick's hands ran over her, claiming her. One perfect touch took her over the edge, threw her into the eye of the storm as Nick's muffled shout echoed in her mind.

Draped over her, Nick breathed heavily, his heartbeat slowing from the frantic beat. His hot face against her throat, Nick smoothed her hair, cupping her cheek. "You could have given me notice," he whispered unevenly.

"Nah. It's more fun this way. You're so predictable," she said as she patted his bare bottom.

"Predict this," Nick muttered, hauling them both to their feet and lifting her in his arms. He carried her into his bed and lowered her carefully. Though his body was aroused and needing hers, the softness in his eyes stunned her. Silver welcomed him into her arms, her knight, her lover—Nick, real and honest and giving himself to her once more.

The woman dressed in a navy business suit and slacks, gold bracelets on her wrists and gold hoops in her ears, wore Nick's ring, the rubies flashing in the Celtic design. Silver's cropped black hair gleamed blue-black in the light of Palladin, Inc.'s Denver conference room, her body lithe as she pointed out the bottle design, the marketing potential for the Celtic coin, the unique fragrance that would be Palladin's Silver's Signature Fragrance. The scent was both sensual and as fresh as the pine trees on Tallchief Mountain, as moody as Tallchief Lake, and the presentation had the magic of legends, of whimsy, of romance. Silver's primary presentation would begin the marketing and production wheels, and she would consult and add to the promotion, complete with television appearances.

Nick sat quietly at the conference table, listening to Silver's smooth, feminine voice point out the advantages of the unique scent curling around the room, which could be used in soaps, shampoos, massage oils— He sank down in his chair a bit, watching the males in the room who were sniffing lightly. He glared at them; one too many sniffs and he'd— Nick sucked in his breath as Silver's smoky gray gaze locked with his and a flash of sensual heat passed between them, a reminder that their second loving had been even more intense. A feminine woman, her fingers flowing lightly over his body, Silver did have those nice little savage edges—ones where she demanded and taunted and greedily took her fill. He shifted uneasily in the conference chair, willing his body to settle.

As though sensing his thoughts, Silver said, "I wore the scent this morning with good results. Someone with experience noted the scent—"

"Aye!" Joel and Rafe said together, grinning down the table to Nick. He lowered his head and fought the damning flush moving up to his cheeks. Silver immediately crossed to his chair and smoothed his hair reassuringly. She straightened his tie and leveled a look at Joel and Rafe that caused them to look innocent, straightening in their chairs.

Mamie wiped a tear from her eyes with a leopard-printed handkerchief. "Continue, my dear."

Silver continued, pointing out the unique honey color of the liquid which would deepen the hues of the blue-green bottle, the unique stopper. This professional woman did not resemble the woman prowling his house in his discarded T-shirts and shorts, with socks flopping overlong at her toes. Nick cherished that look, but admired her sleek business look now.

Under him, straining for breath, for the pleasure they sought together, Silver had cried out his name. She wore his ring, and yet Nick feared she would leave him. This morning she had been high on success, taking him as her trophy. He rather liked that friendly little pat on his bare backside when she had bounced from the bed. Nick had managed to drag himself into the shower, and Silver had stepped into it with him— For the moment, the chest and Silver's legend had been forgotten.

But the chest lay unopened, waiting... He respected her, a thorough woman, set upon her course, and yet he feared that the chest—that life—could tear her away. Silver had created a scent for Palladin, Inc. on site, just as she had promised. She had begun the marketing wheels, and she was a woman who would complete her life. Nick prayed that he would be in it, when she found all that she wanted—the pearls and peace with her sister's death.

After the meeting and congratulations, Nick noted the circles beneath Silver's eyes and tugged her from the room, carrying her briefcase and presentation case. "You're going home and you're going to rest. But first—"

She resisted his shove, his hand at the back of her waist, looking up over her shoulder to him. "There you sat, glowering at me. You're not exactly in a good mood."

"Oh, I'm in a mood, all right. I wasn't prepared to have to have them sniffing your new fragrance. It seems too—intimate."

Silver's black winged brows lifted. "Nick, the scent is for women...first to please them and then possibly to attract men. A fragrance is meant to be sniffed—"

"In here." To reassure himself that he hadn't dreamed this morning, Nick shoved Silver into a darkened office supply room.

Silver crossed her arms in front of her, eyeing him. "I detest being shoved—"

He locked the door, lifted her to sit on a counter and reached for her, moving between her legs. "I want you."

"My, my." Then she grinned, curling her legs around his hips, and Nick's body pounded, hardened instantly. His skin was too hot and tight, hunger too strong to deny, primitive instincts rising in the need to claim her, Nick sank into the scent and feel of the woman he loved deeply. His mouth fused to hers, his hand found her breast, cupping it, treasuring it. In a quick agile movement, Silver stripped off her hose and briefs and leaped upon him, meeting his passion as though she feared Fate would haul them apart.

"You realize that you have begun sniffing me. Just that bit at my ear and my throat, as if you can bring me into you. You've begun to make me very self-conscious, and I think you can tell when I want you desperately…. I'm not going home with you, Nick," Silver whispered unevenly after he had lowered her to the floor and she lay soft and wilted against him, his hand treasuring her freed breast.

His other hand brought her left hand to his lips, treasuring her. His voice was stripped of emotion as though he'd expected this moment. "You've got the scent you wanted. Mamie has approved it, and now you're going after something, you need something else."

"Yes. I need something else." She eased her torn bra from her blouse and smoothed the missing button on his shirt, kissing his bare chest and looking up into his eyes. "I have something to finish. I'm leaving. Don't call me. I have to do this on my own."

"I'll come if you need me."

Her hand smoothed his cheek; he kissed her palm. "I know."

Nick studied the small, ominous chest that Silver had left in his keeping. She'd walked out of his life easily enough, just two weeks ago. It was now the first of August and hot and sultry with dreams that weren't coming true. Not a telephone call, nothing but business memorandums sent to Mamie, ideas Silver had tossed over the lines, which had been routed to him.

Unable to sleep, to think about anything but Silver, Nick plunged into work in the Denver offices, and finally, under Mamie's amused direction, he'd been ordered away from Palladin's marketing staff. Two members of the team had threatened to quit if Mamie did not peel Nick from them and let them do their jobs. Sent into exile, Nick brooded in his empty house.

Outside, the August sun burned the fields, ripened the tomatoes, and Nick had traced Silver to her parents. That first week, on impulse, he'd flown to Seattle and, for hours, hovered outside their home in the misty night rain. It had taken all his strength to walk away, to leave Silver to do what she must.

He hadn't collected Silver, but two scarred alley toms and a skinny starved puppy had claimed him. Because he felt like an uncollected orphan, Nick had stuffed them into his plane and took them back to his ranch in Amen Flats. After a battle with a country rooster, the city toms were happy in the barn. The puppy slept in his box on the sunlit porch, amid torn socks and an old chewed boot.

The second week, Silver had stayed at Mamie's, working on the signature scent, which would be launched in March of the next year. Mamie had sent a directive that she and Silver were very busy with promotional work, and when she needed her grandson's presence, she would notify him—the order had been a professional cease and desist, hands-off and stay away. Nick did not doubt that Silver had made the request to Mamie.

Fine. Silver wanted him apart from her private life. What had he expected? What had he given her? How could he protect her, if she needed him?

The empty house, filled with her scents, her panties in his laundry room, the bed they had shared, mocked him. Whatever Silver sought—his gaze swung to the small chest—it wasn't him....

Nick found the Tallchief cradle in the shadows, newly refinished, a task he had enjoyed. Silver deserved to have bits of her Tallchief heritage; she had inherited talents—

She hadn't asked for tenderness, for courtship, and he hadn't provided— In a short time, he'd given her nothing, pushed her into exhaustion, challenged her. Bred from magic and love, Silver had known a loving family; he'd sprung from greed and passion and a dark life. He knew how to take, to survive, but did he know how to give? He didn't have a drop of magic to offer her, his life stripped and cold without her. A taste of delight, of Silver, and he knew the difference—

I love you...I love you...I love you.... The memory mocked him, tore at him painfully.

He touched the cradle with the toe of his boot, rocking it. Made by Tallchief to support his growing family, the cradle was meant for babies and dreams, not a pretty decoration stuffed with dolls or magazines. Nick inhaled sharply. What would he know of softness, of holding his own child close against him, of seeing his baby nurse at Silver's breast—

In the next heartbeat, a storm hurled through him, leaving him cold and furious...and wounded, if he admitted the truth. Damn her. She'd left him. She hadn't called. He wanted anger and instead fear came creeping—would she come back?

"Aye. There is the chest, after all. She'd wager her life for that. And to take it from me, she'll have to come back." He quickly drained the iced tea, and in a violent movement flung the glass into the fireplace. After a moment, the buzzing of a small plane overhead caused him to go outside. He walked into the herb garden Silver had loved, bending to claim lavender and sweetwood and thyme.

He glanced at the small herd of Appaloosa horses, newly purchased and grazing in the field. The mottled stallion was already nipping at a mare, showing off for the other females. At least one male had female interest, Nick thought darkly, slapping his Western hat on his head and bracing his boots apart. Two weeks without Silver's scent had made him growl, and he'd noted people avoided him, which was just fine with him. Two major contractors for Palladin, Inc. had complained to Mamie, who seemed quite happy with Nick's surly mood.

Silver would come back one day, to claim her chest, her laboratory equipment and her four-poster bed. But she'd return his ring and leave his dreams behind— He'd found a woman, bred in romantic legends, who needed moonbeams and magic, and he'd given her raw sensual need and his hunger. He'd tried to lash her to him, thinking he could buy time to court her. Negotiating contracts and business problems did not work when the scent of a woman stirred him, made him reach out to take greedily. He never thought he'd be a greedy man, a selfish one, but when Silver— He studied his open hands, the scars across them, big enough to hurt and bruise, and saw them open, claiming her pale, shimmering breasts, saw again the smoldering fire in her darkened eyes as he took the tempting mauve tips into his mouth. At night, he ached, remembering her curled next to him, trusting him.

The floppy-eared puppy, as yet unnamed, began yipping. To keep him safe from the rooster and prevent him from wandering off, Nick had made a protective barrier on the porch. Nick had just reached for him, feeling the need for a cuddle, when a small fast red plane ripped across the clear blue Wyoming sky. As Nick straightened, it circled and slowed, and a banner unfurled behind it— *Nick Kisses Good.*

"Joel and Rafe haven't changed. It looks like they've forgotten a few things from the last time we tangled—" Nick inhaled sharply, his heart racing as the puppy began to bark excitedly. In the next moment, Nick's heart stopped as the small plane circled again and began lowering for a landing—right on the road leading into his ranch. "Holy—"

Landing neatly, cruising slowly up to his ranch yard, the engines cut. Nick ran for the plane, grabbed for the door, jerked it open and opened his mouth to serve the pilot hell.

Silver, dressed in a silver flight suit, leaped out into his arms, knocking him to the ground. Before he could catch his breath, she was lying over him, holding his face and kissing him hungrily there in the dust and the sunlight. Straddling him, she sat up suddenly and tugged down the zipper on her jumpsuit, revealing the lack of underclothing. Her nipples pushed tautly against the metallic material.

Nick's hands locked on her hips, his body ready. Because his logic was somewhere else and a grin seemed wrapped around him, he said, "You've mashed my herbs."

Uncertain of his next move with the unpredictable woman hovering above him, he smoothed her hair, the sleek, thick strands seducing him. "What do you mean, flying in here like a red bullet? Don't you know you could get hurt?"

"You'll have to check the merchandise to find out, won't

you?'' She grinned at him and scampered to her feet, running toward the house. Nick, recovering quickly, his mouth drying at the sight of her quivering hips, leaped to his feet. He ran to catch her, swinging her up into his arms. For a moment, they stood there in the sunlight, staring at each other, and the world spun around them, unnoticed.

The puppy began barking again, and Silver glanced down at him. ''I saw you out there in the rain, Nick. Standing like a guardian, asking for nothing from me. I saw you pick up the cats and the puppy and walk away with them into the night.''

She placed her hand along his cheek. ''I know how hard that was for you, a man used to protecting others. To moving into their lives and helping. It cost you to walk away. But I wasn't done with what I had to do, and I couldn't come to you then. I wanted to. You looked so lonely. If I had, I could have never let you go. You can't fix my life for me, Nick. Not this.''

For just a moment, there in the sunlight with the scent of herbs and tenderness hovering between them, Silver smoothed his cheek. Then, slowly, she placed her arms around his neck and settled her head on his shoulder.

''Nick. I'm home. Aye…I've come home to you,'' she whispered in a soft, longing sound that cruised straight into his heart as he carried her to his bed.

He arranged her carefully upon his bed, and came to lie beside her, treasuring the soft look in her eyes, the curve of her lips. Fearing he'd heard wrong, splashing his dreams and wants and needs into reality, Nick ran a finger across the cropped, feathery, blue-black hair on the pillowcase. For a man who had pitted his will against others, who kept others safe, he was now uncertain— ''You came back for the chest.''

''Aye,'' she whispered solemnly, tracing his brow with her fingertip and drifting the trail to his lips. ''I did, because there are answers in it. But most of all, I came for you.''

Eleven

The first time they loved, it was with hurried hunger, bodies damp, pitted against each other, Silver's nails digging into Nick's shoulders, her cry flying through the night as he spilled into her, giving himself to her, coming to rest, braced upon her. She held him close, a part of her, safe in a world of their own where the past couldn't tear them apart.

His comforting kisses and caresses began another loving, Nick still buried within her. This time they loved gently, softly, sweeter—filling themselves with each other.

Silver awoke in the night to see Nick braced on his side, facing her, his fingers tracing her mouth. In the shadows, his hair was rumpled, still damp from his shower, his face angular, jutting, fierce—his lashes shadowing his cheekbones, a cord, defined on his throat, pulsing. Silver placed her fingers on it, feeling the life inside Nick, the heat, the desire for only her. "I was afraid," he whispered unevenly, "that you wouldn't come back. Not like this...here with me."

"You're in my life, Nick, a part of me." She traced his lips, long and sensuous and fascinating. She'd also hidden what haunted her, and she knew what the admission cost him, a man, raised street-tough and tormented by older brothers and a brutal father. While Rafe and Joel protected Nick as best they could, they also sought to help him, by teaching him to shelter his emotions from a father who fed on diminishing others.

He breathed unevenly, the effort lifting his chest, his broad shoulders gleaming in the moonlight passing through the open window. Slowly, so slowly, he eased away the sheet covering her. He studied her face, her shoulders, her breasts, and placed his open hand on her flat stomach, then lower, cupping her for a moment. He eased back slightly, sweeping his hand to her hip and the back of her knee, his thumb stroking the sensitive skin there. His gaze met hers as he circled her ankle with his fingers, then swept to caress her sole.

"I didn't think I'd be in a life, not with this intensity, this amount of—depth."

Silver traced the lines between his brows. "We'll fight, you know. I can't have you shoving me around without pushing back and wanting to do my part in keeping you safe."

Nick's teeth gleamed in the shadows as he smiled slowly, sexily. "I like how you push back."

"I don't know," she teased, biting his shoulder. "You're big and bulky and tough, but not that agile—"

His answer was dry, a reminder of their day on Tallchief Mountain. "I'll try to keep up."

She bent to quickly suckle his flat nipple, and Nick's tall, powerful body jerked as though slammed by a heavy, hot punch. He groaned, unevenly, desperately. "You're getting really good at that."

"You're so easy." She smoothed back the wave crossing his forehead, this man who was both lover and friend, who knew who she was on a level that no one else dared to enter. A man who would shelter orphaned puppies and cats, and guard those he loved, careless of himself. A gentle man, one with heart and soul—an enticing male puzzle, a man to cherish and battle and love for a lifetime. "I understand what you mean about being in a life, not circling it…I've been so driven that I didn't think this could happen for me…not this intimacy with a man, feeling a part of him. You thought you'd always live on the borders of your brothers' lives? And have nothing for yourself? Then suddenly before you can breathe, before your heart can pound one more time—''

His lips curved against her instep. "Something like that. I've found I'm greedy…for you."

"Ah, what are you doing?" she whispered unevenly as his mouth smoothed her ankle.

"It's soft and intimate here, like silky ylang-ylang." The heat of his breath brushed the backs of her knees, sending a wave of heat rippling over her. Their loving had been conventional, predictable, beautiful— He took her arm, placed his lips upon the creases of her inner elbow, smoothed her skin with his open mouth, his tongue flicking gently. He nuzzled her skin with his nose. "A little exciting here, like citrus tempered by rose…frangipani, too."

Nick, set on a course to devastate her, had started her heart slamming against her chest. When he gently nipped her restraining hands and wrapped them around the bedposts. Silver gripped the posts, strained to keep her body still and whispered, "You've been doing your homework."

"Hush. Hold still and stop squirming. That only stirs the scents, and a man has his limits." His smile curved along her waist. "Myrrh, here…Moroccan…harvested at the peak time."

Silver managed to suck in necessary air as Nick kissed her inner thigh. "Sandalwood, a necessary essential oil on satin."

He placed his hand on her stomach, smoothing her legs, which had begun to quiver, heat pouring through her. "There's bergamot…ambergris…rose with just a bite of rosemary," he said, moving lower.

The intimacy of his mouth caused her to cry out— "Nick?"

"I'm studying your pulse points, sweetheart. You're on fire and—" He inhaled abruptly and touched her intimately, "very hot and tight and the scents are incredible—"

"Oh, my," she whispered shakily, stunned at the intimacy of his mouth and his uneven words, breathed against her skin.

"Patchouli...damp...very sweet. Your heart is racing, as though it's trying to be free—"

"Nick, you're shaking..."

"So are you, and your heart is racing like a hummingbird's." She shuddered, caught by the passion driving her. "I don't feel that delicate now, darling. In another minute—"

"You're interrupting my scenting experience. Hush." Sinking his fingers into her hips, Nick shifted her slightly, tracing her hipbones with his lips. "Mmm. Cinnamon and ylang-ylang here."

"You're driving me crazy...."

"You wouldn't want to ruin all my sleepless nights doing homework, would you? Let's see if I can pass the test—"

"Oh, you're passing it, all right...."

His mouth moved on her navel, his tongue swirling, flicking lightly. "Vanilla and rose, just a touch of clary sage."

He nuzzled her with his nose, before moving onto her waist. She cried out as his face burned her skin, his mouth opened finding her throat as he settled over her. One quick, dark flick of his gaze swept down to where his chest met her breasts, the pale softness melding gently upon his rough texture, the hard planes. His hands gripped her hips, fingers pressing possessively into the lush softness. He rested there on her, shuddering slightly, his face damp against her throat, until he moved to the area behind her ear, nuzzling her. "This is the best—rose...a bite of ginger, secret, intimate, feminine and yet edgy, and very feminine.... Ah, there's that lavender and sandalwood."

His breath, uneven as her own, swept across her hot cheeks, an effort to breathe as the pleasure rose. Nick began to undulate above her, nuzzling, never letting her capture his mouth, that wonderful, fiery, busy mouth. A dip of his head and he found her breast, took it into his mouth and bit gently. When she moved to draw him closer, he held her wrists at her sides.

"Nick!" The beat pounding at her, Silver smoothed the taut muscles of his back, explored the hard ridges and cords, and, suddenly, Nick's hand took her spinning, the touch perfect, exquisite. Then he was moving down her body again, his beautiful mouth causing her to cry out desperately.

Nick turned her and held her to the bed scented of their lovemaking as he began kissing her calves, her thighs, the base of her spine and up to her shoulders.

Silver gripped the pillow with her fists as Nick came to lie on top of her back, his warm cheek against hers. His fingers shackled her wrists, lightly, caressing.... "You're so warm, throbbing, so alive. Is it true?" he asked fiercely, demanding now, his heart racing against her back, his body powerful and sensual above hers. His lips slid to hers, the flick of his tongue asked and she gave, turning slowly beneath him, facing him now.

Nick's arousal pressed against her and yet his kisses wouldn't—she couldn't— "It's true…we're a part of each other…that's what you want, isn't it? This…claiming."

Nick's hands slid under her waist, cupping her bottom, tugging her higher. "You are mine."

That flicker of vulnerability, that she would leave him, tore into Silver. She reached for his jaw, drew him down for him and kissed him thoroughly. "And you are mine."

They stared at each other, hearts racing, and each knew that gentle loving would come later, but for now— Silver dug her fingers into Nick's strong shoulders, anchored herself to him and caught his legs with hers. He filled her, stretched her, and gloving him, she gave herself to his scents, to his loving, to the heat and where she began and he began, and the hunger of his mouth.

There deep inside her, where pulses met and pushed and poured, she took him as surely as he took her, flying higher until stars burst and savage pounding pressed on, slowing, easing, and yet went on—

Nick's cry echoed with her own, pushing her beyond the burst of pleasure, quivering, easing and finally, shuddering and damp, Nick eased himself down on her.

Silver settled herself comfortably beneath the drape of the man she had mated with, had always known she would take into her heart and into her body. She smoothed his damp back, kissed the heavy pulse in his temple, kept him warm and safe against her.

He moved heavily as though to escape her and she held him tight. "Silver, I'm too heavy."

"Stay. Don't leave me."

This was Nick's claiming, she thought drowsily, and one he would pay for when she could manage the strength. "You've got wonderful pulse points. Just wait until I'm back in fighting position—" she whispered, holding him close.

His hand skimmed down her shoulder, found the curve of her waist and caressed her hip. "Your position is perfect."

"You're so predictable. We'll have to change that. Nick, you're sniffing—"

"It's the scent of a woman, my woman, here, now, in my heart and in my arms."

Mist layered the dark predawn morning and dew lay on the bed of lavender as Nick prepared to embarrass himself. The woman sleeping in his bed, exhausted after lovemaking, shouldn't lack for anything, and Nick hadn't courted her. He intended to correct that deficiency. Though they'd met in late May, the span of May to August had changed his life, and there had been no time for wine and roses.

Nick bent to pluck a lavender stalk and tuck the multiple purple blooms over his ear. With his instincts telling him to push for marriage, he would give her what he could. Once, caught in their lovemaking and drenched in champagne, Silver had said she loved him. She had also wanted to hear him play the bagpipes, and now he'd give her that.

Those long, sleepless nights away from Silver, Nick had played the wood-and-cloth musical instrument. The sound of a lonely wolf howling at the big silver disk of a moon suited his mood. At night in the meadow, the sheep and the Appaloosas barely noticed when he'd played to them. The puppy had howled at his feet, and distant farm dogs had picked up the whine, yowling as if their ears hurt. He tucked the bagpipe's windbag beneath his arm, placed the blowpipe into his mouth and his fingers over the chanter's holes. He would move quickly, thoroughly, and give Silver romance. Or laughter. Cowboy ballads didn't exactly suit the bagpipe, but Nick's musical background was limited.

He cast show-time fear into the soft dewy scents of the darkness and began to play.

"I think Palladin, Inc. is pleased with the signature scent. Or at least Mamie is delighted. It's my best work, and with the launch in March, there's a lot of work ahead of us." That afternoon, Silver had sorted through the handwoven basket of herb starts she had collected from Elspeth's garden, treasuring them. An expert herbalist, Elspeth had learned from her mother, and from Una's journals. At the Petrovnas', amid the clutter of weaving shuttles, loops of dyed wool and a spinning wheel, the basket of herbs was perfect.

In the basket, Elspeth had placed a bouquet of fresh roses, of every color, and had wrapped the cut stems in a damp cloth, secured by a ribbon. The fiesta of petals and mixture of scents were perfect for the day, after she'd been awakened by Nick's bagpipes. Silver bent to nuzzle the fragrant, silky petals and smiled, hoarding the way he'd looked out in the herb garden by her window—a long-legged, jean-clad Westerner, his chest bare, except for the bagpipe, mist curling around him. There were the lovely strips of red, those enticing suspenders she couldn't resist—

She'd smiled then, too, pleasantly lazy, hoarding his desperately sweet lovemaking inside her as she listened. The howling puppy had only endeared Nick more, his voice gentle as he hushed the puppy. The Tallchiefs had called, grumpy and drowsy, with wives purring sleepily in the background—the dogs howling keeping them awake.

Amid Elspeth's colorful rose bouquet, Silver's smile grew. Nick was so predictable; he was making his move, and she intended to enjoy every moment—unless he tried to keep himself from her. That wouldn't do. Silver frowned slightly. Nick was just contrary enough, wicked enough, to want all the perfect trimmings of their relationship. Well, he could think again, because she wasn't waiting, not now, now that she had her life settled and was hunting a new one. Nick didn't stand a chance. She didn't intend to wait for the slow courtship he'd begun so romantically this morning.

Silver stroked a pink dewy petal thoughtfully. She'd worked for an entire week at Mamie's, exhausting long hours to clear the way for her relationship with Nick. The promotion for Palladin's Silver's Signature Line wouldn't need her for a time—or him. And now, Nick was within her grasp, such a lovely man to grasp and hold on to—

Elspeth came to stand beside Silver as her parents and John drove into the Petrovna ranch yard. "You've settled it, then. What runs between your parents and yourself and your brother," Elspeth noted quietly.

"I have." Fighting tears, Silver walked from the weaving room to meet her parents and John. Jasmine would always be with them, but now with Nick's help, they realized that she could only be herself, not Jasmine.

Her mother was crying, tears were in her father's eyes and John had locked himself into a fierce expression that said he fought revealing his emotions. They hugged each other and Silver's mother quietly passed a box to Elspeth, who nodded.

In the meadow, Duncan and Sybil and their children, all packed into a covered buggy, came toward the house, sheep and cattle scurrying from the path. Calum and Talia, Lacy and Birk, Fiona and Joel, Rafe and Demi, and all their children arrived at once, either on horseback or in wagons. As the children hopped to the ground, dressed in Tallchief kilts; the adults hustled them into tartans, straightening them. Long-legged, tall Westerners dressed in kilts hurried to do their wives' bidding, carrying dishes into the house. Elspeth hurried to pass a basket filled with woven flower wreaths around to them. "It's a family day," she explained breathlessly and reached out to nab a child who had just snatched an extra flower coronet for the dog.

As Nick rode closer, Elspeth stuck a small basket into Megan's chubby hands. "Be off with you. Give your dad and the other men one flower each. Give your uncles a kiss, too, Meggie. And Silver's mother and father and John.''

"I didn't know today was a gathering-of-the-clan day, Elspeth," Silver said quietly, as the child skipped away. She sensed from the sparkle in Elspeth's eyes that something merry and secret was afoot.

"Aye, the Tallchiefs are stirring, and you're one of us now, your mother and father and brother, too," Elspeth stated firmly. "You feel that stirring, yourself, don't you? And look over there. Who do you suppose that is?"

Silver glanced at the cowboy driving the small herd of mottled Appaloosas toward the Tallchiefs. She looked again, staring, and placed her hand over her racing heart.

There in the mid-August sun, Nick rode Montoya, sitting very straight and stern in his dress white shirt, a Tallchief tartan and kilt. "He's wearing his red suspenders, and he knows how I can't resist them— Oh, my, he has lovely knees," Silver heard herself exclaim.

"That he does. We claimed him for our own the moment we saw him. He gives so much to others and never thinks of what he needs...until you. He needs you very much, Silver.... Joel and Rafe pushed the kilt upon him, making him suffer with them. They're quite fond of their younger brother and worried about him. You know as well as I do," Elspeth whispered quietly, a hand on Silver's shoulder, "that he's not waiting. Since you've come to us, your senses are getting stronger and you've let yourself begin to feel when you'd closed them out before. Nick has come for you, Silver, and you'd better hurry. Your bridal shift and tartan are waiting—"

But Silver's feet were locked to the earth. "Those horses are meant to be—"

"Aye, the bridal price. They'll be kept at Nick's ranch, if you agree. Nick wanted you to have everything that your heritage entitles you to. He's a romantic, you see. And once he's found the woman he loves, he's decided to move fast. It's an instinctive thing with men...and when done right and in love, the claiming is beautiful. You sense it as well as I do, or perhaps you might scent it.''

Silver sniffed delicately, finding herself drenched in a shower of sunlight and rose petals. A bagpipe melody curled around her heart. ''He loves me? When did he tell you?''

''It's in his eyes every time he looks at you.''

''I knew he was up to something. He was too innocent and docile. This morning he agreed to everything I said. I couldn't forage one thing out of him— He'll pay for this,'' Silver whispered shakily, rocked by the emotions slamming into her.

Elspeth laughed aloud. ''And he'll enjoy every minute. Nick's life until he met you has been far too dull.''

Fear tore through Silver as the Tallchief men came to stand around Silver's father and brother, preparing to accept the bridal price, the lovely horses. ''I can't give him anything. I have nothing to give— I won't marry him now.''

''You've given him more than you realize. He's found dreams and magic, and his heart is opened. He never thought that life's beauty would come to him, and now he's got you. Along the way, you'll think of something else to give him. But if you're not marrying him, you'll have to tell him by yourself and quickly. Meanwhile—ah! Here comes the minister in that lovely black surrey—and look over there, Mamie's rig has fringes and, my, that black sequined gown will be perfect for the wedding. There's something we've made, the Tallchief women, especially for you. It's inside.''

The bridal shift was new, a doeskin replica of Una's, decorated in sky blue beads and softened by fringes. Elspeth's hand settled on Silver's waist. ''We wanted you to have something new…just for you, apart from anyone else, but with the best of the past Tallchief weddings. You can wear Una's, if you like, but this is just for you.''

Silver skimmed her hand down the shift, treasuring it. She knew that Elspeth and the rest knew what losing Jasmine had done to her life. ''You made this for me.''

''Just for you.''

''I can't make this easy for Nick, you know,'' Silver stated as the other Tallchief women came into the bedroom, wearing their tartans and kilts. Their expressions were soft, filled dreams and love and hopes for her.

Silver sniffed delicately, fighting tears. "You all smell so nice, and you're mine," she whispered.

"We've always been and will be. You have an impatient man waiting for you, Silver. You can have your father refuse the bridal price. You can refuse Nick," Sybil said quietly.

"And let a man like that, with knees like that and wearing red suspenders above his kilt, get away? He plays the bagpipe, you know. Oh, no. He's not getting away from me." Silver grinned at Elspeth. "Is there a way to the roof?"

"There's a ladder in the barn," Elspeth said, and her look met Sybil's. "I'm certain two tall men could manage to secretly bring it around to the back, going by way of the hedge."

Sybil nodded and hurried outside. Minutes later, Nick had dismounted and had asked for Silver's hand in a way that recognized her heritage. Her father accepted the horses, though they would be Silver's.

Nick inhaled slowly and glanced at the Petrovna porch where Silver—if she wanted to marry him—should be waiting. She wasn't. He locked his hands behind him and rocked on his heels. One more minute and he'd— Oh, no, he wouldn't. Silver had to make the choice, though he was pushing her. He braced himself for her refusal and damned himself for his need to claim her, to tether her formally, bond her to him. He pushed his hand through his hair and realized it was trembling.

A nudge from Joel and one from Rafe caused Nick to follow their stares—up on the wood shingles of the house, Silver stood, a huge bouquet of roses in her arms.

Nick backed up two steps to see better, already in terror that she would fall, that she would break that lovely neck. "Get a ladder, someone," he said quietly, not taking his gaze from Silver's. "Silver, don't move. I'm coming up."

"You go up that ladder and your backside will show," Joel stated with a grin, glancing meaningfully down at Nick's kilt.

Nick studied Silver, hair gleaming blue-black in the August

sunlight, beautiful and proud in the fringed doeskin shift that denoted her heritage, the legends that had kept the Tallchiefs safe. His cool logic went sliding into the sunlight, and he felt like one big glow from head to brogan. "What do you want from me?" he asked finally, bracing his hands on his hips, his legs apart.

She met his question with a demand, calling down to him. "Was I worth only five horses?"

"I'd give one or two more." He'd give his soul, his life.

"Where is the cradle? You meant it for me, didn't you?"

"I did. You've been busy." Nick swallowed painfully. He'd wanted to give her the cradle that waited in the bridal tepee and make light of his dreams—so as not to frighten her away.

"Don't think you can hide your dreams from me, Nicholas Palladin. I can smell them pouring off you, even from here. You'll play the bagpipes for me again?" she asked, and Nick glared at his brothers who had begun to snicker—until the application of their wives' elbows in their ribs stopped them.

Nick met Silver's gaze and nodded. "I will. You'll have what you want and need from me. I give it gladly."

"I know who I am and what I want, and sometimes I'll want to give to you. You'll have to allow for that, and accept nicely."

Nick nodded. He understood; Silver wanted him to know that she had left the past behind.

"I think you are the loveliest man I know."

"Does that mean yes?" Nick's heart pounded as he waited for her answer. "Is that a yes?" he demanded again, anxious for the answer he needed. He eyed the trellis against the house, followed it up to the rain gutter and—

"I wouldn't," Joel murmured, putting his hand on Nick's shoulder.

"She's agile and fast. She'll be gone before you can catch her," Rafe added quietly. "And she's lighter."

"I'll get her, all right—"

"Can you smell dreams, Nick?" Silver called down to him, grinning as she threw open her arms.

Without thinking, Nick threw open his. "I do, my fair lady."

In a lithe movement, the fringes flying around her, Silver

leaped off the porch into his arms. Nick reeled back two steps with the force of her body, holding her tightly. His brothers braced him, pushed him to stand upright with Silver in his arms. A slender fingertip, scented of roses and dreams, stopped his reprimand. She grinned up at him. "Aye, I do."

Fearing that he had caught her too tightly, Nick forced his hands to relax. The woman he wanted was here in his arms, and he couldn't believe it. He kissed the finger that had just eased back the wave across his forehead and traced his scowl. "I know I'm pushing, and this is unexpected, but—"

"Aye, that you are and now, you'll have to stand and fight—or at least marry me." Silver placed her head on his shoulder for just a moment to comfort him, and then leaped lightly to the ground. She stood on tiptoe to kiss him, and when he reached for her, she stepped back, fringes dancing and promises in her silvery gaze.

Minutes later, the bouquet of roses and lavender grasped tightly in her hands, the Tallchief tartan draped across the replica of Una's treasured shift, Silver walked slowly toward Nick.

His green eyes ripped down the bridal shift, then back up to her face. With the summer wind gently twining in his waves, Nick was scented of dreams, smooth, predictable notes, then leaping, exciting ones. He stretched out his hand as she came nearer, the Tallchiefs lining the way. Mamie had looped her arms through Joel's and Rafe's, their wives curled to their other sides.

Silver pulled in the scents, hoarding them. Love, trust, delight, wistful bits of wives and husbands remembering their own weddings.

When Nick drew her close, he bent to kiss her lips lightly. "The words are here, in my heart," he whispered unevenly, drawing her hand to his heart, "but for now—"

He placed a small silver mirror within her hand, turning it to her. The handle was exquisite, tiny flowers and vines curling around it and the frame for the mirror. It was heavy enough to last for centuries, and fitted perfectly into Silver's hand. The sunlight hit it and blinded her, then she saw herself, hair gleaming blue-black, silvery eyes soft and rimmed with damp, spiked black lashes. She saw a woman who had been thoroughly loved in the night, her cheeks still flushed, and a woman who had listened to a man playing the bagpipes in the morning mist. She saw a woman on her wedding day, her love standing behind her and her future spreading before her. The girl was gone; the shadows were gone.

"This is who I see," Nick said softly against her cheek. "You. The woman I love."

She turned to him and caught the shimmering dampness in his meadow green gaze as a rush of scents and dreams curled up from the bouquet between them.

The bridal tepee behind him, Nick shoved his hands into his jeans back pockets and stood behind the woman he had just married. Her scent carried to him, sorted from the lush grass and pine surrounding Tallchief Lake. With her Tallchief tartan draped around a newer shift, made by the Tallchief women, Silver stood in the moon-kissed night staring out at the dark lake. Nick tugged his hand from his pocket and shoved it through his hair. Words, lovely words, were locked inside him, words he wanted to give to Silver, to make her understand how he felt.

He jammed his hand back into his pocket and waited for her either to come into the bridal tepee as his wife or to mount Montoya and ride off. It was a damned pushy thing to do, ramrodding a woman like Silver into marriage before she escaped his clutches. He closed his eyes and remembered how she looked, silvery eyes shimmering with tears, her face turned up to his, promising her vows with his. She'd settled the past and had begun mending the distance with her parents, but would she give herself to a future with Nick?

Nick wiped away the unfamiliar dampness on his lashes. Her leap from the porch roof had panicked him and later, Silver had been too quiet. Without a word and with a blush rising in her cheeks, she'd allowed him to place her behind Montoya's saddle, and he'd swung up in front of her. His lungs had almost burst with holding air as he'd waited for her arms to come around him.

They had softly, firmly, and when her cheek rested against his back, Nick had allowed himself to release his breath.

Well. There was that pinch on his rear to let him know that she wasn't exactly happy…that she thought he was high-handed.

He hadn't expected her shyness, those quick curious glances when she thought he wasn't looking nor the furious blushes when he'd shown her the bridal tepee waiting near the lake. He hadn't expected her silence, the methodical way she ate the picnic dinner and drank the champagne. He'd expected— What had he expected? Happiness? From a woman he'd shoved into marriage in front of her relatives?

When she'd taken her vows, Silver's voice had been firm, her gaze clear and soft upon him. She hadn't let go of Elizabeth's mirror from the moment he'd given it to her. In those two lonely weeks, he'd dived again into the cave and found the small silver mirror. Pried from its grave, the metal, enhanced with flowers and vines, had come to life instantly, and Nick had replaced the mirror. Would Silver hurl the mirror into the lake with her new wedding ring?

"You want to know if I'm going to throw my rings into the lake again, don't you, Nick?" she asked so quietly that the frogs chirping along the waterline almost drowned her words. "It crossed my mind. But then you might throw yours, and I want you reminded of your vows…. You're afraid I'll be disappointed in the chest. You fear for me and you want to protect me. You brought it, didn't you? In case I would want to open it?"

"I did."

"I think Elizabeth would like it opened now."

In the moonlight, the chest looked tiny and as deadly as a viper. Nick couldn't bear for Silver's quest to end in pain. His hands shook as he tried to force the brass bands away from the soft, ancient wood, the lid falling apart. He glanced at Silver, kneeling beside him, her hand on his arm, still clutching Elizabeth's mirror. She'd hunted for years for the pearls, and if the chest were empty—

One fierce tug and the bands snapped and the brass studs came free, tumbling into the bits of decomposed litter in the chest. With her fingertip, Silver probed the hard, crusted lumps, and from the mass, lifted a single huge black pearl into the moonlight. "It's all true then. These are Elizabeth's pearls."

And then, Silver began to cry softly as though a precious part of her had been torn away. "Oh, Nick. It's finally over," she whispered against Nick's shoulder as he lifted her in his arms. "Jasmine can rest. I can let her go...."

Before dawn, Nick's hand reached for the woman who had wept softly against him until she slept. She'd held the mirror in her fist, protesting drowsily when he would have taken it away from her. Now, he came quickly awake, searching the dark, empty tepee for her. He'd had the night to fear for his wife and what the dawn would bring; he'd had hours to clean and polish the pearls, stringing them when she finally slept. Then he'd returned to their bed, drawing her against him, needing to protect her, and now his arms were empty.

Nick gripped the pearls in his fist and pushed out of the tepee. Mist curled around his naked body. The steady sound of a swimmer cutting through the water caused him to scan the lake. He moved toward the shore, and out of the shimmering mist Silver stood in front of him, wrapped in her Tallchief tartan.

"I know who I am and what I want," she repeated simply before he could lecture her about the dangers of swimming alone, before he could tug her into the safety of his arms. She dropped the tartan at her feet and stood before him, her long, generous body wrapped in mist. She sniffed delicately. "You're angry, of course. Your scent has that dark bite."

Rather than reach for her, claim her roughly in his joy and anger, Nick thrust out his hand, the strung pearls gleaming on his broad palm. Silver touched them with her fingertips. "You strung them with fishing line and made a clasp from wire. I watched you last night, sitting naked beside me, in that slit of moonlight. You glanced at me now and then, fearing for me. That's what you do, isn't it? Taking care of others? That will have to change, Nick. You'll have to let me do my share of the running, pampering you."

"Pampering," he snorted arrogantly, as though she'd asked for him to wear daisies at a board meeting. "You go running off again and I'll—"

She smiled softly and touched his lips. "I know. Come after me. You're so predictable." She glanced downward at his aroused body. "Very predictable. I can count on you. I know from the way you're sizzling now, that quick hard thrust of your hand through your hair, that you want to pick me up and carry me off to your lair—to have your way with me, of course...to our mutual satisfaction."

"You think so? Maybe I've got other plans."

"Change them."

Nick studied her, a smile lurking around his lips and in his eyes. "You're feeling better. And cocky. I'm delicate right now. You know, the new groom thing. I can't be easy."

"Oh, blast," she said, teasing him. "You're bashful."

The dark heated look he shot her told her that he wasn't. He tilted his head, studying her. "What happened yesterday? You were quiet and shy of me."

"I've never had a husband before. The implications were overwhelming. I don't know how to cook. Here I was, married, riding off on a horse behind an old-fashioned, very gallant man—my prince, so to speak...and I don't know if I can hold up the wifely end. You surprised me, darling. I was expecting to gear up for the event, then make my takeover move. I was planning how to hunt you down and bag you. You didn't stand a chance."

"Thanks," he murmured dryly. He reached to place the pearls around her throat, and Silver placed her hands over his, trapping them at her throat, on the pearls. Nick searched her face, frustration on his expression. "Sweetheart, it's important that you sort through this."

She placed her hand along his cheek. "I cried last night because it was all so lovely and I was leaving one life and beginning another. With you. Thank you for the wedding, for yesterday."

The pearls were warm from his hands and Nick bent slowly to give her a long, slow, tender kiss that caused her heart to stop, then flip-flop with joy. *He'll be a fine beast of a man, haughty and proud and strong as a bear...claiming her with wicked eyes and the pearls nestled in his hand. If he places them upon her, warmed by his flesh, and gives her a sweet kiss, the pearls will be her undoing....*

She realized that she'd come undone the first moment she saw him standing in her shop, the Palladin guardian, the man sent to claim her. In a short time, Nick had undone the darkness shrouding her, giving her light and dreams and scents of more....

"Thank you for the mirror. I didn't have anything for you."

"I wasn't expecting a present," Nick stated roughly.

"But I'm giving you my heart, darling. It's the only one I have. Please don't refuse it." Locking her gaze with his, Silver drew his hands to her face, kissing them. "Love me, Nick...."

Epilogue

"Aren't the scents incredible?" Silver asked, settling back against Nick as they stood in the living room of Tallchief House.

After a huge Christmas Eve dinner, the entire family, Tallchiefs and Palladins, had settled into the living room. Amid opened toys and handmade gifts and dressed in their kilts and tartans, with sleepy children in their arms waiting for Santa Claus, the Tallchiefs and the Palladins were at ease.

The huge Christmas tree, the most beautiful one on Tallchief Mountain, had been selected earlier by a scouting party of women, out for a day of fun, away from worrying husbands and teething children. Draped in twinkling lights, ropes of cranberries and popcorn and an assortment of children's ornaments, the tree still had room for the original ornaments. Una, Elizabeth, LaBelle and Pauline—the five Tallchiefs' mother—had added their touches. The evening the tree had been decorated, the men had been too precise, and the wives had given up, exasperated.

The winter wind howled around the log-and-stone home, but inside, before going to their own homes, the families had come together—the sons of Lloyd Palladin had made their peace, and the Tallchiefs, not unused to a hard life, had welcomed them.

Nick cuddled Silver against him, nuzzling her glossy hair, longer now and as sleek as a raven's wing. She sighed, contented with the scene before her, the dreams in front of her, and leaned back against him. The Montclair-Tallchief pearls gleamed on her white frilled blouse as she placed her hand over his large one that had slid beneath her tartan. Nick's hand opened over their child, coming in the spring and nesting in the tiny taut mound of her stomach. Silver turned her head to kiss Nick's jaw, and he moved slightly, meeting her lips in a long, sweet kiss that promised forever. Then Silver nuzzled Nick's jaw, and he smiled, aware of her inhaling his scents. "Don't start anything," he warned, and knew that once they were home, he couldn't refuse Silver—

Her sensual smile set his heart racing. "You can't hoard yourself from me and worry about our baby for months, Nick."

"You're not going to promote Palladin's Silver's Signature Fragrance while—"

Silver's slender hand bearing the rubies intertwined in the Celtic design slid beneath the red suspender crossing his chest, resting on his white dress shirt. Nick, stunned as always when she touched him possessively, stopped talking and didn't disguise the heat in his look at her. Silver smiled, a tender predator who knew her sizable and lovable prey. "I adore these and you know it. It's your fault if you're so tempting, not mine. Mamie agreed with me. You'll take care of me and I'll take care of you and the baby. Just as I did when you were going through morning sickness. The Palladin scent is the best work I've ever done, mostly because you wouldn't let me settle for less. The formula captures a sensual excitement, a stirring subtlety of the Tallchiefs…it's very feminine and timeless. I think I'm even more sensitive to scents when I'm pregnant, Nick, and definitely more creative. We'll have to do this more than once, you know, the pregnancy thing. Mamie and I are already thinking about adding a black pearl line—"

"I'm not happy about this," Nick muttered, ...nt gathered Silver closer.

"You'll be wonderful and you know it. And I have ... Demi and Fiona that Rafe and Joel didn't fare that easily with morning sickness, either, but don't you dare tease them," she added. "Look—"

The blazing fire in the rough-hewn fireplace lit the scene— tall, rugged men who had fought to keep the ones they loved safe, and the women who loved them, who gave them children and love. There were Duncan and Sybil, Calum and Talia—who preferred her Hessian boots to brogans, Birk towering over his petite curly-headed wife, Lacy, Elspeth and Alek Petrovna—a man who had come hunting Elspeth—Fiona and Joel Palladin, Rafe and Demi Palladin. The five Tallchiefs had found their loves, their lives, their happiness, and with them, the Palladins. Children of all ages and sizes draped across their parents' shoulders, and cradled in their arms—children with the black glossy hair of Tallchief and the gray eyes of Una, the Scotswoman, captive bride of Tallchief. Then there were children with brown wavy hair and startling dark green eyes, with tiny clefts in their chins, drowsy now with food and dreams of Santa Claus filling their Christmas stockings. Like a queen, Mamie sat Joel's baby daughter and a teddy bear in her arms, her expression at peace, the shadows gone.

With the sound of the crackling fire, the scents of love and his wife's unique, incredible one curling around him, Nick met his brothers' gaze, each filled with words that didn't need to be said aloud—they'd found their lives, twined with the Tallchiefs, their dark legacy placed in the past.

Silver had found peace with Nick, sometimes uneasy and stormy as he worried about her and the baby, but a sturdy foundation and bond ran through the heated passion, the quiet loving. At times, she looked too long in a mirror, and Jasmine's shadow swept across her face, then she'd turn to him and place her sister in another part of her heart, one to be remembered.

Silver placed her hand on his chest and looked up into his

eyes, whispering the legend that had brought them together.
"He'll be a beast of a man—"

Nick grinned at that, smothering the grin inside him, for it
isn't do for his brothers to see him blush.

"Haughty and proud and strong as a bear," Silver continued
and grinned as Nick's blush began to rise. "You did test me,
claim me with wicked eyes—such wicked, wicked, lovely eyes—
and the pearls nestled in his hand. If he places them upon her,
warmed by his flesh and gives her a sweet kiss—" Silver kissed
Nick softly, promising him her love. "The pearls will be her
undoing. Then their hearts will join forever."

Nick inhaled slowly, treasuring the scent of a woman, his perfect fit, his love, his wife.

* * * * *

Bestselling author Cait London revisits the
powerful Blaylock family in her all-new,
emotional MAN OF THE MONTH *love story,*
Blaylock's Bride,
coming in April 1999 from Silhouette Desire.

Take 2 bestselling love stories FREE

Plus get a FREE surprise gift!

Special Limited-Time Offer

Mail to Silhouette Reader Service™

P.O. Box 609
Fort Erie, Ontario
L2A 5X3

YES! Please send me 2 free Silhouette Desire® novels and my free surprise gift. Then send me 6 brand-new novels every month, which I will receive months before they appear in bookstores. Bill me at the low price of $3.49 each plus 25¢ delivery and GST*. That's the complete price, and a saving of over 10% off the cover prices—quite a bargain! I understand that accepting the books and gift places me under no obligation ever to buy any books. I can always return a shipment and cancel at any time. Even if I never buy another book from Silhouette, the 2 free books and the surprise gift are mine to keep forever.

326 SEN CH7V

Name	(PLEASE PRINT)
Address	Apt. No.
City	Province	Postal Code

This offer is limited to one order per household and not valid to present Silhouette Desire® subscribers. *Terms and prices are subject to change without notice. Canadian residents will be charged applicable provincial taxes and GST.

CDES-98

©1990 Harlequin Enterprises Limited

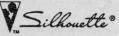

For a limited time, Harlequin and Silhouette have an offer you just can't refuse.

In November and December 1998:

BUY **ANY** TWO HARLEQUIN
OR SILHOUETTE BOOKS and

SAVE $10.00

off future purchases

OR BUY ANY THREE HARLEQUIN OR SILHOUETTE BOOKS
AND **SAVE $20.00** OFF FUTURE PURCHASES!

(each coupon is good for $1.00 off the purchase of two
Harlequin or Silhouette books)

JUST BUY 2 HARLEQUIN OR SILHOUETTE BOOKS, SEND US YOUR
NAME, ADDRESS AND 2 PROOFS OF PURCHASE (CASH REGISTER
RECEIPTS) AND HARLEQUIN WILL SEND YOU A COUPON BOOKLET
WORTH $10.00 OFF FUTURE PURCHASES OF HARLEQUIN OR
SILHOUETTE BOOKS IN 1999. SEND US 3 PROOFS OF PURCHASE AND
WE WILL SEND YOU 2 COUPON BOOKLETS WITH A TOTAL SAVING OF
$20.00. (ALLOW 4-6 WEEKS DELIVERY) OFFER EXPIRES
DECEMBER 31, 1998.

I accept your offer! Please send me a coupon booklet(s), to:

NAME: _____

ADDRESS: _____

CITY: _____ STATE/PROV.: _____ POSTAL/ZIP CODE: _____

Send your name and address, along with your cash register
receipts for proofs of purchase, to:

In the U.S.	In Canada
Harlequin Books	Harlequin Books
P.O. Box 9057	P.O. Box 622
Buffalo, NY	Fort Erie, Ontario
14269	L2A 5X3

PHQ4982

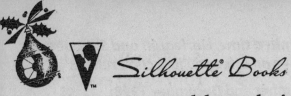
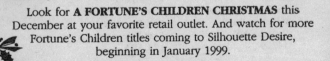

COMING NEXT MONTH

#1189 BELOVED—Diana Palmer
Long, Tall Texans

Beguiling Tira Beck had secretly saved herself for Simon Hart, January's *10th Anniversary Man of the Month*. But this long, tall Texan wouldn't give beautiful Tira the time of day. And she wasn't about to surrender her *nights* to the stubborn-but-irresistible bachelor…unless he became her beloved!

#1190 THE HONOR BOUND GROOM—Jennifer Greene
Fortune's Children: The Brides

His prestigious name was the *only* thing formidable businessman Mac Fortune was offering pregnant, penniless Kelly Sinclair. But once this dutiful groom agreed to honor sweet Kelly, would he love and cherish her, too?

#1191 THE BABY CONSULTANT—Anne Marie Winston
Butler County Brides

Father-by-default Jack Ferris desperately needed instruction in baby-care basics. And Frannie Brooks was every toddler's—and every virile man's—dream. Now, if Jack could only convince the sexy consultant to care for his child…and to help him make a few of their own!

#1192 THE COWBOY'S SEDUCTIVE PROPOSAL—Sara Orwig

A simple "yes" to Jared Whitewolf's outrageous proposal and Faith Kolanko would have her dream: a home *and* a baby. But she wanted a husband, too, not some heartbreaker in a ten-gallon hat. Could a ready-made marriage turn this reckless cowboy into a straight-'n'-narrow spouse and father?

#1193 HART'S BABY—Christy Lockhart

Zach Hart wasn't about to open his ranch to sultry stranger Cassie Morrison just because he and her baby shared a strong family resemblance. He had to beware of fortune seekers…and their adorable, chubby-cheeked children! Then again, what could it hurt if they stayed just *one* night…?

#1194 THE SCANDALOUS HEIRESS—Kathryn Taylor

Was the diner waitress really a long-lost heiress? Clayton Reese had fallen so deeply for the down-to-earth beauty that he wasn't sure if Mikki Finnley was born into denim or diamonds. This lovestruck lone wolf had no choice but to find the truth…and follow his heart wherever it might lead.